Crumbling Truth

RACHEL FITZJAMES

ISBN: 978-1-967700-07-3 (Paperback)
ISBN: 978-1-967700-06-6 (Ebook)

Library of Congress Control Number: 2025920379

Book Cover by Maldo Designs

Editing by Melissa Rotert – Wordplay Copy & Line Edits

A note to readers

Each book in the Spruce Hill series features on-page, open-door steamy scenes, along with swearing and some degree of suspense. There may be a limited amount of on-page physical violence as well as the threat of peril facing one or more characters. Specific content in this story that might be of concern to readers includes emotional abuse (historical), frank discussions about food allergies and allergic reactions (historical), and threats involving allergens. As a general reassurance, no animals or children are ever harmed in my books.

Food allergies are not a joke. They are not a punchline. The reactions detailed in the story are based on my own family's lived experiences, and all individuals are different. There are no depictions of anaphylaxis in this book and no on-page allergic reactions occur in the text. I will include chapter numbers for specific content warnings on my website, if you need them. I firmly support protecting your mental health, especially if you or a loved one are newly diagnosed.

For more details, please visit my website or use the QR code below.

*To my firstborn, whose allergies inspired the bakery
I wanted to call The Nutless Wonder, even if
it only exists in fiction now.*

Contents

Chapter One

THEO

YOU COULD ABSOLUTELY GO home again—I just didn't want to.

Driving across the town line convinced me that Thomas Wolfe's famous line was utter bullshit. Spruce Hill looked exactly as it had when I left.

The twenty years I'd been gone had barely touched the place, aside from a facelift on the Starbucks that rocked the town's inhabitants when it first opened back in the nineties. Most of the landscape hadn't changed one bit in all that time, from the lampposts lining Main Street to the tidy little yards and minivans parked along roads named after various trees and flowers. Not even a few tall, modern buildings at one end of town, featuring trendy restaurants at street level and luxury condos above, could dispel the bizarre time warp I was experiencing.

The familiarity of it threatened to tear my chest wide open.

I pressed a fist to my sternum to quell the ache, but it did no good. I even tried not to flinch when I passed the high school—so many of my memories here centered around that red brick building, the stone benches out front, the soccer fields tucked behind. For a moment, I felt like I was drowning in them.

As I paused at a red light at the corner of Magnolia, I caught sight of a purple food truck by the edge of a parking lot. My stomach rumbled, and I decided my parents' cat could wait an extra twenty minutes while I grabbed something to eat.

I parked my pickup at the end of a row, shoved my hands in my pockets, and strolled over to join the line leading up to the window, hoping for a burrito or something to tide me over.

The name painted along the side of the truck in swirling pink script read *The Nutless Wonder*. I snorted a laugh and the young blond guy in front of me shot a dirty look over his shoulder, but he quickly turned away.

The line was long enough for me to scan the menu board—an array of cupcakes, cookies, and pastries that the fancy chalk script professed to be free of milk, eggs, and nuts—but the guy in front of me lingered, chatting with the person behind the counter. My mind drifted to all the reasons I didn't want to be back in Spruce Hill until he finally left, then I had only a split second to realize it was my turn to order from an outrageously beautiful woman wearing a tee that matched the truck.

"Sorry." I cleared my throat. "I'll take a couple of apple turnovers and a chocolate chip cookie."

The woman, whose nametag said *Queen of Sweets,* grinned at me. She had dark hair pulled into a bun, golden skin even though it was the beginning of November, and eyes of the palest green, practically seafoam. I was grateful for her unfamiliarity—it was a balm against the flashbacks brought on by my drive into town.

"First time, huh?"

I grimaced. "Is it that obvious?"

"I can't say any of my regulars would order a single cookie," she teased, moving to the display case to put my turnovers in a brown paper bag.

"How many should I get?" I asked.

She paused, scanned me top to toe in a way that shouldn't have warmed my body the way it did, and said, "At least four, but probably half a dozen."

"Then I'll trust your professional opinion and take six."

I almost asked for her number as she swiped my card, then reminded myself my stay here was the very definition of temporary. Getting involved with a woman from Spruce Hill would be an act of idiocy—not only because I'd be leaving in two months to go back to Asheville, but also because there was almost no chance that my parents wouldn't hear about it.

Instead of flirting, I took my items, thanked her, and bumped straight into the same dude who'd ordered before me but now stood weirdly close behind me. He skirted around me to get to the window, cooing about forgetting something. I rolled my eyes as I trudged back to my pickup.

Before pulling out of the parking lot, I grabbed one of the cookies and groaned into the silence of the cab as the perfect blend of chewy and crispy goodness melted against my tongue.

The Queen of Sweets had earned herself a newly devoted customer.

I shoved the rest of it into my mouth as I drove to my parents' house, too caught up in thinking about a beautiful stranger and her phenomenal cookies to feel more than a twinge as I made each familiar turn.

The house looked as unchanged as the town itself: immaculate landscaping, because not even retirement could keep my father from doing what he loved, clean white siding above red bricks, pale green shutters and a cheerful yellow front door. A pumpkin or gourd sat on each of the concrete porch steps, the only traces of Halloween that remained after the calendar changed over to November.

When I pulled the key from under the welcome mat by the side door, I paused and stared down at the keychain. It was shaped like the Spruce Hill Lighthouse and made of cheap plastic, but it caused my lungs to seize.

I knew it predated my high school years—this ring had held our spare key for as far back as I could remember, a memento from some field trip in elementary school—but I couldn't believe they'd kept it.

Nor could I believe my response to a piddly piece of plastic.

It was only when I heard the breath wheezing from my own chest that I forced myself to swallow the reaction and go inside.

Toni, my parents' fluffy ginger cat, sat barely three feet from the front door, staring at me with huge golden eyes. This creature was, ostensibly, one half of the purpose of my return to Spruce Hill. For a moment, we simply stared at one another, her steady feline gaze against my own, then I let out a laugh that startled the cat into flicking her plumed tail and stalking toward the kitchen. Hoisting my duffle bag over one shoulder, I followed her.

My grandmother in Miami had broken a hip at her last salsa class, and since my parents had both retired in the past year, they'd decided on an extended vacation down south to take care of her during the recovery period. My brother was local, but he was incredibly allergic to cats. Mom had always wanted one, and she finally adopted Toni after Alex moved out.

Toni was her baby now. At least, that was how she'd spun the whole situation, and I'd uprooted my ass to ensure my mother's feline wouldn't suffer any irreparable distress in her absence.

So here I was, taking care of the cat and the house. Most importantly, according to my mother, my purpose here was to ensure the widow renting their guest house apartment didn't have to deal with any emergencies or shovel on her own when the snow started to fall.

The cat I could have refused, but an old lady who needed someone to keep an eye out for her? My parents definitely knew how to exploit my sympathies.

There had been no other vehicles in the driveway when I arrived, so I assumed she wasn't home. After I freshened Toni's water and refilled her food dish, I peeked out the kitchen window toward the guest house. It was tucked toward the corner of the property, framed at the back and one side by the giant oak and maple trees. In the thick of summer, the leaves on those trees gave the little cottage a fairytale feel, but in November, the bare branches made it look desolate.

Now that I thought about it, I knew very little about this tenant. She was a widow with some classic old lady name. Edith? Agnes? Something like that. I imagined a sweet, doddering retiree who needed someone around to help out when the snow came, as it inevitably would at this time of year.

If the idea of returning to my hometown hadn't been so terrifying, I probably would have thought to ask my mother for more details. Instead, I'd numbly agreed to the arrangement, taking advantage of the slow season for my landscaping business down in North Carolina in order to spend two months living in my childhood home while my business partner, Billy, handled everything back in Asheville.

I still wasn't convinced it was the right choice, but my mother had laid it on thick and I hadn't had the heart to refuse.

Maybe twenty years of hints and pleading had finally demolished my resistance.

Fortunately, my parents had turned my childhood bedroom into an office and their guest room had a newly renovated ensuite bathroom. No matter how many times they suggested I use the master bedroom while I was there, I couldn't stomach the thought of sleeping in the bed where I'd been conceived.

"Oh, fuck," I whispered, lifting my elbows from where I'd braced them on the kitchen counter.

My parents had been alone in this house since my younger brother left home a few years after I moved away—that was plenty of time for them to christen every surface in the house. God knew my father was a randy bastard, even in his sixties. He never missed an opportunity to touch Mom's hip or even ass, if he thought he could get away with it. I'd seen him kiss her neck and whisper something blush-inducing into her ear too many times to doubt he'd made good use of their privacy once their sons had flown the nest.

My first order of business would be to scrub down every horizontal surface.

On the plus side, my father was also a neat freak, which made my job significantly easier because there was a stash of various cleaning supplies in the pantry that could last me an entire year in this house. Under Toni's watchful eye, I set to work, wiping down counters, tables, and desks. By the time I finished, the surfaces gleamed in the afternoon sunlight and I wondered if there was any food in the house.

I shouldn't have questioned it, because of course my mother had stocked each cabinet and every square inch of the refrigerator.

Nibbling on another cookie, I fired off a text to the little group chat my parents had created before they left the house that morning, thanking them for the sweet but unnecessary gesture and wishing them safe travels. In response, they sent back an awkwardly framed selfie in front of a palm tree at one of the welcome centers along their route to Florida.

Two months wouldn't be so bad, even if Spruce Hill held more bad memories than good. With a glance toward the orange tabby staring into my soul like she knew exactly what lay within, I sighed.

"I guess it's just you, me, and the old lady, Toni girl. Let's hope things go more smoothly than the last time I was in town."

To my surprise, I didn't meet my parents' tenant in the three days after my arrival. She drove a beat-up green sedan that had seen better days and she was gone from before I got up in the morning until sometime in the late afternoon, though she never returned home at the same time. No matter how often I peeked out the window, I never managed to catch her actually coming or going.

It seemed odd for a little old lady to be so active, but maybe she volunteered at the library or hung out at the little senior center across town.

By Thursday, I was starting to wonder if I should check in on her, see if she needed me to pick up groceries or something. Why hadn't my mother given me more details about this woman before dragging me home to take care of the cat?

Apparently summoned by my uncharitable thoughts, Toni was perched next to the kitchen sink when I walked into the room. "Yeah, yeah," I muttered, then spooned cat food from a can according to my mother's very specific instructions.

Just as the timer sounded on my reheated casserole, a text popped up on my phone. Though I tensed, afraid it might be from my brother, since he had to know I was in town by now, the message was from Oliver Jimenez, my childhood best friend.

Heard you were in town. When are we grabbing that beer you owe me?

I laughed—trust Ollie to call in a six-year-old bet from his sister's wedding in the Finger Lakes. That was the closest I'd been to Spruce Hill since I first left town after graduation. I was still smiling as I sent back a reply.

Name the time and place, I'll be there.

If Ollie knew I was here, it was only a matter of time before his sister Sofia, the queen of gossip herself, found out. Then reality would truly hit as news of my arrival made the rounds among her social circles. Word traveled faster in this town than any place I'd ever been. The holidays might make it better by distracting everyone with their own families and traditions...or they might make it worse by inspiring everyone who'd ever wondered about my abrupt departure to invite me to join them for Thanksgiving or Christmas.

Oh, shit.

My stomach clenched at the thought. I had no intention of spending the holidays with anyone, least of all the busybodies of Spruce Hill. Though I did want to see Ollie, even the Jimenez family wasn't enough to tempt me away from solitude. It'd be like turning back the clock, going back to middle school again—absolutely out of the question.

As I dug into the casserole, I wondered what the old lady in the guest house did for the holidays. Did she have family in Spruce Hill? My mother had made it sound like she'd be here the whole time, but if she didn't have any relatives locally, she might go out of town at some point. I couldn't remember my mother ever mentioning the woman's late husband, either. Had he been a local?

Toni had no answers for me, but Oliver just might. I finished my dinner and grinned down at my phone when Ollie suggested we meet at The Mermaid the next day after lunch. Maybe I could learn more about my mysterious neighbor, after all.

I walked into the restaurant a few minutes before one, trying hard not to openly stare at the updated decor. The restaurant itself had opened before I left town, but its current state was not at all like the tidy family restaurant I remembered. It was...well, hip. Trendy. I greeted the hostess and was directed to a long, gleaming oak bar at the back of the restaurant, where Ollie was chatting with the bartender-slash-owner, Jake, who'd been a couple years behind us in school.

The trek from the hostess stand to the bar felt like running a gauntlet. The crowd wasn't comprised of only familiar faces, but I caught everything from curious smirks to furtive whispers as I made my way past the tables. I tipped my head to those I recognized and hoped like hell no one would try to pull me into conversation.

In nearly twenty years, the town must have moved on to fresher scandals.

"This place looks nothing like I remember," I said as I claimed the stool beside my friend.

Jake slid a beer across the bar. "I'm going to take that as a compliment. Good to see you, man."

When he moved away to serve another customer, Oliver laughed and clasped my hand before pulling me into a one-armed hug. "You've been away too long, buddy. God, what do they feed you down in Asheville? You look like a wall of muscle, you dick. What happened to the scrawny little jerk I used to pin down in the mud at the end of recess?"

"Physical labor will do that to you, I guess. And Ollie, bud, you pinned me once. One time, then I kicked your ass the next time you tried it."

"Yeah, whatever," Ollie muttered, but he couldn't hide his grin. "It is so good to see you, man."

For the first time since I arrived back in Spruce Hill, there was no trepidation, no regret marring any pleasure at being here. Ollie and I met in kindergarten and stayed friends through high school and beyond. We were closer than brothers. Only Ollie knew every detail about why I had left town—and why I hadn't come back.

"How are things with you and Julian?" I asked.

Oliver's grin was as infectious as ever. "Wonderful, actually. We've got our eyes on a house, across town from my folks. My mom just sent Julian a listing for a house on their street, though. I begged him to pretend the email got lost."

"Probably for the best," I said, lifting my bottle to clink against Ollie's. "Congratulations. Give me a warning when I should expect a wedding invitation, will you?"

"Maybe we'll elope," Ollie mused. "After Sofia's wedding, I'm not sure my parents would mind."

I laughed. "It was sure something."

He sent a sly look in my direction. "And you, my friend? Anyone special in your life?"

"Nope. Single and happy about it, as usual. Good thing, too, for my parents' sake, since I was free to come up here. You can bet your ass I wouldn't have agreed to this if I had someone in my bed back home."

"In your bed," he repeated. "Not your heart."

As my best friend, he knew I didn't let myself get attached—and why. Even if we hadn't discussed it in years, he knew every one of my deepest fears, and until now, he hadn't tried to meddle.

No one else was going to get hurt on my watch.

I rolled my eyes. "Man, we've talked about this. I know you're all loved up with Julian, but not everybody is waiting for Cupid's arrow to hit."

"No, but most people aren't as adamant about avoiding it as you. That shit was a long time ago. You deserve a chance at happiness."

"I'm happy," I said tightly, sounding anything but.

"Right, right. Single, happy, and cat-sitting. How's that going?"

I shrugged, grateful he'd let the subject of my love life drop. "As well as can be expected, I guess. It's weird being back at the house, though."

After taking a long swig of beer, Oliver blinked at me with a feigned innocence that made me immediately suspicious. "Have you met Esther yet?" he asked.

"Esther," I echoed, taking a sip of my own. Not Agnes or Edith or Edna. "No, I haven't even seen her. She's pretty busy for an old lady. She's barely ever home."

Oliver's sudden guffaw drew the attention of half of the restaurant. When my eyebrows shot up, he cleared his throat, thumped a fist against his chest, and said, "Yeah, guess so. Well, I'm sure you'll run into each other soon."

"My mom made it sound like she was basically housebound," I muttered, shaking my head.

"No, not quite."

Something in his tone caught my attention. "What aren't you telling me?"

"Nothing," he replied as he smiled and finished his beer. "Only that you might hear some rumors around town about Esther and her late husband."

"What kind of rumors?"

That jovial smile broadened and he said, "Oh, just that she murdered him."

Chapter Two

ESTHER

I MANAGED TO SLIP home while my landlord's son was still out, though I heard his truck pull into the driveway barely half an hour later. It was silly to try to avoid him, but I wasn't ready yet.

Then again, I'd probably never be ready. Maybe it'd be better to give in to the inevitable and get it over with.

Anita Vasquez-Silver was one of my closest friends, even if she was more a mother figure and mentor than a peer. I owed her a great deal after she'd swooped in to help me when my husband died, but I'd spent weeks rolling my eyes at her little comments about her handsome eldest son. I had encountered the younger one, Alex, several times in the years since I'd moved in, but Anita had never attempted to play matchmaker between the two of us.

Apparently the son who'd moved away was a different story.

He'd left town years before I moved here from Oakville for college. Though Anita spoke of him often and I knew she and Lou went down to visit him a couple times in the years since I'd moved into their guest house, he never came here.

Then again, my parents lived one town over in my childhood home and I didn't visit them, so who was I to throw stones?

The only thing I knew about him was what I'd heard from Anita: he ran a successful business of some kind down in North Carolina, he was handsome and clever, and he was clearly enough of a sucker to let her convince him to come cat-sit over the holidays.

Though I told her I could feed the cat, Anita insisted the feline would be too lonely at home by herself and I couldn't have Toni around while I was baking, so here we were.

Besides, nothing had been clearer than just how badly Anita wanted her firstborn to return to Spruce Hill, even if she wouldn't be there to welcome him. It didn't seem like the best time to butt in and foil her plans.

Once I finished updating my accounting spreadsheet, I rose to start a pot of water for pasta, but a knock at the door froze me in place for a solid minute before the soft sound came again. I forced my limbs to move toward the door, bracing myself as I swung it open to reveal the handsome stranger who'd bought turnovers and cookies the other day.

For a breathless moment, we stared at each other in shocked silence.

He was the perfect combination of his parents: Anita's rich brown hair and eyes the color of dark caramel, Lou's chiseled jaw under a close-cropped beard that looked soft and lush. Thick waves fell over his forehead and his broad shoulders filled the doorway.

How the hell did I miss the resemblance when he came to the truck?

No, I knew how. I'd been caught up on the arrival of a new face—a gorgeous one that topped a muscled frame stretching somewhere over six feet, with the kind of deep voice I wanted to read me to sleep every night of my life.

While I blinked at him, taking in all that made up this beautiful man, his lips curved up into a sheepish smile, revealing a flash of straight white teeth. "You."

"And you," I replied, shaking my head a little to get my thoughts in order.

"You're Esther?"

Stupidly, I glanced down at myself like I needed to check. "I am."

"I'm sorry to barge in on you. I just wanted to introduce myself, since our paths haven't crossed yet. Or, I guess, since I thought they hadn't. I'm Theo."

He held out a hand—a big, capable hand—and I ignored the fizzle of sensation that zipped along my veins when I shook it. His palm was rough and warm and I found myself staring down at how it dwarfed my own instead of responding.

"I swear I'm not trying to be a creep, but I pulled out a container from the freezer to make for dinner and found this," he continued as he released my hand to pull an index card from his pocket.

"Oh," I replied, wincing inwardly at the inanity of the word as I took it.

This is Esther's favorite. Invite her to have dinner with you. Assure her I followed all the allergy protocols she's taught me. Do NOT screw this up.

A strangled noise caught in my throat. For a second, I considered refusing, but I couldn't be sure he wouldn't turn around and tell Anita that I was an ungrateful wretch. Instead, I sighed and handed the card back to him, meeting his amused gaze as his fingers brushed mine again.

"Your mother is a meddling pain in my ass," I muttered.

Startled laughter lit his expression, the dark amber of his eyes sparkling with mirth. "That much we have in common, then. Will you join me for dinner? I'm not sure what her punishment will be if I fail, but I imagine it will be swift and severe."

My lips parted to say no and my fingers tightened on the edge of the door, ready to close it in his face, but beneath the glimmer of good humor and the quirk of his broad lips, I saw a loneliness so profound that its twin deep inside me responded immediately.

His smile faltered ever so slightly and that waver crumbled the rest of my resistance.

"Yes, okay," I said quickly, and my reward came in the form of a grin so wide it was nearly blinding.

"Phew. Thank you. My mother would never let me hear the end of it if I failed in this, believe me. And I'd be eating pot pie for a week. I don't know why she thought I needed so many frozen casseroles. I do know how to cook. Seriously, I owe you one for this."

I started shaking my head even as laughter bubbled up inside my chest. "Believe me, it's your mother who owes me. Let me just grab my coat."

Theo waited in the doorway with his hands shoved into the pockets of his battered jeans, looking like the world's most sheepish vampire. He probably could've pulled off the sexy, brooding version if not for the tiny, self-deprecating smile peeking out from his beard. Well, and the deep bronze of his skin that spoke to both his parentage and hours spent in the sun.

Before I could get too lost in those daydreams, I grabbed the first jacket I found on the rack and threw it on without a second thought. It was my favorite, a dark purple trench coat with a flared skirt, and I normally saved it for special occasions when I was wearing something dressier than leggings and an oversized tee. Though it was swiftly stifled, I didn't miss the quick flare of Theo's appreciative gaze as I cinched the belt around my waist.

We stepped out into the evening without another word. The guest house I'd been renting since my husband's death was about twenty yards behind the main house—far enough to give me the illusion of total privacy, but close enough that Anita regularly invited me over for coffee when our schedules allowed.

Crossing the distance with Theo beside me made it seem like a chasm between safety and the unknown.

Lou and Anita were amazing people and I didn't doubt Theo's motives for a second, not after reading Anita's note, but running the food truck sapped so much of my social energy that I hadn't done anything more exciting than having brunch with this man's mother in the past year.

As we passed his pickup truck—not the shiny proof-of-masculinity kind so many guys his age drove around here, but an older model, slightly battered from clearly being used for actual work purposes—I snorted when I saw the writing on the side of it.

THE LAWN RANGER: LANDSCAPING SERVICES.

"Hi ho, Silver?" I asked, lips twitching. Anita and Lou both had a great sense of humor, but this flash of comedy was unexpected.

Theo grinned. "Might as well have fun with it, right?"

"Given that my business is called The Nutless Wonder, I can't really argue with that," I replied.

The deep chuckle that erupted from him was surprisingly satisfying. "Seriously love that name. And you were absolutely right about going for more cookies."

"I'm glad you enjoyed them."

"My mom's note mentioned allergies, are you allergic to all the things listed on the truck?"

"Just peanuts now. I was allergic to milk and eggs as a kid, but I outgrew those two. Everything in the food truck is free of milk, eggs, peanuts, and tree nuts, though, and obviously fish and shellfish. Most of it is soy-free as well. The demand for it is growing, and it's gratifying to help kids with food allergies enjoy the same things other kids do."

For fuck's sake, I was babbling. When was the last time I'd babbled at a strange man? I highly doubted Theo cared about my medical history, but he hummed thoughtfully, as though maybe he *was* actually interested. I forced myself to stay silent until he opened the side door, then ignored his warm smile as I toed off my boots in the mudroom before walking into the kitchen. Its homey familiarity comforted me and I tried to pretend I was just here to have coffee with this stranger's mother.

Of course, my attempt to play it cool lasted a total of seven seconds before he noticed my socks, which were patterned with brightly colored mathematical equations.

"Ahh, I see now why my mom likes you. A math nerd, huh?"

I scowled at him. "Numbers are beautiful, and these were a gift from your mother."

My expression didn't deter him at all. Theo sent me a broad, friendly smile and asked, "Can I get you something to drink? Water, beer, wine?"

It was a stupid little question, certainly not worth the sudden clench of anxiety in my stomach, but the memory of Steve flinging insults at me on the drive home from a colleague's house after I spilled a glass of red wine on my dress hit me like a softball to the chest, forcing the air from my lungs.

Standing there under the bright kitchen lights with a man I barely knew, I couldn't stop myself from reacting. My mouth opened and closed a couple times before I snapped it shut in order to try to regain control over myself.

"Hey," Theo said softly. "You okay?"

His voice was gentle, and that sliced through the rush of panic rising in my throat. I blinked a few times, focusing first on his beard, then on the hair tumbling across his forehead, then finally on those caramel eyes, filled with concern.

Slowly, my lungs inflated again and the tension seeped out of my limbs.

"Esther?" he murmured, though he didn't come any closer to me.

If he had, there was a distinct chance I'd either flee or throw myself into his arms. The fact that both seemed equally likely was disconcerting.

"I'm okay," I said finally. God, I was mortified, but I was definitely okay.

Theo studied me for a long moment before he gestured to the fridge. "Can I get you something to drink?" he asked again.

"Water would be great."

When he set a glass of filtered water in front of me, he didn't look pitying or morbidly curious or even annoyed—all expressions I'd seen on people around Spruce Hill whenever they'd caught me in a weak moment. Even Anita, only once in the years we'd known each other, but it was less pity and more motherly sympathy.

Theo had been gone for so long, though, that maybe he had no clue what exactly he'd missed. The fact that I'd been married to a narcissist and had spent the years since his death relearning how to trust my intuition, especially around men, was not likely a topic Anita would have brought up to her out-of-town son.

The pot pie smelled amazing as it thawed in the oven, settling my nerves moment by moment even while Theo and I sat in awkward silence. I took another sip of my water before I glanced up and caught him studying me with a rueful smile playing across his lips.

I arched a brow. "Why are you looking at me like that?"

"You're not what I was expecting, that's all."

"What were you expecting?" I asked, curious.

I hadn't grown up in Spruce Hill, but I'd lived here since I started college. After all these years, I was used to everyone knowing practically everything about everyone else. It felt strangely freeing to realize that Theo didn't fall into that category—even more so when I realized I knew next to nothing about him, aside from the fact that he was handsome as hell and had just a touch of a southern drawl after spending half his life in North Carolina.

He stretched out his long legs as he leaned back in his chair and tipped his head to one side. "This is going to make me sound like a first-rate idiot, so I'd be very grateful if you would refrain from telling my mother about it, but I will admit I was under the impression my parents' tenant was an old lady."

Oh, this was *good*.

I burst out laughing because I could absolutely imagine how vague Anita would have been in telling him about my existence. Even in a town full of busybodies, she never stooped to gossip. Her respect for my privacy was one of the biggest reasons I had taken her up on the offer of renting the guest house rather than finding myself an apartment.

"Did you, now?" I asked finally, still grinning. "If it's any consolation, I'm actually ninety-three, you know, but I made a deal with a swamp hag to keep me looking young and spry."

"Top notch swamp haggery, if I may say so. I shouldn't have made assumptions. Being back here is throwing me off my game, I'm afraid."

I wasn't sure if that was an opening to question him, but I would never have taken him up on it even if it was. Instead, I simply hummed and offered a smile as a token of forgiveness for his mistake. The oven timer saved me from having to figure out how to respond without sounding like I was digging for information.

Theo waved away my offer to help serve dinner in a gesture nearly identical to his mother's. As I settled back into my chair, I watched him move around the kitchen with an easy sort of grace, the kind that came from being comfortable in one's own skin. Part of me wished Anita had been speaking from a place of motherly love rather than objective observation when she'd described her firstborn son.

He really was beautiful.

With nothing else to occupy my mind, I reflected on the little that I knew about him. By the time I started college here, Theo had been gone for several years already, so the rumor mill had mostly moved on by then. Respect for Anita, one of the college's most beloved professors, reduced the chatter even further. All I really knew was that *something* had happened in his senior year of high school and that he'd left town immediately following graduation. From what I gathered, this was the first time he'd come back.

When Theo set the plate in front of me, he narrowed his eyes. "You're smiling," he said cautiously.

"I do that sometimes," I replied, shrugging.

In truth, not very often, but I wasn't going to tell him that.

He sat down across from me and shook his head. "No, there's something going through that head of yours. What is it?"

"I was just thinking that it's funny, us sharing a meal," I replied.

"Why is that funny?" Theo asked, cocking his head at me.

"Because we're two of Spruce Hill's greatest mysteries, sitting right here in one room."

Chapter Three

THEO

ESPITE THE DRY HUMOR in how she said it, I almost fumbled my fork.

Aside from Oliver and my parents, I hadn't spoken to anyone about the events leading up to my abrupt move to Asheville. No matter how close my mother might be to the woman across the table, I couldn't imagine she'd given Esther any details about it, either.

Before I could respond, she grimaced, the expression almost comical set against her beautiful features. She was stunning, really, so different from the elderly widow I'd imagined living out there in the guest house that I was still in shock. With her long black hair falling halfway down her back, those beautiful moonlit eyes, and flawless, glowing skin, she was about as far from an old lady as she could possibly be.

I figured she must be somewhere around thirty, maybe a couple years past. Petite and curvy, she'd barely reached my shoulder as we crossed the distance between the houses. Even dressed casually in a t-shirt, there was something calm and collected about her, a self-possession that made her seem wise beyond her years.

Christ, she was young to be a widow. I'd immediately discarded Ollie's comment about her killing her husband, but I wondered what the hell had happened to start a rumor like that.

She was right, though—we represented two separate eras of Spruce Hill legend, apparently. The difference was that no one brought up my history, not anymore, and here I was, wishing she'd bring up hers.

Not so I could pry, but because I wanted to know what was lurking behind her quiet beauty. Gorgeous or not, she struck me as a little too solemn, a little too serious.

Those lips had looked so sweet when they curved into an unconscious smile only moments before, but now they were pursed and tight. It was a harsh contrast to the rest of her body, soft and generously rounded.

"I'm sorry," she said quietly. "That was...indelicate."

I snorted at the word and shook my head. I didn't want to talk about the past any more than she probably wanted to talk about her dead husband, but I didn't want her to feel bad about bringing it up, either.

"Nothing to apologize for. Tell me about your food truck. How did you get into that? Did you always want to own a bakery?"

"Well. No," she admitted, flashing me a sheepish grin. "I like baking. When I was a kid, my mother was always making something or other for me to bring to birthday parties or on field trips. She didn't want me to feel like I was missing out. I never intended to make a living from it, though. My degree is in math."

It was a little ridiculous how suddenly fascinated I was by this woman. "I guess baking involves a fair amount of math, huh?"

She shrugged. "Like I said, I enjoy numbers. I had no real plans for what to do after college. When my husband died, I started a tiny little baking business on the side, mostly just word of mouth. I didn't realize how much demand there was out there for things made in a completely nut-free home by someone who knows about cross-contamination. Overhead is crazy for an actual bakery, and renting kitchen space doesn't really give me control over what allergens are present in the facility, hence the truck. I love the freedom it gives me, so I'm sticking with it."

"That's amazing," I said, leaning toward her slightly. "So you met my mother through your math classes?"

"Yes, she was my academic advisor and taught quite a few of my courses. She encouraged me to go into teaching, but that was never my passion. We compromised and she got me into an accelerated program where I got both my bachelor's and master's with just one extra year of college."

"So you're a brainiac, like my mom." I grinned at that.

"I guess so." A tiny smile curled her lip, then it faded as she went on. "After Steve's death, I was getting ready to sell the condo and she must've heard about it from somebody in town, because the next thing I knew, she was offering up the guest house."

"Doesn't surprise me in the slightest."

"I wasn't sure what I was going to do with myself, and your mother encouraged me to use some money from the sale of the condo to start the truck. My baking orders were taking off, so it was the next logical step."

In a sudden flash of clarity, I could see it, the friendship between Esther and my mother. This woman was clever and bright and clearly driven, all things Mom appreciated, but underneath the capable exterior that would've drawn my mother to her in the first place, there was also an air of loneliness.

I saw it because I'd experienced the same thing, and I was sure my mother saw it, too. She was too perceptive to miss it. If she'd helped to ease that wound for Esther, I was happy for them both. I knew firsthand how it felt to trudge through the mire alone.

Of course, Esther herself raised a brow at my sudden silence and I got the impression she probably didn't give a shit about my opinion. I cleared my throat and flashed a smile, though she looked equally unimpressed with that.

"So," I said, searching for a safe thread of conversation, "where's the truck now?"

"I park it at Mr. Ankarberg's plaza most of the time, though your parents don't mind me parking it in the driveway when I need to. I try to limit that so the neighbors don't complain."

"People complain?"

She lifted a shoulder. "The name isn't everyone's cup of tea. My parents hate it."

Something in the way she said it convinced me she didn't want to discuss her family, so I just nodded and we fell into a less awkward silence as we ate our meal. All the while, I wondered how much she knew about my family's past, whether my mother had told her anything about why I left. Now that I knew a bit of Esther's history, it seemed like she was a kindred spirit. In those odd, silvery-green eyes, I saw the kind of pain that resonated inside me, and somehow I knew she'd understand if I confessed everything to her then and there.

Fortunately, common sense—or self-preservation—kicked back in before I could lay those years of conflict before a complete stranger.

Esther refused to be waved off again when she rose to help me clear the table. "Even your mother lets me help with the dishes, you know," she insisted.

"Fine, fine," I muttered, joining her beside the sink.

We settled into an easy rhythm, her rinsing the dishes and me loading them into the dishwasher. Even with Esther joining me for the meal, we still had enough leftovers for two separate containers. I put one in the fridge and set the other on the counter for her to take home.

Strangely, when the time came to walk her out, I didn't want her to leave.

"Will you be at any of the holiday events around town? With the food truck, I mean?"

Her moonbeam eyes widened slightly, but she nodded. "Some of them, yes. November is mostly business bookings and personal orders, but I'm scheduled for the tree lighting and then the Carolcade in December. This time of year gets pretty slow otherwise. Were you planning to go to those events while you're in town?"

I grimaced, unable—or unwilling—to lie to her. "No, I wasn't, but if I don't go, certain Spruce Hill residents will be all over me for locking myself away and I'll end up bullied into joining them for Thanksgiving and Christmas."

"The horror," she replied with a shudder.

Though I laughed, there wasn't even a hint of a smile on her face when she said it. Either this woman was extraordinarily good at poker or she was as uneasy about being roped into socializing as I was. That suspicion touched something deep in my chest, another flash of connection between us.

"I'll have to stop by and get some more baked goods," I said, inwardly kicking myself for the stupid phrasing.

Esther didn't seem to mind; she offered a smile, broader than any I'd seen from her so far, with the barest hint of a dimple appearing at one corner of her mouth. It hit me like a fist right in the center of my chest. She was stunning anyway, but that smile—shit, I hadn't responded like this to a smile since high school. The reminder of where that particular smile had led crashed over me like a bucket of ice water.

"I'll set something aside for you. I usually sell out in the afternoon," she said, slipping her boots and jacket back on as I stood there and watched, my entire body practically frozen in place.

"Thank you," I managed, though the words sounded a little hoarse. "For joining me tonight, I mean."

"Have a good night, Theo."

The simple words were uttered without much warmth, as though she'd sensed my withdrawal and accepted it as some sign of dismissal. Before I could even attempt to respond, she was walking along the paved path to the guest house. For a long moment, I stood there, watching the distance between us grow and wondering what the hell I'd been thinking, agreeing to come back here.

I was off-kilter, that was all. Under normal circumstances, I'd never have been so affected by a woman's smile, so awkward at conversing with a stranger that I fumbled the conversation like I was thirteen again.

Beautiful or not, she probably wasn't interested in me at all, and I damn well shouldn't be interested in her, either.

Just after she disappeared through the door to the guest house—without a glance back toward me—my phone chimed with a text from my mom. I snorted at her request for a photo of me and Toni, then let myself back into the house. The feline in question wove between my legs as I strode toward the kitchen, poured myself a glass of my father's second-best scotch, and dropped down into a chair, thinking about Esther.

I realized my mother had never referred to the woman's age, only that she was a widow. In fact, it seemed odd now just how emphatically she'd stressed that part. I'd barely even paid attention to Esther's name, but now I had to admit I hadn't been paying close enough attention to the rest of the conversation, either.

The next time I spoke to my parents, we were going to discuss what constituted pertinent information about my current living arrangements.

By the time I finished my scotch, I decided Oliver also owed me an explanation and hit call on his contact in my phone.

"Hey, man, miss me already?"

"Ollie, what the fuck?"

For a beat, he was silent, then he started laughing. "You met Esther," he guessed.

"Yes, though technically we met when I stopped at her food truck on my way into town. Why didn't you tell me she wasn't an old lady?"

"I thought this way was more fun."

I sighed loudly enough for him to hear it over the phone. "You owe me."

"Happy to pay up," he replied. "Let me guess—you want intel on the beauty living in your backyard?"

I didn't dignify that with a response, just asked, "Is she from Spruce Hill?" Surely I'd remember Esther if she'd grown up around here.

"Nah, she's from Oakville. Came here for college."

Oakville was the next town over, even tinier than Spruce Hill. They were our biggest rivals in high school soccer, but that was about the extent of my knowledge of the place. I was still trying to regain my equilibrium after all those stupid assumptions crashed down around my ears.

"So you know her?" I pressed.

"It's Spruce Hill, man. Of course I know her. She was Sof's college roommate, actually, and I think they had a lot of classes together. They used to hang out all the time, but Esther got married after graduation and they kind of lost touch."

"Who did she marry?" I asked.

Oliver's tone soured. "Steve Pautler."

The name was vaguely familiar, but I couldn't quite place it. "I don't remember him. Did we go to school with the guy?"

"Nah, he was much older than us. Jesus, probably fifteen years older than Esther. Some kind of real estate developer. Do you remember when the old Randy's Hardware building was knocked down? I think we were juniors."

"Yeah, vaguely. There were protests, right?"

Oliver huffed a laugh. "Tons of them. My mom called Steve a snake oil salesman once and believe me, it fit. Smarmy bastard talked the town council into accepting his development plan—or greased the right palms. You can thank him for the shiny new condos around the corner, too."

Memories started coming back to me, but my brain caught on something else Ollie had said. "Esther married a man fifteen years older than her?"

"Yup. Look, you know I'm not one to gossip," Ollie said, lowering his voice, "but the dude was sketchy as hell. He could turn on the charm when he wanted to, but there was always something creepy about him. Sofia didn't even think Esther liked the guy, then suddenly they were engaged. She called me a couple times crying because she was worried about Steve cutting Esther off from her friends."

I felt a stirring of sadness for her, but I forced myself to re-member the bastard was dead and no longer posed a threat. Still, my fist clenched against my thigh. "You think he was abusing her?"

"It's possible, but Sof didn't think so. Your mom was pretty protective of Esther. She probably would've castrated him with a protractor if she had proof he was hurting her. After Steve died, Sofia's been in touch with her a little more. I think she's been trying to get Esther to go out with a group of them."

"That's good," I said, but Oliver made a scoffing sound.

"Esther shoots her down every time, but gently, I guess. Sof's not offended, just more determined than ever to get Esther back out in the world. She's even more of a recluse now that she's in your parents' guest house than when she was married, according to my sister."

"Hmm." I stared into my empty glass.

"Don't do it," Ollie warned.

I scowled at the phone. "Don't do what?"

"Don't make it your personal crusade to rescue her."

"I'm not on a crusade, Oliver," I ground out.

"She's no damsel in distress and from what I hear, she happily grinds potential suitors under her heel. God knows why your mama didn't warn you herself, but all Esther wants is to be left alone, bro."

"I'm not an idiot. And I'm leaving in two months, anyway." I frowned. "How did Steve die? Even with the age difference, he couldn't have been that old."

"And that, my friend, is the million dollar question. Nobody knows."

Chapter Four

ESTHER

THE WEATHER IN SPRUCE Hill was too fickle to rely on steady business all year around, so winter's impending arrival heralded my slow season for the truck. Fortunately, the little town loved to host community celebrations, so I'd have the two events I mentioned to Theo before settling down to supply allergy-friendly baked goods for individual orders and a couple local restaurants to get me through the winter.

Two days had passed since our dinner together and I hadn't run into him again, though I *might* have creepily watched through a crack in the curtains as he replaced the railing on his parents' deck the day before.

In battered jeans and a red flannel shirt, he looked like the world's hottest handyman. It was almost enough to make me regret my decision to avoid romance for the foreseeable future.

Maybe I'd been alone for too long. That was the only logical explanation for this interest in Theo Silver. No matter how enthusiastically his mother talked him up, he was leaving town again when his parents came back. My life definitely did *not* need that kind of complication.

My husband had died nearly four years ago and, while I couldn't claim to mourn him, I still had no desire to throw myself back into the hell of dating. In fact, that was why I'd taken Anita up on her offer of renting the guest house only a few months after his death, to give myself some space from well-meaning friends and neighbors who thought I just needed a little nudge back into the world.

At the time, that was the last thing I'd needed. Now? I wasn't so sure.

My gaze settled on the windows at the side of the room. It was a gray November day, dreary and depressing. At that point, it suited my mood perfectly.

Why had I let Theo get to me? For a while, I'd done so well, deflecting his comments, rolling with the punches. Then he'd gone from smiling at me like he'd never met anyone so delightful to looking like I'd just drop-kicked Toni into traffic. It was enough to send me reeling off balance, and I hadn't managed to regain my equilibrium yet.

Steve's colossal mood swings had left scars on my psyche. They might have faded, but they weren't gone.

The temptation to talk to him, to actually *connect* with someone for the first time in so long, had been overwhelming.

And he seemed like he needed that connection just as badly, but then he shut down.

I'd always considered myself immune to charm, at least since the first time Steve's practiced smile melted into red-faced rage. Theo's handsome features were a point against him, really, but he was rugged where Steve had been slick, good-natured and self-deprecating instead of smooth. The honesty in his words, even if he was prone to putting his foot in his mouth, struck a chord deep inside me.

It was disconcerting in the extreme. With nothing else to distract me from thinking about my dinner with Theo, I did something I hadn't done in years.

I called my friend Sofia.

She answered before the end of the first ring. "Esther! How's it going?"

"Hey, Sof. Things are good, how have you been?"

One of my favorite things about her was that she never hesitated to take the lead. No matter how awkward I was, she could carry a conversation forward at dizzying speeds. Instead of making me feel worse, it somehow served to bolster me until I was ready to contribute something of value.

As soon as she paused for a breath, I said, "Do you want to get coffee sometime?"

"Are you kidding? Of course I do! I'm free tomorrow morning, if you can do early? I took the morning off for a doctor's appointment at eleven."

"Yeah, early works. Eight? Nine?"

"Nine, Cafe Aroma?"

I grinned, remembering all our college study sessions at the little coffee shop on Main Street. "Yes, that's perfect."

"Good. I'm so glad you called," she said softly.

My heart constricted in my chest. "Me too."

"I have to run, Chase is making dinner. I'll see you tomorrow."

When I ended the call, some of the nerves had settled, but I still felt like I'd stuck my finger in an electrical outlet.

In the morning, as I got ready to meet up with Sofia, I studied my reflection for several long moments, trying to remember the last time I'd gone out with a friend. Looking back, it was easy to see how Steve had isolated me, but even after his death, I'd made excuses, kept to myself. Anita hadn't allowed me to retreat completely into my own little world, but I had tried.

Oh, how I tried.

Sofia was already seated at a little table in the corner of the cafe when I arrived. While I wasn't much of a hugger, she pulled me immediately into an embrace tight enough to force the air from my lungs.

"God, you look amazing, honey! It's been too long," she gushed.

Shockingly, it felt as natural as breathing to simply fall back into my friendship with Sofia. We'd bonded during freshman year of college, long before Steve came into my life, and Sofia had been my closest friend. One of my biggest regrets was letting the bastard drive a wedge between us.

It took approximately three minutes before she asked, "So, have you met Theo yet?"

I wrinkled my nose. "I have, yes."

"And? God, isn't he just gorgeous? Ollie would've skinned me alive if I ever said anything, but I had the biggest crush on him when we were kids. I'm telling you, when he came to the wedding, I was sorely tempted to call it off and beg him to take Chase's place," Sofia said, propping her chin on her hand and gazing dreamily into the distance.

At that, I fought back a flinch—I'd missed the wedding because Steve had planned an important dinner for investors that night, probably just so he could keep me from being Sofia's maid of honor.

It still hurt to think of everything else I had missed.

"You were not," I scolded gently, forcing myself to stay in the present. "You love that man to distraction."

She winked. "Okay, but admit it—Theo is a mighty fine specimen."

For a moment, I simply glared at my friend, but finally I caved. "Yeah, fine, he's beautiful. He's not for me."

The smile dropped from her face and she leaned forward. "I'm sorry, Esther, I swear I wasn't trying to pressure you. No harm in having a nice view out your window though, right? I'll drop it, I'm sorry."

"Sof, really, it's okay. He is definitely nice to look at," I said, smirking from behind my coffee mug so she would stop looking so serious. "He was fixing something on the back deck the other day and looked like he stepped right out of a hot handyman calendar."

She laughed and raised her own mug in salute. "To eye candy!"

By silent mutual accord, we steered the conversation away from Theo and back toward safer subjects. I contributed as much as I could, but Sofia had always seemed to understand that I was more of a listener, content to let her regale me with stories about her students, her husband, and her boisterous but intensely loving family. It made me feel less alone, just hearing about that kind of life.

Eventually, though, she tilted her head and asked, "Are you going to be alone for Thanksgiving? And Christmas?"

"Sofia..."

Holding up her hands to ward off an argument, she said, "I'm just asking, but you know you're welcome to join us. I hate the thought of you all by yourself for the holidays."

I sipped my coffee as I considered my response. "It's okay. Anita always invited me to have dinner with her and the family, but I'd rather be alone. This year, I'm planning to spend the weekend curled up on my couch reading romance novels and catching up on my Netflix queue. I'll be fine, trust me. I do appreciate the invitation, though."

"Well, if you change your mind, just let me know. You know my mother won't have a problem with a last minute addition." Sofia dropped her gaze and pursed her lips, making me immediately suspicious, then added, "But I guess Theo might be alone for the holidays too, since he doesn't speak to his brother."

That little tidbit was news to me, but I scrunched my nose at her anyway. "You're terrible."

She just shrugged, grinning. "Thought I'd mention it, that's all. You're both like family to me and I don't want either of you to be sad this season. You deserve happiness, honey. You've been alone a long time."

I tapped a finger against the tabletop. "I know. I'm not sure I'm ready for more just yet."

"It doesn't have to be serious," she said slyly. "You could have a no-strings affair for a few weeks, kiss him goodbye, and probably never see him again. He avoids this town like the plague."

Though my brain tripped over the *affair* part of that, I forced myself to focus on the final sentence. "Why does he avoid it? His whole family still lives here, right?"

She was quiet for a minute. "There were a lot of rumors flying around at the time. Theo's brother, Alex, is only fifteen months younger than Theo, and I think...I think it was an argument over Theo's girlfriend at the time. Alex and Michelle were in the same grade."

"Oh, shit," I whispered.

"They fought, Alex and Theo. Physically. There was an accident at the lighthouse, Michelle died, and her family moved away the same summer when Theo left."

"She *died?*" That wasn't at all what I'd expected.

"Yes. Ollie insisted it wasn't Theo's fault, but that's all he would say about it. The gossip was awful for a while. Ollie made me swear not to get involved in any of it and not to say anything if anyone asked."

I frowned, knowing just how vicious Spruce Hill rumors could be. I'd spent the last few years fighting my way past my share of them, everything from gold-digger to murderer. This town was as creative as it was curious, and once you became a curiosity, it was hard to shrug off that mantle.

Hell, I was fairly certain a portion of my customers still only came to the truck to see if they could glean any new information from my existence.

Forcing my mind back to the topic of Theo's tragic past, I grimaced. "Sorry I asked."

"Don't be sorry. It sucks, but it does bode well for a fling."

I rolled my eyes. "Why is that? Trauma bonding?"

"No," she protested, laughing. "From what I've gathered, Theo swore off love after that—he dates, but he always ends things before he gets too deep."

"He must have really loved her," I mused.

What a tragedy. No wonder he'd left town.

I had met Alex on occasion, both when he was visiting their parents and around town, but I'd never really interacted with him for more than a brief greeting or impersonal small talk. He wasn't quite as tall or broad as Theo, though his good looks were smoother, more classic. I wasn't sure if my view of him was based on anything more than my own history, though. Alex didn't exactly remind me of Steve, but he possessed a similar easy sort of charm that made me have to force myself not to recoil when he was nearby, at least in the early months after Steve's death.

I blinked, realizing that while I wasn't necessarily relaxed around Theo, I didn't experience anything like that when he was close to me. Maybe his tendency to blurt out such naked truths reassured me with his very awkwardness.

Or maybe my intuition had recovered from those years with Steve. Maybe I was finally able to see true good in someone again, to sense whatever was below the surface.

It was a moment before I realized Sofia was staring at me, waiting for a reply.

"Sorry," I murmured. "What did you say?"

She grinned. "Oh, nothing important. I just wondered if you'll have the food truck at the tree lighting at Town Park?"

"Yes, and thc Carolcade."

If Sofia's brilliant smile was anything to go by, that was exactly what she wanted to hear. "Awesome. If you change your mind about Thanksgiving, let me know. I've got to run, but seriously, thank you for meeting me today. I've missed you, honey."

"I missed you too," I said quietly as she waved and left the cafe.

THE NEXT DAY, I finished boxing up an order of cupcakes for the elementary school's "Welcome Winter" concert reception and set them on the counter to run over to the school that afternoon.

With rising rates of food allergies, school events and birthday parties had become the staples of my winter orders. Happy as I was that kids with allergies wouldn't feel left out of their school celebrations, I was even more glad that I wouldn't have to stick around to witness the chaos of first graders on a sugar high. My job was done once the cupcakes were handed off to the music teacher, and then it would be their parents' job to deal with them.

No matter how hard I tried to focus on the work in front of me, my mind kept drifting back to everything Sofia had told me about Theo.

Part of me wanted to read the entire story for myself, but I managed not to search the internet for that sad moment in history. Now that I knew him, it felt like an invasion of privacy to look him up. Everyone in Spruce Hill knew so many details about my own life—I couldn't quite bear to be another nosy element in his.

So instead of researching ancient history, I grabbed a spoonful of the leftover peppermint frosting.

After years of critical remarks from Steve about my figure, comments that started out subtle until he'd eventually given up even the façade of civility when we were in private, I still found a deep-rooted satisfaction in eating whatever I pleased. I'd learned quickly that sampling my products too frequently made me grow sick of even the sweet smell of frosting, but I made sure to enjoy my favorites when I felt like it—and peppermint was a favorite of mine.

These past few years had finally allowed me the freedom to appreciate my curves, a freedom that I wished had come sooner. Between my sister telling me when I was eleven that I'd clearly been switched at birth, given how my rounded cheeks and sturdy body compared to my mother's and sister's willowy figures, and Steve's snide criticisms about what I was eating, my comfort within my own skin had been a battle.

Just before I plopped down on the couch to savor it, my cell phone rang.

Awkwardly juggling the spoon in one hand and the phone in the other, I answered. "Hello?"

I used my personal number for business purposes, which was probably stupid but it kept me organized. Unfortunately, it meant I couldn't act on my instinct to avoid spam calls and had to answer unknown numbers.

For a moment, there was silence, then a deep sigh and a click as the line went dead.

"Dammit," I muttered, tossing the phone onto the couch before curling up in one corner with my frosting.

I had just tossed the spoon into the sink when I heard Theo's pickup pull into the driveway.

For a heartbeat, I froze there in the kitchen, wondering if I should wait until he was inside the house before loading up my boxes. Then, with a swift shake of my head, I forced myself not to be such a coward. I wasn't the frightened, downtrodden wretch Steve had tried to crush me into. I was a successful business woman making her own way in the world.

I straightened my shoulders and propped the door open before carrying the first of the boxes out toward the food truck.

Should've waited, I thought when I saw Theo grinning at the side of the truck.

He snapped to attention when he realized I was walking down the driveway with my arms full. "Please, let me help," he called.

I nodded my head toward the door at the back of the truck. "If you could open the doors there, that'd be great, thanks."

"My pleasure. Is there more to come out?" He peered curiously into the truck while I secured the boxes.

"Yes, a few more trips probably."

As I went to hop back onto the driveway, he held out his hand to help me down. It was probably just a polite gesture, but the heat of his palm hit me like a bolt of electricity when I laid my hand in his. I blinked at him in the watery November sunlight, hoping I didn't look as startled as I felt. He exhaled sharply and released my hand as soon as my feet hit the concrete.

"I'll help carry them for you."

I nodded, grateful he didn't comment on my reaction to his touch, and led the way back into the guest house to load his arms with boxes.

If I might, perhaps, have noticed the sculpted bulge of his biceps under his long-sleeved gray henley, well, surely that could be excused. It was important that I knew he could handle the weight of six dozen cupcakes.

With his assistance, I had the cupcakes stashed and ready to go in half the time it would've taken me alone. Whether because I had time to spare, because I wanted to thank him for his help, or because I wanted those extra few minutes in his presence, I didn't know, but after I closed the door of the truck, I said, "There were a couple of leftovers, if you want to try one."

His eyes widened slightly, but he nodded so eagerly that I was able to clearly imagine him as one of the first-graders who'd soon be enjoying the bounty I'd made.

"Hell yeah, I'd love to. I mean, if you have enough."

I snorted and headed back into the guest house. "I can only eat so much peppermint buttercream myself, so you're saving me from throwing them out. Usually I pass off extras to your parents."

"My dad must love you," Theo said as I handed him a cupcake on a pretty little plate I'd found at a thrift store. "Mom's an amazing cook, but not such a stellar baker. Do *not* tell her I said that."

"My lips are sealed," I replied.

I decided to join him and was just putting another cupcake on a plate when I heard him groan with pleasure. It sounded so deeply sexual that muscles I'd forgotten all about clenched in response. When I looked at him, his eyes were closed in an expression of pure bliss.

"Oh, Esther," he growled, licking a dot of frosting from the corner of his mouth. "Marry me."

Even though I knew he was joking and rolled my eyes accordingly, I couldn't deny the swift kick in my pulse at the words. "I could be a serial killer, Theo."

Something about the comment had his eyes opening, their dark amber depths studying my face intently. To cover my discomfiture, I bit into my cupcake and kept my attention on the plate in front of me. I had just swallowed when realization struck.

"You've been back here for less than a week and already heard the rumor that I killed my husband."

To his credit, his cheeks grew pink along the edges of his dark beard. "I didn't believe them, if it's any consolation."

It wasn't. I scowled and muttered, "Only because you didn't know him."

For a moment, he went perfectly still and his lips parted, then he grinned as he shook his head. "No, I don't buy it. Maybe in self-defense, but I can't see you as a cold-blooded killer."

"You barely know me," I protested, then wondered why the hell I was offended by not looking like a murderer.

Theo must have interpreted my disgruntled expression correctly, because now he laughed. "I promise, Esther, I definitely believe you could commit murder if you put your mind to it. Especially if you hid poison in one of these tasty little fellas," he said, popping the remainder of his cupcake into his mouth. "But what a way to go."

I huffed a laugh. "You're kind of a weirdo."

"Takes one to know one," he retorted with a wink, then asked, "Do you need help taking those over to the school? It's a lot to unload on your own."

This...this was dangerous territory. I *liked* this guy. He was as attractive as Anita had not-so-subtly promised, he was funny and quirky, and underneath it all, I still sensed the thread of connection that made me want to confess all my deepest secrets to him.

I wouldn't, of course, but the urge was strong, especially when those golden-brown eyes twinkled at me like he knew exactly what I was thinking.

Before I could stop myself, I nodded. "Sure, if you really have nothing better to do."

Chapter Five

THEO

I'D EXPECTED A SWIFT—BUT polite—rejection, so I smiled at Esther like a total fool for a solid minute before I finally managed to say, "Right, great."

Get yourself together!

She raised her brows but said nothing further, not even to tell me I was being weirder than usual. As she locked the guest house behind us and led the way back to the food truck, I wondered what the hell it was about Spruce Hill that brought out my every idiosyncrasy. Down in Asheville, I was calm and collected, polite and professional. People knew me as a reliable guy, prepared for any situation.

Here? I felt like I'd been transported right back to high school, especially when I was around this dark-haired beauty living on my parents' property.

The only thing keeping me from banging my forehead against the side of the truck was the glitter of amusement in her eyes, the tiny dimple that peeped out at me even when she pursed her lips to keep from smiling.

"This is really nice," I said, hoping to cover up my awkwardness once I was in the passenger seat.

Esther grimaced. "It's like driving a big tin box, but it gets the job done. It sucks in the snow. Then again, so does my little sedan."

"I have a hybrid down south and only use the pickup for work stuff, but with the timing of this trip, I figured it might do better in the snow up here." I tapped my fingers on my knee, wondering where the line between curious and nosy might fall. "You didn't grow up in Spruce Hill, right?"

"No, Oakville."

It wasn't effusive, but it was an answer. "Not too far away, then. Is your family there?"

She hesitated, then said, "My parents still live there. My sister moved to Phoenix several years ago."

"Will you be spending Christmas with them?" I asked, hoping the question sounded casual.

From Esther's lips came a sound somewhere between a scoff and a snort. I glanced over and saw her shaking her head.

"No. My parents and I aren't really on speaking terms."

"I'm sorry," I said quietly.

"Don't be." As we pulled into the elementary school parking lot, nearly empty an hour after dismissal, she parked by the doors to the gymnasium and gave me a small, tight smile. "We just need to hand these off to Mrs. Meyers and then I'll get you back to whatever it is you do all day."

It was my turn to scoff. "There's only so much television I can handle, the house has been cleaned top to bottom, and I'm pretty sure Toni hates me."

"Now, I'm sure that's not true," she said, her smile widening. "Don't all pets love the person who feeds them?"

"Not this one. She jumped out from under the bed and bit my ankle when I walked by her this morning. I think maybe she's possessed."

A choked laugh escaped her lips as she hopped down from the driver's seat. When we both rounded the back of the truck, she was grinning. "That cat is just particular, that's all. She attacks your dad all the time, if it makes you feel any better."

"Somehow, that doesn't soothe the flesh wounds she left," I grumbled, but I considered this progress and wanted to keep her talking. "Maybe she just hates devastatingly attractive men."

Esther's response could only be called a guffaw. Maybe a chortle. Either way, it lit her features like a chandelier, brightening her eyes as the corners creased and her lips curved until that dimple was as deep as I'd ever seen it. My heart tripped at the sight, even when she plopped a box of cupcakes into my waiting arms.

"Yup. That must be it," she agreed, grabbing a box of her own and tipping her head toward the gymnasium doors.

I followed obediently behind her, attempting to ignore the sway of her hips for a total of fifteen seconds before I gave in. She looked sweet and cozy today in leggings and a slouchy sweater that slipped off one golden shoulder. Her hair was pulled up into a bun like it had been when I stopped at the food truck on my way into town, exposing the long line of her neck. Little ankle boots with fuzzy trim completed the outfit.

During the minute it took for us to reach the doors Mrs. Meyers had propped open, I'd envisioned an entire scene featuring Esther sprawled in front of a fire, her hair falling in loose waves around that enticingly bare shoulder.

By the time we entered the gym, I had *almost* convinced myself getting involved with her wasn't the worst idea I'd ever had.

Then, as we stepped inside, I was transported back to my childhood. The paper decorations might've been updated over the intervening decades, but the smell of pine floors, rubber kickballs, and youthful excitement was the same. When Mrs. Meyers strode into the room with an armful of disposable tablecloth packages, I felt all of seven years old again.

"Surely these old eyes deceive me!" she exclaimed.

I felt Esther's curious gaze on the side of my face and forced myself to smile at the woman who'd taught me to play Hot Cross Buns on a recorder thirty years ago, much to my mother's dismay.

"Hey, Mrs. M."

With a grandmotherly tut, she said, "You must be old enough by now to call me Cheryl. How sweet of you to help Esther with all these cupcakes! This table over here is for the desserts, if you don't mind, dears."

Though Esther murmured politely, it didn't escape my notice that she barely spoke a word as we brought in the cupcakes. Granted, she wasn't the most outgoing woman I'd met, but it seemed strange to see her even quieter than usual. I wondered if she was simply shy, until I caught Mrs. Meyers laying a gentle hand on Esther's shoulder.

"You should get back out there, darling. It's been long enough," the older woman said kindly.

The lips I'd spent far too much time thinking about since meeting Esther tightened into what I supposed might pass as a smile if I didn't already know what her real smile looked like, and she replied, "I appreciate your concern, Mrs. Meyers."

Apparently, my former teacher knew better than to continue pressing. She just patted Esther's shoulder and sent me a commiserating kind of look. Without another word, I followed Esther out of the gym after giving Mrs. Meyers a brief wave.

Silence had never been my thing.

"Is it always like that?" I asked, frowning at Esther's strained expression.

"Like what?" she shot back, voice tight. "Like everyone in town thinks they're my personal dating cheerleader?"

"Yeah, that."

To my surprise, she huffed a laugh. "Are you always this direct?"

"Yes," I said simply, shrugging. "Look, there are things I don't particularly want to talk about, so I'd be the worst kind of hypocrite to not respect that you probably feel the same about certain topics. You don't have to tell me anything you don't want to. I just...Christ. There are some aspects of Spruce Hill I managed to forget, and I guess the 'nose in everyone's business' thing was one of them."

She sighed, dropping her head against the seatback, then rolled it so she was looking at me. "I wouldn't think that's something you could forget."

"You're right." I scrubbed my hands over my face. "Maybe I just forgot what it was like to see it in action from the outside. It's one thing to know people are probably whispering about you—hell, I'm sure there's been plenty of that going on since I showed back up—but watching it is brutal."

"If it makes you feel better, I haven't heard any whispers about you." She pursed her lips thoughtfully. "Then again, I don't talk to many people unless it's work-related."

"Rumors are one thing. Well-meaning neighbors acting like it's their job to guide you, that's what gets me. It's none of their business if you don't want to date."

"Why do you think I'm such a hermit?" she joked weakly.

For a moment, I had to wrestle down the urge to reach over and touch her cheek. Everything about her screamed of exhaustion, and not the physical kind. Whatever the reality of

Esther's marriage had been, whatever the truth about Steve's death, the realization that more than a few residents of Spruce Hill felt responsible for shoving Esther back out into the world before she was ready just gutted me.

"I'm sorry, Esther. That sucks."

Her forehead wrinkled in confusion. "It's certainly not your fault."

"No, but I feel responsible somehow. I should have told her to back the hell off."

At that, she simply laughed, seafoam eyes alight. It was one of those sudden bursts of pure joy that hit me like a fist to the gut and warmed something deep in my chest. I wanted to see it more often, to make her howl with laughter, to watch her glow with it.

"Will you have dinner with me again?" I asked softly, hoping she wouldn't shoot me down in the way I probably deserved. It was beyond low to take advantage of her in a moment like this.

And yet…she didn't shoot me down at all. I bit back a victorious grin when she rolled her eyes and said, "Fine, but you're cooking. Real food, not some frozen casserole your mother left for you. I'll provide supervision and allergy assistance only."

"Yes, ma'am. I am at your service."

As she shifted the truck into gear, I let the grin spread across my face until my cheeks hurt with it.

Maybe I'd have the chance to soak up more of her laughter, after all.

Chapter Six

ESTHER

I WAS ANNOYED THEO overheard that little exchange with Mrs. Meyers, but I hadn't anticipated his apparent guilt over not defending me, nor had I prepared myself enough to politely decline a dinner invitation. Most people reacted to pity with more pity, or else with explanations and excuses for any unintended rudeness they witnessed. Theo responded with self-deprecation and humor.

It was a certain brand of kindness, I knew, but the man never quite did what I expected him to do.

Stranger yet was the realization that most people in this town knew all about his past, too. Maybe leaving town had served to actually quell the rumors—Sofia said he didn't date, but how would anyone else in Spruce Hill know that?

Not for the first time, I wondered at his mother's comments in the days leading up to her departure. Even after nearly four years of living in the guest house, I could count on one hand the number of times Anita had made *any* reference to my social life. She seemed to understand in a way no one else did that my soul still bore invisible scars needing time—and solitude—to heal.

Then, out of nowhere, she started dropping casual mentions of her handsome firstborn son's imminent return to Spruce Hill. These little hints started off subtle, but somewhere along the way, they became a bit too flattering to be simply informative. There wasn't a coy bone in Anita's body, something we had in common, which meant her efforts to extoll Theo's virtues were glaringly blatant.

When I pulled into the driveway and shifted into park, I felt Theo's amused gaze on the side of my face. I rolled my eyes and asked, "What are you staring at?"

He only grinned. "You looked very deep in thought during our seven minute commute home. Dare I ask what had your mind so occupied?"

"Your mother's meddling," I replied.

"Ah, yes," he mused. "She's something, isn't she? I thought the pot pie was a bit heavy-handed for her. What else did I miss?"

I sighed and turned off the engine. "Oh, just her telling me how handsome and intelligent and single her eldest son is. I swear she knew exactly what she was doing, too, because she'd drop one compliment and then change the subject, so I could never be sure if she was actually trying to make a point about you or if she was just excited about you coming back here."

"Oh, no, please tell me she didn't," he groaned, covering his face with both hands.

Embarrassing him hadn't been my intent, but it didn't seem unfair either, exactly. After all, he'd witnessed my awkward moment in the gym. I decided to roll with it.

"Come on, surely you can't blame her for bragging, not with such a stud muffin for a son."

He choked out a laugh, but his eyes were aglow with mischief when he dropped his hands. I imagined he must have gotten into a great deal of trouble as a child.

And out of it, most likely, with that cheeky grin of his.

"I refuse to believe my mother used the term 'stud muffin,' but if that's how you see me, I'm not going to argue."

"Touché," I conceded. "I guess you're not half bad."

"You know what I'm even more curious about, though?" When I raised a brow in his direction, he said, "I feel like she went out of her way to avoid giving me any details about you. Granted, my assumption that you were an old lady was my own, but it's like she made it a point not to mention your age or occupation or the fact that you're drop-dead gorgeous. Why would she only play matchmaker on one side?"

My cheeks flooded with heat at the casual compliment, spoken as though everyone in Spruce Hill agreed with his assessment. I'd heard them at each stupid event Steve had dragged me to, the people who congratulated Steve on seeing past my looks in order to find the good inside. As the years went on, I recognized more and more of how he'd manipulated me into thinking I was lucky to have him.

Theo was waiting patiently for me to respond. I stared at him for another second, then gave myself a mental shake.

"I don't know. She's *your* mother, why don't you take a guess?"

"I'm not sure, but I'll be thinking about it, believe me. I don't like feeling like a puppet."

I scowled. "You think I do?"

Across his face bloomed a smile so sweet my chest ached with it. "No, Esther, but between the two of us, we'll solve this mystery. Come on, then, let's get cooking."

"You're cooking, I'm supervising, remember?"

His low chuckle roused a thousand butterflies in my midsection. I had to force the reaction down as we headed into the main house, considering the situation instead. Even if I weren't personally involved, Anita was the last person on Earth I'd expect to play matchmaker.

Given what she knew about my life? It seemed even less likely.

Unless...I stopped so suddenly that Theo ran right into me, his entire front pressed into my back as he caught my hips so I didn't pitch forward with the impact. The heat of his body radiated against me, soaking into my limbs.

"What is it?" he asked, sounding slightly panicked.

I turned slowly toward him as I mulled over the idea that had occurred to me. "What if she wasn't trying to tempt me with that information, but to warn me?"

"Warn you against my numerous charms?"

He sounded doubtful, and I couldn't really blame him. The more I thought about it, though, the more sense it made.

"I don't date, Theo. I barely socialize. My late husband was a charming narcissist who had everyone in town fooled except for me, because I lived with him, and your mother, because she's ridiculously insightful. She was probably the only person in Spruce Hill he couldn't win over. He hated her for that."

Theo's dark brows drew down. "And if you weren't expecting my devastating good looks, would my presence have upset you?"

I rolled my eyes at the description, however accurate, then decided I owed him honesty since I'd brought it up. "Yes."

"Esther," he began, still looking troubled. "I'm not like him, I hope you know that."

"If I didn't know that, I would have slammed the door in your face the first time you invited me to dinner," I said sharply.

Maybe I wasn't fully convinced I could trust my gut yet after everything Steve had done to make me feel like my reality was warped to hell, but I'd done enough work in therapy to finally rely on my instincts again.

Theo Silver was as different from Steve as night and day. That much I didn't doubt for a second.

The smile that flashed across his bearded face looked both pleased and relieved, like he realized me snapping at him meant I wasn't as fragile as he feared. I would've been annoyed if his concern didn't kindle a ball of warmth in my belly. After our collision, he hadn't stepped away, so we were still standing almost uncomfortably close.

At least, it would have been uncomfortable had he been anyone other than himself. I didn't want to explore that too carefully just yet.

"Why wouldn't she have told me anything about you, do you think?" he asked.

I shook my head slowly. "I'm not sure about that part."

Still barely half a foot away, Theo swept his amber gaze over my features, from my hairline to my chin. He paused ever so slightly at my lips, then lifted his eyes to mine once more. "Because if she'd told me you were young, beautiful, and clearly quite able-bodied, I might not have let her talk me into coming. By letting me believe you were a little old lady who needed some degree of help, refusing to come up here would've made me into the asshole."

I snorted. "Are you saying Dr. Anita Vasquez-Silver is the asshole here, Theo?"

"No," he protested quickly, lips twitching. "However, she's a mastermind when it comes to playing the long game, and she's spent almost two decades trying to get me to come back into town. I wouldn't put it past her to use whatever weapons she could in order to get me here."

The ball of warmth was spreading upward the longer I spent at this proximity, so I drew a breath and turned to lead us both into the kitchen. "Well, mastermind or not, we're grownups who can handle ourselves, right?" I asked as I sat down at the table.

"We are, indeed," he agreed. "We'll save the mystery for another day. Now, it's time for you to give me a crash course on food allergies so we can get dinner going. I'm famished after all that heavy lifting."

Chapter Seven

THEO

ESTHER WAS AN EXCELLENT instructor, patient and concise. She had a sharp sense of humor that seemed to come out of nowhere, flashes of dry wit that kept me laughing all through the process. I still wasn't happy about the idea that my mother had tried to warn her away from me, but given that she'd done so by complimenting me, I wasn't completely sure I could complain.

Of course, I also believed that if my mother thought Esther would view me as any kind of threat, she would have drilled into me that I was to behave like a perfect gentleman. That was more her style.

And if I couldn't deny the sizzle of attraction when Esther and I were standing so close together? Well, part of me wondered if my mother had foreseen that, as well.

By the time we finished making the pasta primavera—which I assumed she chose in order to go easy on me—Esther had probably said more than I'd heard out of her in our previous encounters altogether. I thought at first that she was nervous, chattering to fill the silence, but it didn't come across that way.

It seemed more like she'd finally deemed me safe enough to trust with her social energy.

"Is it a pain in the ass for you to eat at restaurants?" I asked, frowning as I realized just how much the allergies must impact her life.

Esther shrugged. "It can be. Certain places are better than others. The benefit to such a small town is that people know me and once I find somewhere that's willing to work with me, they get to know the drill."

"What about dating?"

"Like I said, I...don't really date," she said slowly, "but yes, it can complicate things. My first kiss wasn't until college, because I was so worried about making sure whoever I was with hadn't eaten anything with nuts recently."

I frowned at that. "Are partners really not willing to forgo nuts for your safety? Seems like an easy choice."

Esther stared at me for a second before saying, "Thanks, I think?"

As I finished serving up our dinner, I made a mental note to be sure I stopped consuming anything with nuts. Whether it proved necessary or not, I didn't want to do anything that might put her at risk. It seemed like such a small change for me, but it could make a world of difference for her.

Or maybe even *us*.

The thought came out of nowhere, along with the desire to kiss her now that the topic had been raised, but it settled over my chest like a weighted blanket, soothing something deep in my soul. My presence here might be temporary, but that didn't mean Esther wasn't interested in temporary, too.

Still, I'd let it simmer, see how things unfolded between us.

"You said you'll have the truck at the tree lighting the weekend after Thanksgiving?" I asked as I set a plate of food in front of her.

She nodded. "It's one of the few gatherings I actually enjoy, so I'll be open for a couple hours at the start, close up so I can go see them light up the tree, then I usually sell for another hour or until I'm out of cupcakes."

"Do you have any help? Like a sidekick or an assistant or something?"

"Do I have...a sidekick?" she repeated, blinking at me for a beat before her laughter floated around me. "Sadly, no. This might surprise you, but I don't mind working alone."

I was too distracted by the dimple in her cheek and the mischief in her eyes to feign shock, but I snorted. "No way."

"Way. Why, you wanna be The Nutless Wonder's sidekick?"

It was an odd invitation, sure, but it was clearly an invitation nonetheless. I wasn't going to let the opportunity pass. "Absolutely, I do, if you'll accept my help."

"I could be convinced," she said, smirking.

"If you're the Queen of Sweets, what would my name be?"

Her grin turned sly. "That is an excellent question. Eclair? King Cake? Oh, I've got it. Long John!"

"Esther," I gasped, leaning toward her, "was that a dick joke?"

"No, of course not!" A blush crept along her cheekbones despite the denial. "A Long John is a type of donut, you perv."

I continued to stare at her until she dissolved into giggles. The sound did something strange to my chest, flooding me with a giddy kind of pleasure. It wasn't her usual sweet, husky laugh, but something light and carefree, fizzing in the air like champagne bubbles. I wanted to bask in it. At that moment, she looked younger, the way I imagined she must've looked before meeting Steve Pautler.

Maybe this was the Esther my mother had first known, the one she'd taken under her wing.

When she managed to get herself back under control, wiping at the corners of her eyes, I was still grinning like a fool. And staring at her, a fact which had slipped my mind until her eyes widened slightly.

"I like hearing you laugh," I said before I could think better of it.

Another faint wash of rose crept along her cheekbones, but she didn't look away when our eyes met. Even if the feeling of triumph I experienced was unwarranted, that didn't make it any less sweet. The sparkle of humor in those minty depths faded into something warm and a little bit rueful.

"It feels good to laugh again. I'm a little rusty, I think."

"Well," I said softly, "cool sidekick name or not, I'd be happy to help you out at the tree lighting. I worked in restaurants all through college."

She hesitated only a second before nodding. "If you're sure it's not asking too much, I would appreciate the help."

"I have basically nothing to do around here, Esther. I'm not used to sitting on my ass so much. The Lawn Ranger's books have never been so up to date, since that's about all I can do from a distance. Can't say I'd be much good at baking, but I can definitely ring up customers and hand over your delightful cupcakes to adoring fans. And I'd do just about anything for more of those cookies."

"I recently perfected a new brownie recipe that's nice and gooey without being oily. I'm making one last test batch tomorrow. If you behave yourself, maybe you'll get to try one."

My lips twitched and I tried, I really tried, to ignore the way her gaze dipped to my mouth. "Then I'll just have to be very, very good, won't I?"

If I wasn't mistaken, her blush deepened as she turned her attention to her meal, and I was forced to do the same before she caught me staring at her.

Again.

To my surprise, the quiet that settled over us wasn't uncomfortable in the least. It felt like Esther had simply used up her current allotment of chitchat and laughter, leaving her in need of time to recharge. I'd always considered myself fairly outgoing, but for once, I didn't mind the silent camaraderie, either.

As we had before, Esther and I rinsed and loaded the dishes together. While she was pulling her boots on, her phone chirped from a hidden pocket in the waistband of her leggings. My eyebrows lifted as she tugged it free and then grimaced.

"Bad news?" I asked.

Esther shook her head. "No, but Sofia wants me to meet the group of them at The Mermaid tomorrow night for dinner."

Before I could respond, my own phone vibrated and I glanced down to see the same invitation. "Guess I'm invited too."

"Lucky you."

I tapped the edge of the phone thoughtfully against my chin as an idea took root. "We could go together," I mused.

"Together," she repeated. "You want to carpool?"

My lips twitched. "That's not exactly what I meant."

"Like...a date?"

"A fake date."

"Remember how I said I don't date? Sofia will never buy it."

Esther's expression was skeptical, but she hadn't dismissed the idea out of hand. The more I considered, the better the prospect sounded. She was skittish, but it would give us the chance to get to know one another without pressure.

And it would give me the opportunity to see if she was open to more while I was in town.

"Think about it. You and I make occasional appearances together in a social setting. I'll help you in the truck for your events. People in Spruce Hill start to make assumptions, and voilà—a perfect excuse for us both to avoid the inevitable invitations to various holiday dinners."

"I usually just say no thank you," she said dryly.

"That can't be foolproof, right? Especially knowing the Jimenez family. They don't ask half a dozen times, in different ways, hoping you'll change your mind?"

Tipping her head to one side, she conceded, "Okay, true."

"I'm only here until the end of the year, but that's more than enough time to get us past the holidays. It's perfect."

She still looked unconvinced. "Perfect. Except then you'll be headed back to North Carolina and I'll be stuck here fielding questions from every resident in town about what went wrong. What *I* did wrong, because you know they'll blame me instead of Spruce Hill's prodigal son."

That bugged me in more ways than one, the thought that people would assume she did something wrong instead of me, but I was increasingly convinced this would work.

"You can tell them whatever you want," I said, my tone bordering on cajoling. "I'll be the asshole. Tell one person that I had a rabid scabies infection and you sent my ass packing, and I assure you the entire town will know soon enough."

With a choked laugh, she nodded. "It might work."

"Okay, maybe the plan's not *perfect*, but admit it, it's not half bad. I saw how Mrs. Meyers was, and we're only getting closer to Thanksgiving. Eventually, someone's going to try to set you up with their cousin's nephew's stepbrother. Don't tell me nobody else in town tries to convince you to join them for a holiday meal?"

"Only your parents," she muttered, then added reluctantly, "And Sofia. Everyone else tends to hint at it instead of asking outright."

I gave her my most convincing smile. "Just think about it, okay? If we spend the holidays together, we can turn down everybody else."

For a moment, I thought she was going to tell me to go straight to hell, but then she nodded. "Fine. But there will be rules."

Shock rocketed through me—no matter how confidently I'd pitched the idea, I didn't expect her to agree. Fuck, I hadn't been this excited about anything in a long time. A smile split my face as I nodded like a fool.

"Rules, yes. Anything you say. You're the boss."

"No Christmas gifts," she said, frowning like I'd argue.

I inclined my head graciously. "No gifts. What else?"

"We only attend social occasions of my choosing," she added. "I haven't done a whole lot of socializing in recent years and I don't know how much I can handle."

"Esther, I hope it goes without saying that I have no desire to make you uncomfortable in any way. You absolutely get final say on anything we agree to go to."

She sucked in a breath. "I don't want to discuss my marriage."

"I'd rather not talk about why I left town," I countered. "I'm happy to shut down anyone who tries to bring up either topic, okay?"

"Okay." The word was quiet, but firm.

"Any other stipulations?"

"I'm a terrible liar, Theo. If someone asks straight out if we're really dating, I'm going to have a hard time with it."

"Then you can put your air of quiet mystery to good use, and I'll field as many inquiries as I can," I said, relieved when she snorted a laugh.

"And when your parents hear about it? Because you know they will."

"I'll tell them that my mother's 'warnings' piqued your interest and you asked for a low-commitment, scorching hot fling with an expiration date."

Esther rolled her eyes, but she couldn't hide that dimple. "Lovely."

"It'll be good, Esther. For both of us."

"And just how touchy-feely are you expecting us to be in front of people in order to sell this charade?"

I hesitated, partly because I wasn't sure what answer she wanted to hear and partly because there was a flare of challenge in her eyes that made me want to throw caution to the wind. It took a second for me to control the urge to tell her I wanted everything she would give me.

"Whatever you're comfortable with," I replied, keeping my tone soft.

She dropped her gaze to the phone in her hands for a long moment, then those pale eyes lifted to meet mine. Her dimple winked at me as she held out a hand to shake on it.

"Okay, Long John. I'm in."

Chapter Eight

ESTHER

I T WAS A BAD idea. I knew that even as I agreed to it, especially with Sofia's suggestion echoing in my mind, but he was right—there *were* some advantages to be had. I just hoped they'd outweigh any possible repercussions.

If the radiant smile on his face was anything to go by, Theo didn't share my reservations.

As we reached the door, he followed me out onto the driveway. "I'll walk you home," he said when I shot him a curious look.

"You know, it's only twenty yards from your door to mine," I pointed out.

He only hummed a little, the sound vibrating into the night air between us. I tried to hide the shiver that trembled up my spine, but he slanted a glance in my direction as we walked through the dark toward the guest house.

"So, I guess I'll tell Sofia we'll be there tomorrow?"

"Only if you're okay with it, Esther." He sounded so serious that I stopped walking to turn toward him. "I know I can be a little overenthusiastic at times, but seriously, if you don't want to do this, I understand. I didn't mean to pressure you into agreeing."

I scowled at him. "Look, I said yes, and I meant it. If you're going to second-guess me every ten seconds, fake dating isn't going to work because I'll be forced to fake break up with you or for real kick your ass."

Theo's startled laugh broke through the tension that had formed between us. His broad shoulders relaxed as his lips curved into a sheepish smile. "Sorry, sorry. I promise I will trust you to be honest with me about what you want and what you can handle."

"Good," I said, struggling to maintain my grumpy expression. He looked so earnest that I gave up after a few seconds. "Then I guess you'll be a decent fake boyfriend."

When we reached the door, Theo slipped his hands into his pockets. "It'll be good for us both, Esther. I'm sure of it. And if anything goes haywire, you can punch me in the nuts."

Choked laughter burst past my lips. "With that kind of guarantee, what could possibly go wrong?"

Under the light of the two lamps on either side of my front door, Theo's hair shimmered with golden highlights. Nothing

Anita had told me about him could have prepared me for the reality that was Theo. It wasn't his handsome face. It wasn't even that deep, honey smooth voice. There was something so inherently *good* inside him, something so reassuring. I hadn't known him long enough to trust him, not really, and yet...I wanted to.

"Let me know the details for tomorrow. I'll drive, if you're comfortable with that," he said after a minute, still smiling faintly.

I let myself enjoy the simple pleasure of it for another second, then nodded. "Give me your phone, I'll add my number."

Theo's eyes brightened even further as he dug it out of his pocket and handed it over. I didn't let myself think too hard about what that meant. When I passed it back, those long fingers brushed over mine, sending another shiver up my spine. Even in the chilly evening air, his hands were warm.

I fought the urge to grip that rough palm with my own, to let his warmth envelop me against the cold, and forced myself to push the door open instead. "Thank you for your help today, and for dinner."

"You're very welcome. I'll see you tomorrow."

With a nod, I closed the door behind me, but I couldn't stop myself from leaning back against it as I tried to slow my whirling thoughts. Then, silently, I turned around and peeked through the peephole.

Theo had started turning as though to walk back to the main house, his hands tucked into his pockets again, but his head was tilted back as he gazed up at the night sky. Though his features were somewhat distorted by the tiny bubble of glass, his expression appeared utterly serene, almost blissful.

For longer than I cared to admit, I watched him with one eye, trying to soak up some of the peace he exuded. After he finally lowered his head, shook himself loose from whatever reverie he'd been lost in, and headed toward his parents' house, I took a single step away from the door, then another.

"He's only a man," I whispered.

It wasn't as fantastic a reassurance as I might have hoped.

HALF A DOZEN TIMES during the following day, I considered backing out of dinner with Sofia's crew. My stomach had tied itself into knots so tight I thought I might vomit. By mid-afternoon, I was on the verge of hyperventilating.

My phone rang twice as I got dressed, each time from an unlisted number, but both calls ended without a word on the other end.

Before Theo arrived at half past five, I'd stress-baked two separate batches of brownies, frosted a dozen of my favorite Mississippi Mud cupcakes, and downed several antacids in an attempt to settle my stomach. The guest house smelled amazing and I couldn't even appreciate it in my current state of agitation.

Theo, however, looked like he was ready to propose marriage again when I opened the door for him.

"Sweet mother of Christ, what is that heavenly aroma?" he asked, closing his eyes on a deep inhalation. When he opened them, the radiant smile on his face slowly untangled the tension in my gut.

"Dessert," I answered, taking the time to look him over.

Instead of his usual lumberjack chic, he wore dark pants and a gray dress shirt. His hair was still damp from a shower, curling around his collar, and I was fairly certain he'd trimmed his beard. I wondered if it was as silky as it looked.

"You look stunning, Esther."

I flushed. "Thank you. You clean up pretty well yourself."

Despite the frequent college outings Sofia dragged me to, eyes had always been drawn to her, not me. Even Steve had expressed his interest with restraint—after all, it wasn't my body he wanted, but someone to subjugate. I wasn't used to being scoped out or ogled.

Theo's slow, appreciative perusal knocked the breath clear out of my lungs.

I'd chosen a black dress that flared from the waist to swish just above my knees, black tights, and low-heeled ankle boots. The dress had long sleeves but a plunging neckline that revealed far more skin than anything else in my closet. Theo didn't let his gaze linger, though, just lifted it back to my face and smiled warmly. I grabbed my coat from the hook by the door in a frantic attempt to keep from babbling.

"Ready?" he asked, offering his arm.

I nodded and slipped my hand through the crook of his elbow. "Ready as I'll ever be."

The temperature had been steadily dropping and the air smelled like that first frigid whiff of snow. I drew a deep breath, savoring the pristine newness of it, and Theo shot me an amused glance. In response, I shrugged and watched my breath crystallize in the night.

"I like the cold, is that a crime?"

Theo tilted his head back and forth, like he was considering it. "No, I just didn't realize you were such a weirdo."

I sputtered indignantly. "I am not a weirdo!"

He winked at me as he opened the passenger door of his pickup. "I suppose you'll just have to prove it, Esther."

"Hmph." I bit back a smile when he climbed into the driver's seat. "Remind me again why we're doing this?"

One hand froze on the gear shift as he turned to look at me, his eyes glittering black in the darkness. I might appreciate certain aspects of winter, but the early sunsets were not among them. Theo seemed to be searching my expression for something.

"It's not too late to change your mind," he said finally. When I opened my mouth to reiterate my threat from the previous evening, he held up his hand to stop me. "I trust you to know what you want, Esther, but I'd hate for you to feel like you should do this just because logic says it will work in our favor. We can show up as friends or neighbors or whatever makes you more comfortable, and I'll tell them all to back the hell off. I just want you to know I've got your back, however you want to proceed."

It shouldn't have surprised me that a man raised by Anita and Lou would be as kind and perceptive as he was attractive. I nodded slowly as I let that observation sink in.

"Okay. I think we should stick to the plan."

A slow smile curved his lips and, before I could react, he lifted his fingers to brush lightly over my cheek. My skin heated under his fingertips and my brain stalled as I met his gaze. There was nothing about him that reminded me of Steve. Hell, there was nothing unsettling about him in the least, aside from the unexpected warmth I felt pooling in my belly when he looked at me with that faint smile tugging at his lips.

For the first time in a long time, I *wanted.*

I stared at him in shocked silence until he dropped his hand and said, "It'll be great, Esther. You'll see."

I couldn't match his confidence, but the lingering trails of warmth from his caress bloomed under my skin until I was grateful he couldn't see me blushing in the dark. My reservations about this plan had been simple—now I wondered if there was a greater danger than the Spruce Hill gossip mill.

Under no circumstances could I allow myself to fall for this man. I could play the part, pretend to be casually dating the town's prodigal son, but this farce had an end date. Theo had fled Spruce Hill almost twenty years ago and never looked back, not even to visit his amazing, loving parents.

If I let myself fall in love with him, even a little, it would end in the kind of heartache that had been blessedly absent upon my husband's death.

No, falling in love was out of the question.

Chapter Nine

THEO

I SHOULDN'T HAVE TOUCHED her. What the hell was I thinking?

Esther was so quiet during the drive that I was convinced she was going to explode by the time we pulled into the restaurant parking lot. Hell, she'd probably punch me straight in the throat the minute she stepped out of the truck. I couldn't even blame her for it.

Instead, she slipped her hand into mine when I reached her side. I felt the faintest tremor in her fingers, then she lifted her face and summoned a brave smile.

"I'm ready. Let's do this."

Shock short-circuited my brain, so I just squeezed her hand and headed toward the front door of The Mermaid. As we passed the signature golden statues on either side of the entrance, Esther let her free hand graze over one's intricately carved fins. A surge of need coursed through my veins, startling in its intensity, as I imagined her fingers trailing over my skin like that.

Shut it down, I told myself firmly. This wasn't a real date.

Even though I'd already been to The Mermaid with Oliver since my return, the place blindsided me again with its cool, slightly hipster atmosphere. While the hostess led us to a big booth in the back corner, I took in more of the details than I had last time. Local art adorned the walls and the lighting was low without making the place seem sketchy, giving every wooden surface a warm gleam.

Our friends were already seated, leaving me and Esther to slide in at the end. Though I was going to let her have the outside seat in case she felt the need for a quick exit, she willingly positioned herself between myself and Oliver's sister.

Unlike me, still pondering that bolt of lust, Esther had her game face on. She greeted everyone with a friendly smile, joked a little with Sofia about accepting the invitation, and then nudged her leg against mine beneath the table for reassurance.

On the other side of Sofia sat her husband, Chase, followed by a pair of women introduced to me as Melody and Theresa, who had apparently gone to college with Sofia and Esther, then Oliver and Julian. It was a small group, thankfully, and Esther didn't appear outwardly uncomfortable.

Just when I started to think this might not be so bad after all, Oliver piped up with, "So, you two."

I froze, startled into silence, but Esther snorted softly and elbowed me in the ribs.

"Us two," I repeated finally, causing the rest of them to stifle their laughter.

Julian caught my eye, then hissed in Ollie's ear, "Jimenez, zip it."

With her boisterous brand of assistance, Sofia jumped in to turn the conversation to the upcoming tree lighting—Spruce Hill's official kickoff to the holiday season. When asked if I was attending, I mentioned helping Esther with the food truck and we were met with a chorus of "awws" from the entire table.

I glanced at Esther, who grimaced but winked at me, and I finally gathered the courage to drape my arm along the back of the booth behind her. To my surprise, she shifted slightly so that her side brushed against mine, like she'd simply been waiting for the invitation.

We managed to get through dinner without receiving any pointed invitations for Thanksgiving gatherings, though Sofia shot me a look when we were saying goodnight that I took as a warning we weren't off the hook just yet. Watching each of them embrace Esther, one after another, filled me with a soft sort of warmth. Maybe it was seeing her surrounded by friends, maybe it was the connection of my past and my present, but either way, it made me intensely happy.

As I drove us home, Esther sighed contentedly. "That was surprisingly tolerable."

"Admit it. You had at least a tiny bit of fun."

"Maybe a little," she agreed, rolling her head against the seatback to smile over at me.

"I'm glad you had a good time. I'm even more glad I didn't have to kick Ollie's ass for getting all up in our business."

Esther laughed. "Well, my money's definitely on you if it comes to a brawl."

It was a silly, offhand sort of comment, but it felt like more. She'd trusted me enough to enter this arrangement, ventured well out of her comfort zone tonight, and, if my speculations were correct, had lowered her guard at least a little bit throughout the evening. I wasn't stupid enough to believe that was my doing, but I could certainly appreciate it nonetheless.

By the time we pulled into the driveway at home, Esther had gone silent again, but it felt softer somehow. She was no longer buzzing with nerves or taut with tension, just cloaked in quiet. I was about to thank her for coming out with me and bid her goodnight when she made a little sound and swiveled toward me.

"Oh, dessert! I almost forgot. I have brownies and my favorite flavor of cupcakes, if you have room for dessert."

Would this woman ever cease to surprise me?

"If there's one thing you should know about me right now, Esther, it's that I *always* save room for dessert."

Instead of going home to my lonely couch and Toni's judgment, I followed Esther back into the guest house. It felt a little like winning the lottery.

"I just need to change. Make yourself comfortable," she called over her shoulder as she tossed the keys onto a table by the door.

My last trip inside to help carry out cupcakes had been brief, so I followed more slowly, taking in the changes that had been wrought over decades. The guest house was once a woodworking shop housing the original homeowner's handmade furniture business. By the time my parents bought the property, the little outbuilding was in a state of disrepair. They'd converted it into something of an office for my mother, who loved us desperately but often needed an escape from our rambunctious crew in order to get some work done.

A handful of other renovations had taken place since then, including the addition of a decent-sized kitchen, a storage loft, and a full bathroom. The bedroom off the back had been completed during the final stage of redesign—I always thought my parents hoped one of their sons would choose to stay close to home for a while, but both of us left after graduation.

Alex, however, came back during every semester break and long weekend, while I had resolutely refused to return.

The place wasn't large, but it felt homey and comfortable now. A variety of soft blankets lay draped over the loveseat and recliner in the small living room, colorful area rugs lined the wood floors, and artwork and a few knick-knacks broke up the studious nature of several overflowing bookshelves.

There wasn't a single photograph anywhere to be seen, with the exception of a small framed image of my mother and Esther at her college graduation. I trailed a finger over the edge of the silver frame and wondered if it was a gift from my parents.

"Sorry, I don't get a whole lot of company," Esther said as she returned from the bedroom in a pair of loose pants and a blue sweatshirt. She grabbed two plates from the cupboard and set them on the small dining table.

I frowned. "Have you had *any* company here?"

"Does your mother count?" She glared at me before gesturing for me to sit.

"Definitely not. She's family," I said, nodding toward the photo. "I have one just like that back home from my high school graduation. Clearly, she considers you one of her own."

Esther bit her lip before responding. "Then no, I haven't had any company here."

I nodded, unsurprised. "That's nothing to be ashamed of, Esther. I wasn't teasing you about it, just asking."

"Are you always this earnest?"

The way she said it, like she was utterly baffled by my attitude, made me laugh. "Is that a bad thing? I'm a straightforward kind of guy. The whole foot in mouth thing seems to be a terrible side effect, but it's never been quite this bad before."

Esther narrowed her eyes. "So you just say whatever comes into your head."

"Pretty much," I said with a shrug. "Though I'll admit it usually doesn't sound quite as stupid as half of what I've said to you so far. I don't know what it is about you, but I apparently have no filter when I'm around you."

"I don't—is that a compliment?"

"If I hadn't already asked you for a do-over, I'd request one right now. What the hell is wrong with me? I've been back in town for a week and I feel like I've been sucked back into middle school."

"You don't look like any middle schooler I've known," Esther muttered under her breath, but my head snapped up.

"Was *that* a compliment?" I demanded.

She made a point of looking around the room. "Do you think your mother knew how this was going to play out and planted cameras here?"

At that, I laughed. "I like you, Esther. I'm glad you're not ninety."

"You and me, both," she replied. "I really wanted to dislike you, you know."

"Just to spite my mother?"

"No. Well, maybe a little. I've done a damned good job of sticking to myself for the last four years and you snuck right past my defenses." She scowled at me, but there was still a hearty dose of humor sparkling in her eyes.

I flashed a wide grin at her, the kind my father always used to charm my mother whenever he messed up. "Well, I'm sorry my mother roped you into things, and I feel obligated to inform you that I'm almost positive she's hoping to convince me to stay in town."

"So I'm the lure?"

No turning back now. I lifted a hand to tick off each point on one of my fingers. "You're the most beautiful woman I've ever seen, clearly as scary-smart as my mother, tough as hell, more than a little bit mysterious. They couldn't have orchestrated a better trap for me if they'd tried."

Esther smiled at me, this time a bit sadly. "I appreciate your honesty, but having been trapped myself, I won't be anyone else's bait."

"Esther, I didn't mean..."

I trailed off, wishing I could rewind that moment into the compliment I'd intended it to be. The invitation for dessert had felt like more progress than holding her hand as we walked into the restaurant; I still wasn't sure if that concession had been borne of the need for reassurance or the desire to make our little act appear convincing.

Being welcomed into her inner sanctum seemed a more conscious choice, and now I was afraid I'd ruined everything.

"It's fine," she said quietly, rubbing her forehead with one knuckle before turning to fetch a plate of baked goods from the kitchen counter. When she sat down across from me, she tucked one leg under her and gestured toward the desserts between us. "Bad news for you. I'll need you to try at least one of each."

I rubbed my hands together, rolled up my sleeves, and stretched my arms like I was preparing for a sporting event. Her eyes looked almost topaz against the royal blue of her sweatshirt and they followed the line of my forearms just long enough to convince me she wasn't as indifferent as she might seem.

"You're the boss. Which of these beauties should I sample first? What kind of cupcakes are they?" I asked.

Esther waved her hand magnanimously. "Guest's choice. These are Mississippi Mud. It's a mocha cupcake with cookie chunks mixed in and coffee frosting with a fudge swirl."

"Oh, Esther," I said gravely, placing a brownie and a cupcake on my plate before peeling the paper wrapping from the latter. "Where have you been all my life?"

Though I expected her to laugh, she only leaned forward a little, her gaze intent on my face as I took a bite from the cupcake. Even if I hadn't been playing it up for her sake, I couldn't have held back the moan of absolute bliss. It was amazing—soft and moist, the frosting fluffy and light, the flavors perfectly complementary. I was no expert on food allergies, but even the small sample I'd had of Esther's other confections hadn't prepared me for this.

"Well?" she demanded, scowling at my silence.

"I've never tasted anything this delicious in my entire life."

She huffed like she didn't believe me, so on the next bite, I closed my eyes and tipped my head back to savor it. By the time I finished the cupcake, I was ready to propose marriage again. I opened my eyes to find her watching me.

"You, Queen of Sweets, are an artist," I said, letting appreciation color my tone.

Pleasure crept across her features, tugging at the lushness of her mouth and brightening her eyes. It was like watching a flower bloom. For the second time that day, I wanted so badly to reach out and touch her that it became a physical ache, but I managed to refrain this time.

As my mother had always drilled into us: interest didn't equal invitation.

Clearing my throat, I picked up the brownie. "Right, moving on. These are the ones you were still testing?"

"Yes," she replied, taking one off the plate in the middle of the table.

I watched, captivated, as she tore off a corner, popped it between her lips, and chewed thoughtfully. When she made an impatient gesture in my direction, I did the same. A long sigh of pleasure escaped me as soon as I swallowed it.

"These are amazing. They're going to be a hit."

"You think so?" she asked, breaking off another chunk. "They're a little crumbly, but that was the payoff for reducing the oil."

I scoffed and ate the remainder of my own brownie in two big bites. "Who cares? Besides, since the tree lighting and the Carolcade are both at night, no one is going to notice a few crumbs."

"True. You're an excellent sidekick, Long John."

"We're a good team." I paused, studying her tranquil expression. "I think it went well tonight."

She wrinkled her nose and said, "Yeah, it did, but I'm sure Sofia isn't going to bite her tongue for long."

"You don't think she bought it?"

"I don't think she's going to believe we're dating, but..."

"But?" Curious, I raised my brows and waited for her to continue. A faint wash of pink crept over her cheeks and I clenched my fist when her straight white teeth sank into the plump rose of her lower lip.

"But she'll probably assume we're sleeping together."

The words seeped right through my skin, settling deep inside me in a way that was both intensely arousing and oddly satisfying.

My voice was hoarse when I asked, "How do you feel about that?"

She drew a slow breath, met my gaze straight on, and said, "I think it's a rumor I can live with."

Chapter Ten

ESTHER

Long after Theo left that night, I was still thinking about the molten heat in his eyes when I told him I could handle my closest friend assuming we were having the very hot affair she'd recommended. I was still thinking about it the next day when Sofia texted me about meeting up for drinks that weekend.

Drinks at Botticelli's Sunday night? Bring lover boy.

Staring down at my phone as I paused in the middle of scooping out a batch of cookies, I sighed, washed my hands, and sent a text to Theo to see what he thought.

He didn't answer right away, so I focused my attention on getting the tray into the oven. Just as I set the timer, a knock sounded at the front door. Out of habit, I checked the peephole, and the sight of Theo in a blue plaid shirt and worn leather jacket knocked me back half a step before I swung the door open.

"Hey," he said, his gaze dipping to my neck before lifting back to my eyes. "You've got flour just...here."

One thumb brushed over my collarbone, warm against the cool air outside and sending tendrils of fire along my veins. I forced myself to hold still, though I couldn't prevent my lips from parting as I stared silently back at him.

"I haven't had anyone to talk to all day except the cat, so I figured I'd come over instead of texting back. Am I interrupting something?"

"Oh. Just baking. Come on in."

I stepped back to let him through and pretended not to notice the way his shirt molded to the muscles of his back and shoulders as he shrugged off his jacket and hung it on the hooks by the door. He lifted his head like a wolf scenting the air.

"Cookies?" he asked, lips curving into an eager smile.

"Behave yourself and you can have some fresh out of the oven."

With a deep, rumbling chuckle, he winked at me. "Esther, I'd do just about anything for your cookies."

"I'm not sure shameless flirting constitutes good behavior," I said dryly as I led the way back into the kitchen.

"What about offering to help with anything you need? I'm an expert at dishwashing."

I huffed out a laugh and waved at him to sit at the table while I scooped dough onto one last tray. "Just relax, I'm almost done. So. Are you ready for another date?"

When he didn't immediately respond, I glanced over my shoulder and caught him watching me. Heat blossomed under my skin, even when his gaze drifted to my face. There was something soft and inviting in his eyes, but his expression was serious.

"Absolutely," he said quietly. "Are you?"

I blinked at him for a beat, then nodded. "Yeah, drinks won't be that big a commitment, right? I think if I put her off, she'll badger me about Thanksgiving. I'd rather make an appearance that we can escape from easily than get roped into a meal that will stretch for half the day."

"Mrs. Jimenez takes holidays very seriously," he said, grinning. "I think half a day might be underestimating her."

"I'll tell Sofia we'll be there," I said as I turned back to the cookies.

Theo stayed quiet as I pulled the first tray from the oven, but he cocked his head at me when I turned to face him.

"Everything okay?" he asked.

"Yes, I just...I don't know what to wear to a place like that."

His eyebrows shot up and he rose to his feet, moving toward me. He paused a few feet away, leaning against the counter, and said, "I'm probably not the best judge of that, but I can ask Ollie if you don't want to involve Sofia. I've seen you dolled up and casual, and believe me when I say no matter what you wear, you're going to be gorgeous."

"Thank you." I cleared my throat and moved a handful of cookies from the cooling rack to a plate before handing it to him. "Can I get you a drink?"

"Water is fine," he replied.

The gentleness of his tone threatened to unravel me, but I managed to keep my hands steady as I filled two glasses from the filter and nodded for him to sit back down at the table. I took the seat across from him, careful to keep my knees from brushing against his.

"They're best when they're still warm," I told him, grabbing a cookie off the plate.

That was all the invitation he needed—he lifted one to his mouth, closed his eyes as he took a gooey bite, and released a guttural sound of satisfaction that had me clenching my thighs under the table. Right before he opened his eyes again, I dropped my gaze to the plate and shoved the cookie into my mouth.

"You're right," he said. "These are even better than the first ones I tried, and I thought those were the best thing I'd ever tasted."

"You have a pretty strong sweet tooth."

He shrugged. "Guilty as charged."

"So. What else should I know about you besides that, if we're going to convince our closest friends we're dating?"

"Or banging," he muttered.

A startled laugh burst from my lips. "Or banging."

"I don't think anyone is going to quiz us, Esther," he said gently. "Especially because they know us both and it's going to be obvious this is temporary."

The reminder should have doused me with ice water, but instead it made me square my shoulders and nod.

Temporary. Right. I could do this. I *wanted* to do this. Maybe a fake relationship would help prepare me for another real one.

Someday. Down the road. When I was ready.

"Yeah. Still. I'm afraid Sofia is going to question me and I'll just freeze up," I said.

He ate another cookie, rubbed a hand over his beard to check for crumbs, and leaned back in his chair. "Crash course, then. I'm thirty-eight, I have a degree in business management, and I co-own a landscaping company with a guy named Billy. I used to help my dad out when I was in high school and fell in love with the prospect of both being my own boss and creating beautiful gardens for customers."

I nodded. "And I assume you don't have a girlfriend down in North Carolina?"

"Definite no. I wouldn't have agreed to come up here for two months if someone was waiting for me back home."

The desire to ask about his aversion to relationships welled in my chest so strongly that I had to clench my hands together in my lap. "Right, okay. Any hobbies?"

"I played on a sort of bar league adult soccer team for a while, but when the business took off, I couldn't commit to enough practices," he replied. "You?"

I shook my head, then shrugged. "I like to read. I do some yoga, but I decided against classes because I got tired of everyone staring at me when I showed up."

"This fucking town."

My eyes widened at the vehemence of the words. "It's not that bad."

With a humorless laugh, he leaned his elbows against the table and said, "Esther, even when you *want* to get out of this house, you're sent scurrying back because every busybody in Spruce Hill feels the need to be up in your business."

"I don't scurry," I protested, scowling.

"You know what I'm saying. Why do you stay here?"

I took a sip of water to put off responding, then sighed. "The memories aren't all good, obviously, but I never fit in when I was growing up. Spruce Hill is the first place that's ever felt like home. Leaving feels like...letting Steve win. I love my customers, I love your parents. This is my refuge."

His gaze swept over my features and I caught the moment he recognized my sincerity on the issue. "Okay."

"It doesn't matter. I don't mind being alone, Theo."

"You're not alone now."

"I guess you're right," I replied, then bit my lip. "You really think we can pull this off?"

He laid his hand on the table, palm up, and waited until I hesitantly laid my hand on top of it. The warmth of his fingers curling around mine was both unsettling and reassuring, summoning up all kinds of feelings I thought I'd locked away long ago.

"Esther, Queen of Sweets and goddess of cookies, I have the utmost faith in us."

Chapter Eleven

THEO

B Y SUNDAY NIGHT, I was pretty sure Esther did *not* have faith in our ability to pull off the dating charade. She answered the door looking scorching hot in a sheer black blouse over a dark purple tank top and skintight black jeans, but her eyes were wide and panicked.

"I'm sorry, I just need a second," she said in a rush, bolting back toward the bedroom while I stepped inside the guest house and closed the door.

A minute later, she returned wearing dangly, glittering earrings and boots with heels that brought the top of her head nearly to my chin. Before she could reach for her coat, I caught her hands in mine and waited for her to meet my gaze.

"Hey," I said gently. "It's going to be fine. Even if we leave after twenty minutes, that's fine. Breathe for a second, okay?"

The breath she sucked in was shaky, but the panic slowly leached from her expression. "Sorry," she whispered.

"Nothing to be sorry about. As your fake boyfriend, am I allowed to tell you that you look outrageously beautiful tonight?"

She wrinkled her nose at me. "Yeah, yeah. Let's go before I decide this is a terrible idea."

I laughed and helped her with her coat, pleased to note that the tension in her shoulders eased while she tied the belt at her waist. When I offered my hand, she rolled her eyes but took it, holding onto me like I was a lifeline.

The drive, fortunately only a few minutes through town, was mostly silent. I'd never been to Botticelli's, but Oliver told me it catered to a slightly older crew than some of the college bars nearby, offering craft beers from local breweries and cocktails with pop culture references in the names.

"Should we come up with a signal in case one of us needs to hightail it out of there?" I asked as I pulled into the parking lot.

"Yeah, I'll run screaming toward the door."

Laughing, I parked the truck and turned to face her. "I'd like things to not reach quite that level of emergency."

"It'll be fine," she said quietly. "It can't be that much different than dinner with the crew, right?"

"Right. Let's go."

In theory, it wasn't much different—in reality, it seemed likely that walking into a noisy, crowded bar the last weekend before Thanksgiving was Esther's worst nightmare.

And mine.

People I only vaguely recognized stopped us every few feet from the minute we walked in the door, which meant the trek to the back corner where Sofia, Chase, Ollie, and Julian had secured a high-top table took a solid fifteen minutes. Esther smiled politely, murmuring noncommittal responses to direct questions, but her fingers tightened painfully around my hand until we broke free of the final group of interested citizens.

"I'm sorry," I whispered against her ear, catching a hint of vanilla and peppermint drifting up from her hair.

"It's fine."

I knew enough to recognize it was definitely *not* fine, but this wasn't the place to argue, especially when one of her conditions for this entire act was that I trust her word. We eventually reached the table, greeted our friends, and ordered our drinks from a passing server.

Esther perched on the tall stool beside me, so close I was afraid I'd elbow her in the ribs. I wrapped my arm around her waist to avoid that and rejoiced when she relaxed against my side. Both Sofia and Ollie were watching intently—I wouldn't have been surprised if little hearts came floating out of their eyes.

Fortunately, no one asked any personal questions. Sofia dropped a few pointed hints about us hooking up, including a comment about a handyman calendar that left me baffled but drew a fierce blush and a choked giggle from the woman at my side.

When I sent a questioning look in her direction, she just burrowed under my arm and muttered, "Tell you later."

I was ready to declare the entire outing a success when an older man wearing a bolo tie passed the table on his way back from the bathrooms and did a double take when he saw Esther.

She went stiff and my entire body snapped to attention.

"Esther, how lovely to see you," he cooed, his pale blue eyes lingering on the hint of cleavage above her tank top. When she didn't respond, he smirked. "If I'd known you were going to settle for a loser like this, I'd have made a move sooner."

"Do I know you?" I asked, striving for a polite tone and falling short by a mile.

He sneered at me. "No, but everyone in Spruce Hill knows about you and your little...accident."

Anger pulsed through my veins at this asshole making light of the moment that changed my entire life, but I forced down my reaction. Esther deserved a peaceful night out, not her fake boyfriend throwing down with a stranger in a bar.

The tension radiating from her shifted in a way I couldn't quite read until I glanced down and saw fury written across every inch of her face. I opened my mouth to reassure her that nothing this jackass said was worth expending any energy on, but she beat me to it.

"Now is when you take your sleazeball ass far away from here, Tyler," she spat, "unless you want the whole town talking about how you've spent your entire life enabling abuse. I'm sure the truth won't impact your career."

I looked back toward the man just in time to see the blood drain from his face, then he stormed past us to grab his date by the elbow and propel her out the door.

Every one of us stared at Esther, who heaved a sigh and threw back the rest of her drink.

"I think it's time to call it a night. This was fun," she said in an even tone, as though the disruption had never happened. "Let's do it again sometime."

Sofia blinked in surprise as Esther hopped down from her stool. "Yeah, for sure."

I followed suit, clasped hands with Ollie, Julian, and Chase, kissed Sofia's cheek, then looped my arm around Esther's waist to shelter her as we pushed through the crowd.

When we reached the parking lot, she shifted away, though she took my hand instead of retreating completely. Her fingers were cold, trembling against mine, and the tiny puffs of her breath in the night air came at unsettling intervals.

"Let me guess, he's a friend of Steve's?" I asked as I opened the passenger door.

"Business partner. Do snakes have friends?"

I laughed, releasing her hand so she could climb into the seat, then jogged around to the driver's side. "Other serpents, maybe."

"God, I hate that guy."

"Has he messed with you before?" I swallowed back a ball of hot fury at the thought.

"Pretty much on a weekly basis during the length of my marriage. Steve had him over all the time, probably because he knew I hated the guy."

My jaw clenched hard, but I managed to loosen it enough to ask, "Did he ever touch you?"

"Besides trying to grope my ass at the grocery store a couple years ago?"

I watched my knuckles turn white as my fingers tightened around the steering wheel. "Please tell me you're joking."

"Nope. He said Steve told him how hot I was before I stopped 'putting out' and he'd been waiting for his turn. I believe he offered to remind me what a real man is like."

"He's the one who needs a reminder," I growled.

Her hand settled on my thigh and I glanced at her in surprise. Under the street lamps, I saw her lips twitch into a tiny smile.

"Please don't get into any fistfights on my account."

I laughed, covered her hand with mine, and said, "If he gets near you again? No promises."

She left her hand there until I pulled into the driveway and I felt its absence like an icy dagger between my ribs. When I shifted into park and turned off the engine, she made no move to get out of the truck, so I stretched my arm along the seatback and rotated my body toward her.

"Tyler aside, that was less terrible than I expected," she said quietly.

I grinned at her. "Just once, I'd like one of our dates to be better than *not terrible*. Think we can make that happen?"

When she turned her head, the smooth silk of her hair slipped across the back of my hand, tantalizingly lush and soft. I lifted my left hand to cup her cheek and watched her fight back a flinch. Dropping it back to my lap, I sighed.

"Can I ask you something?"

Esther's nose wrinkled. "If you must."

"You don't owe me any information and I won't ask for anything more, but even as a fake boyfriend, I feel like I need to know one thing." I waited for her to tell me to piss off, but she just gave a quick nod, so I steeled myself for the answer and asked, "Did your husband hurt you?"

Surprise washed over her features. "Oh. No. Not physically."

It wasn't the reassurance I'd hoped to get, so I just repeated, "Not physically."

Esther sighed. "He was...manipulative. He isolated me from my friends, even somehow managed to win over my parents so they wouldn't help me get a divorce."

"Are you shitting me?"

"No. He spent years systematically breaking me down, criticizing everything about me, flying into a rage over anything he perceived as a mistake."

I wondered why she hadn't left him, hadn't gone to Sofia for help if her parents weren't willing, but I stopped myself before I could make the mistake of speaking that aloud. Hell, I'd read enough about the psychology of abuse to know it wasn't that simple. Esther was brilliant and resourceful—if she'd felt trapped, it was because of what her asshole husband had done to make her that way.

Even without speaking a word, she caught the look on my face and shook her head like she was disappointed in me for thinking it.

"You're right. I should never have let it get to that point."

"That's not what I was going to say, Esther."

She made a disbelieving sound. "It doesn't matter. He's dead, and I'm free. Dickheads like Tyler have no power over me anymore."

"Esther," I said softly, "I'm sorry I brought it up. Even if he wasn't abusing you physically, emotional abuse is still abuse."

"Yes, it is. Does that answer all your questions?"

Briefly, I closed my eyes. "I'm sorry for asking, but I needed to know. This doesn't have to be real dating to involve real issues and I don't want to hurt you with some misstep. I had a girlfriend years ago who'd been in an abusive relationship. She didn't want to tell me about it, but her roommate mentioned it once a few weeks in. I wished I'd known sooner."

"Right. Well, it was a long time ago, but I appreciate your concern," she said, unbuckling her seatbelt.

"Esther, hang on. I didn't mean to upset you."

She flashed a bright smile that was so clearly fake, I felt my chest cave in a little. "I'm fine. I'll touch base with you in a few days about our next public appearance. I should get to bed, I have a lot of work to get done this week."

Fuck.

"Please wait," I begged, but before I could even open my mouth to continue, she shook her head.

"It's fine, Theo. Really. I'm just tired."

Though I wanted to take back every word of the last five minutes, it was too late for that. I was a fool for pushing her so soon and the worst kind of hypocrite, given that I hadn't opened up to her in the same way.

With a sigh, I waited until she finally glanced at me again to offer the gentlest smile I could manage.

She didn't smile back, not even a fake one, just gave a jerky nod and practically fled from the truck, disappearing into the guest house before I even set foot on the driveway.

All I could do was hope the memories of the rest of the night—apart from the interaction with her dead husband's asshole friend—would outweigh the debacle of its ending.

Chapter Twelve

ESTHER

G UILT SLITHERED THROUGH ME the minute I closed the door, enveloping myself in the silence that had been my companion for so many years but now felt hostile and lonely.

I braced my arms against the kitchen counter and drew several shuddering breaths until the risk of bursting into tears finally diminished. My limbs trembled as though I'd run a marathon instead of sitting at a bar with a handsome stranger.

A stranger I was pretending to be involved with in order to avoid holiday invitations that, in my case, were barely even a threat after all these years.

Why the hell had I agreed to this?

He's a nice guy and you're doing him a favor, I told myself sternly, but then a voice at the back of my mind—probably the voice of the therapist I'd been seeing since the week after

Steve's death, at Anita's urging—reminded me that I had my own self-serving motives as well. I didn't need the shield of a love interest to protect me from being inundated with holiday cheer.

I was, however, sick and tired of being alone. On weekends. On holidays. On quiet evenings at home.

Despite my sister being the golden child of the family, I always thought I'd had a decent relationship with my parents. They weren't overly affectionate people, nothing like the Silver family, but they were involved, encouraging. Of course, they didn't love that I didn't become a doctor like my sister or a lawyer like my father, but I at least felt like I was still part of a unit, like there was someone I could go to when the entire world went to shit.

I was wrong.

That fantasy came crashing down two years into my marriage when I showed up on their doorstep, sobbing uncontrollably after Steve screamed at me for nearly an hour, then shattered a wine glass—full of red wine—against the wall in the living room. My father was an insurance attorney, but I'd thought he could connect me with a colleague to help me start the process to divorce Steve, make an effort to save me from the misery that had become my married life.

Instead, my parents patted me on the head, told me marriage required work on both sides, and sent me back to him.

Looking back, that was the beginning of the end of my relationship with my family—and of my marriage, as well. I set the idea of divorce aside, not because my father was right, but because that moment taught me that the only person I could rely on was myself.

Instead of serving Steve with divorce papers, I went home to his familiar series of apologies and let them bounce right off of the newly formed armor around my heart. When he tried to kiss me, I told him if he ever touched me again, I would kill him in his sleep.

Apparently raw fury lends credence to that kind of thing, because he took me at my word.

It didn't stop any future manipulations or his continuous stream of filthy insults, but it kept him standing silently aside while I moved my things into the guest bedroom. It didn't eradicate his threats or his pointed reminders that he held a great deal of power over me, but it prevented him from trying to coerce his way back into bed with me.

It hadn't kept him from telling his closest friend about my "betrayal," either. After that, Tyler was around more than ever.

With a broken sob, I pushed away from the counter, shut off the lights, and crawled under the covers. When Steve's contemptuous sneer flashed through my mind, I summoned up an image of Theo instead. The only way to keep the memories at bay was to focus as hard as I could on tiny details, so I envisioned the soft, curling beard that surrounded his mouth, the way his fingers felt wrapped around mine as we walked into the bar, the solid warmth of his body beside me. I remembered that growling moan as he sampled my baked goods, the blissful sigh, the deep rumble of his voice, the solid strength of his arm draped over my shoulders.

With the comforter cocooned around me, I squeezed my eyes shut and thought about Theo until I fell into a fitful sleep.

J UST AFTER SEVEN THE next morning, I jerked awake from a distinctly explicit dream featuring my very attractive fake suitor. I reluctantly peeled my eyes open, staring up at the ceiling as I tried to slow the pounding of my heart. The images receded slowly, leaving trails of fire along my veins even once I recognized it was only a dream.

Holy hell, was that actually what Theo would look like naked?

I groaned and buried my face in the pillows for a minute before forcing myself out of bed. The ghosts of the previous night had dissipated, and in the weak morning light, all that remained was a burning sense of shame.

Theo had ventured into dangerous territory for my sake, not his own. He'd only been trying to make sure he didn't inadvertently press any buttons during this charade, especially after Tyler's little digs, and I fell apart over it.

I needed to apologize, definitely. But first, I needed time to process, to figure out what to say and how to proceed.

Since I did my best thinking while baking, I scarfed down a quick breakfast and got straight to work. Instead of beginning the preparations needed for my upcoming orders, I sat down at the table with a cup of coffee and my color-coded binder of recipes. Some of them were specifically for the business, others were personal favorites. One section was for recipes I hadn't gotten around to trying yet, and that was where I started.

I considered Theo's reactions to the items he'd tried already, thought back through our conversations for any clues about what he might like. After ten minutes of deliberations, I consulted the fridge and the pantry, then decided on a peppermint cheesecake. He might love my cookies, but it was the groan of pleasure brought on by peppermint frosting that echoed in my brain.

While I made the chocolate cookie crust, I considered the best way to apologize for ditching him so abruptly. I could've answered him without any details, but instead I'd grown defensive and sullen. That was why I'd suggested that rule in the first place, knowing I wouldn't be able to stay calm during the discussion, but maybe that had been a mistake.

Fake dating or not, we were spending a lot of time together. Maybe we'd set ourselves up for failure by not sharing pertinent information. Maybe we needed to discuss some amendments to our original agreement.

Once I started preparing the filling, my mind wandered back into the dangerous waters brought on by that dream.

Except...maybe they weren't as dangerous as I'd thought.

Sofia's suggestion of a torrid love affair took root in my mind. God knew I'd had my fill of long-term relationships already. Maybe something temporary—and scorching hot, if the dream was any indication—was just what I needed.

We were both consenting adults, weren't we? Granted, he might not want a fling while he was here in town, but if he did, what was stopping us? How better to convince the town that we were together than to actually enjoy the fruits of our labors?

Of course, that was assuming he was interested in such an arrangement. I thought he might be, but I admittedly didn't know him all that well.

I put the cheesecake in the fridge to set and took a long, hot shower as I debated how to broach the subject with Theo. Should I devise a plan? Speak from the heart? Wait for him to take the lead?

"No," I told myself firmly as I rinsed the conditioner from my hair. "You are not going down that road again. If you want something, you're going to trust yourself and ask for it."

Now *that* spurred a number of even more X-rated images in my mind. I was just going to blame my non-existent sex life for these lapses.

I braided my hair to get it off my neck, pulled on jeans and a kitten-soft gray sweater, and stared at my reflection in the mirror. My cheeks were still rosy from the heat of the shower, but I looked good, I thought. Steve had always pressured me into dresses and makeup and expensive jewelry when he was entertaining investors or colleagues. After his death, I'd donated every stitch of clothing Steve had liked, pawned every piece of jewelry, and turned to clothes that made *me* happy.

The way Theo looked at each new outfit, even the most casual of them, stirred a ball of warmth deep in my belly.

With a fortifying breath, I peeked out the front window to be sure Theo's truck was still in the driveway, then pulled on my boots and grabbed the cheesecake from the fridge. I tucked a stray wisp of hair behind my ear and summoned every ounce of courage I possessed.

When I opened the door, a cellophane-wrapped bouquet of snow white lilies sat on my front step. I blinked down at it, wondering who on earth would deliver flowers without ringing the bell.

Maybe Theo, too, wanted to make amends for how things had gone last night?

I stooped down to grab them, grimaced as their cloying perfume hit my nose, and hurried back into the kitchen to set them on the countertop. The last person to give me flowers was Steve, and that had been during the whirlwind courtship when he was still striving to convince me I'd never find anyone who loved me like he did.

It took a long time for me to recognize that for the lie it was.

There was no note attached to the bouquet, and the longer I stood there, the more unbearable the aroma became. "Sorry," I muttered aloud to the flowers as I came to a decision and stuck them into the back hall where I wouldn't be able to smell them.

If Theo was the sender, I'd find a way to gently tell him flowers were not really my thing, and hopefully he wouldn't be offended.

In the meantime, I had dessert to deliver.

"You can do this," I told myself one last time, though my heart hammered so hard I was afraid I might pass out before I even reached his door.

I'd survived things far worse than apologizing to a kind man who I also happened to find devastatingly handsome, hadn't I? And if I managed to gather my wits and proposition him, the worst he could say was no. I wouldn't be irreparably harmed, even if it might be embarrassing as hell.

Embarrassment be damned. It was time to be honest about what I wanted.

Chapter Thirteen

THEO

PUTTING MY FOOT IN my mouth was not a new phenomenon for me. I'd experienced plenty of awkward moments over it, but never before had I been so terrified that I might've permanently ruined something beautiful. I spent the night tossing and turning, wishing I'd managed to stop myself before bringing up her asshole husband.

By morning, I'd resolved to apologize again and pray she'd forgive me. I decided to wait until after lunch, hoping that giving her time would help my case, but I picked up my phone half a dozen times to text her before tossing it aside when I thought better of it.

Just before I set it down again, the phone rang, startling me out of my skin.

The hope that it was Esther died as I saw my mother's picture on the screen. "Hey, Mom," I said as I answered the call, rubbing my forehead with my other hand.

"Hi honey, just checking in. How's everything going?"

"I haven't destroyed the house or thrown any keggers yet, but there's still time. How are you and Dad? How's Nana doing?" I asked.

"Oh, we're fine. Everyone's enjoying the sunshine. Nana starts PT tomorrow. How are you and Toni getting along?"

"Just fine. She says she misses you—no, wait, I misinterpreted. She says she's going to kill me in my sleep."

My mother laughed. "And how are you and Esther getting along?"

My eyes narrowed as I glanced down at my phone. "You know, I'm beginning to suspect you meant for me to think she was some doddering old lady when you asked me to come keep an eye on her. I'm pretty sure she wouldn't appreciate being treated like she's helpless."

"No," Mom agreed readily enough, "she would not. I certainly hope you haven't been treating her that way."

"Fortunately, I was raised better than that. We're getting along just fine, too."

There was a beat of silence where I was certain my mother was picking apart every nuance of that sentence, but then a knock at the door sent my spirits rising.

"Someone's here, I better go. Take care, Mom. Give my love to everyone."

"Love you, honey. Tell Esther I said hello!"

The call ended before I could decipher if she thought it was Esther at the door or if she meant it more generally.

Sure enough, though, there stood the woman in question when I threw open the side door, looking achingly sweet and holding a pie plate in her hands. The pale gray of her sweater morphed her eyes into huge silver disks, blinking up at me like she'd forgotten what she was going to say.

"Esther, hey. Come in, it's freezing out there."

I held open the door for her to step past me and watched as she steadied herself, then turned to offer me the plate. It looked like some kind of pink pie with a chocolate crust and pieces of candy cane crumbled across the top.

"It's peppermint cheesecake," she said in a rush. "I just...look, I'm really sorry I flipped out on you."

My mouth dropped open for a second. "Esther, Jesus, I'm the one who's sorry. I've been wracking my brain trying to figure out how to apologize for being such an asshole. Sometimes my mouth starts going before my brain catches up."

One shoulder lifted and fell. "It's okay, really. You were trying to protect me. I overreacted."

"I shouldn't have brought up the one subject you asked me not to. Now that we've established our mutual regret and forgiveness, please tell me you'll stay and enjoy some of this with me?" I ventured hopefully.

With a soft, shy smile, Esther nodded. "I will, sure."

"Come on. This looks amazing."

As she followed me into the kitchen, she said, "You didn't drop off flowers earlier, did you?"

I paused, brows drawn down in confusion. "No, I didn't. Someone sent you flowers?"

"Maybe? They were outside my door, no card. I don't know who they came from, but the smell is a little overwhelming. Since they're not from you, I can safely tell you I hate lilies."

"Who do you think sent them?" I asked, rubbing my hand over my beard. It was stupid to feel a quick flash of jealousy at the thought of some secret admirer making a move on Esther, but I couldn't quite control the instinctive reaction.

"I don't know. Nobody who knows me would send flowers, because I hate them, but sometimes customers give me little things as a thank you."

"I assume chocolates are probably a no go with your allergies, and so are flowers. Noted."

I didn't like the idea of someone else sending her gifts like that—it annoyed me in a way I couldn't deny, but she didn't seem overly concerned about it, so I tried to let it go. Maybe Sofia had dropped them off for her, maybe my mother was meddling yet again—but if they were close enough to know she wouldn't like receiving a bouquet, why would either of them send it?

Sleazy Tyler and his bolo tie flashed through my mind, along with his comment about making a move, but why bother if he wasn't going to include a note to take credit for it?

I shook off my unease and sliced into the cheesecake, serving it up onto my mother's favorite little plates, the ones covered in flowers and edged with gold. Instead of sitting at the table, though, I nodded my head toward the family room where I'd been spending most of my time. I didn't want the dining table between us, not when she was clearly willing to breach the chasm of last night's disaster.

Esther curled up at one end of the plush sofa, tucking her feet underneath her so she was angled toward me. I caught a glimpse of her fuzzy pink socks and my lips twitched.

"What?" she asked primly. "I like cozy fabrics, is that a crime?"

"No," I replied, thinking about just how much I'd like to cozy up to her. Everything about her today looked soft and welcoming.

From the way her gaze jerked to my face, I suspected my tone conveyed that more clearly than I'd intended, but she bit her lip to hide a smile. I wondered what exactly was going on in that beautiful head of hers. She dropped her eyes to her plate and I watched as she placed a delicate bite of the pink cheesecake between her lips.

Holy hell, I thought with an inward groan. I shifted subtly in my seat and dug into my cheesecake as a distraction.

"Holy hell," I muttered aloud this time, shoving another hunk into my mouth. "Is there no end to your talent?"

She laughed. "I'm glad you like it. I wasn't quite sure what to make."

"This is phenomenal, so you picked a winner."

The room settled into silence as we finished off the cheesecake, but I gestured for her to stay put while I put our plates in the sink. When I came back into the family room, Esther was just as I'd left her, aside from resting her head against the cushioned back of the couch. She smiled at me as I resumed my seat, but it faded quickly as her brow furrowed.

"I'm sorry," I said again, grimacing. "I broke one of our only rules last night."

"Actually, I wanted to ask you about something. An amendment to the rules. Or a couple of amendments, maybe."

My eyes widened. "Anything. I feel like I owe you after last night."

"You don't owe me anything, so please don't let that influence your answer. I need you to be honest."

"Of course," I agreed easily, leaning toward her.

"I think making our pasts off-limits might be a mistake. Not that I need you to spill all your secrets or anything, but I guess we probably shouldn't tiptoe around the things that have affected us like that."

I swallowed my immediate panicked reaction, forced myself to take a second, then nodded. "I think that's fair."

"Right, okay."

"What else?"

She sucked in a deep breath and let it out slowly. "I wondered if you might be interested in...not...fake dating."

I blinked in confusion. "Meaning you don't want to do this anymore?"

"No," she protested quickly. "I mean I—I want more than just fake dates."

Startled by a crashing wave of desire at her words, I stared for a moment before I could summon the powers of speech. "You want to actually date me?"

Though she flushed with embarrassment, she said, "No. I mean, sort of. We can keep up the fake dating, but I want more."

There was that word again, stoking a fire in my chest. I studied her expression, traced the wash of pink coloring her cheeks as I wondered if she felt it too. "More?"

"I want you to sleep with me," she said in a rush. "If you're interested, I mean."

"You...what?"

My brain tripped over a series of images—beautiful, glorious, tempting images of things I'd tried not to let myself think about. Esther in my bed, all bare skin and soft curves, that dark hair spilling across the pillows. Feeling her. Tasting her. Making her mine, even temporarily.

Every muscle of my body clenched in reaction.

"Nothing, forget it." She jumped to her feet, but I caught her at the waist before she could run past me.

"No, it's not nothing. Not even close to nothing. You want to add sex to the agenda, is that what you mean?" I searched her expression, afraid I'd find reluctance or trepidation, but she bit her lip against a shy, breathtaking smile.

"Yes," she whispered.

My fingers flexed, pressing in against the softness of her hips. Every inch of my body perked up at the word, my pulse jumping into overdrive. It felt too good to be true, like there must be some hidden catch. The need to confirm what she wanted overwhelmed me.

"Esther." Her name sounded like a prayer on my lips. "You want me to fuck you?"

The bald honesty of the words made her breath come faster, her pupils dilating until only a ring of silvery-green surrounded them. That tantalizing blush in her cheeks crept across her chest until it shadowed the neckline of her soft sweater.

"Yes." It was barely audible, but her body shifted incrementally closer until she was standing between my knees.

"You want me to make you feel good." My hands slid down until my pinkies swept over the lush curve of her ass. At her nod, I grinned. "Because believe me, Esther, I am completely on board with that."

"You are?"

"Are you kidding me? Why wouldn't I be? You're incredible. Beautiful and intelligent and strong," I replied, brushing my thumbs back and forth along her hip bones.

"No strings," she said, still sounding a little breathless. "Just sex."

An icicle of doubt pierced through the haze of desire. "This isn't because you feel bad about last night, right?"

"Jesus, no." The protest was immediate and firm—and exactly what I needed to hear.

"Okay, good, because you don't need to feel guilty. You're sure about this?"

Esther nodded again. Those soft pink lips parted as my gaze zeroed in on her mouth. When a tremor ran through her, I tugged her down onto my lap, lifted one hand to cup her cheek, and traced my thumb along the curve of her lower lip.

"It's been a long time for you?" I asked.

"Years." A soft puff of breath grazed my thumb as she spoke.

I didn't like the thought of her going without for so long, but after our conversation last night, I couldn't blame her for it, either. Determination to make this arrangement benefit her as much as it did me crashed through my chest.

Still stroking her lip, I said, "I suspect you're a very different woman than you were all those years ago. Tell me what you want from this. How do you see this going?"

"It stays casual. This is just our current arrangement plus sex."

"Right, okay. No catching feelings," I agreed.

That was an easy one. I liked Esther, respected her, certainly desired her—but I didn't do long-term relationships, even if we had lived in the same state.

No attachments meant no pain.

She tilted her head, considering. "At the end, we part ways amicably. I don't want things to be awkward with your parents."

"Agreed. I had no intention of sharing details with them, anyway."

The thought that my mother had a hand in this was a little unsettling, but I doubted she'd anticipated anything blatantly sexual between us. She obviously knew I was approaching forty and hadn't introduced her to a girlfriend since high school, but we didn't discuss it.

Not now, not in the years since I left Spruce Hill. Not since the early days after the accident.

Esther bit her lip. "No sleepovers. For now, at least. I'm used to being on my own."

"We can take that part slow and reassess if you want to. Anything else?"

A shuddering sigh coasted over her lips before she said, "I want to feel free again. Like there's no dead husband weighing me down, no whispers or rumors or nosy townsfolk keeping tabs on me."

"I'll do everything in my power to shield you from that. Even from our friends. Do you trust me?"

"I think so," she whispered.

"Good. The only rule I want to add is that you come first in this." A choked laugh escaped her at my phrasing and I grinned, shaking my head. "Yeah, literally and figuratively. Anything you're not comfortable with, anything that doesn't work for you, I want to know so I can change it."

"Yeah. Okay. Definitely." The words tumbled from her lips and I bit back a smile.

"Good. Now, I haven't eaten anything with any nuts since we talked about it. I wasn't assuming anything was going to happen, I just wanted to keep you safe."

Surprise and pleasure flooded her features as she slid her hand around to the back of my neck. "That's good. I think you should shut up and kiss me, then, if that's all right with you."

"Christ, yes," I muttered, and I cradled her jaw as I dropped my mouth to hers.

If her desserts were delicious, then her lips were beyond anything I'd ever tasted. A faint tang of peppermint graced her tongue as she opened to me, hints of sweetness lingering along the curve of her bottom lip. I hadn't let myself envision what it would be like to kiss Esther, but now that I knew, I couldn't imagine wanting to do anything else ever again.

A low sound purred from her throat as she shifted, tugging me over her as she reclined against the arm of the sofa. When the planes of my chest met the welcoming softness of her belly and breasts, I groaned quietly, drawing back just enough to kiss a path along her jaw.

"Is this what you want?" I murmured as my teeth grazed her earlobe. "We're not moving too fast?"

She scoffed, arching to offer me more room to tease my lips along her throat. "It's been a long, long time for me. I think you're underestimating just how much I need this."

"Oh?" I lifted my head to look down at her. Her lips were plump and rosy, her eyes slightly glazed but still blazing up at me with such desire that my heart jolted in my chest. "Christ, do you have any idea what you're doing to me?"

"Not really, no. But if it's half of what you're doing to me, you must be getting pretty desperate," she replied, then she tangled her fingers in my hair and pulled my mouth back to hers.

She was absolutely right.

Chapter Fourteen

ESTHER

T HEO WAS AN EXPERT kisser. There was no doubt in my mind, even knowing my experience was severely limited and plenty outdated. He used his lips and tongue like tools, delicate and precise, like he was decorating a wedding cake that required both artistry and skill.

By the time we came up for air, my limbs were noticeably trembling.

Smoothing my hair back from my flushed cheeks, he trailed his lips down to my chin and along the curve of my jaw. When he nipped lightly at my earlobe, I gasped, overwhelmed by a desire so strong and pure it knocked the air from my lungs.

On its heels came a shock of fear. As his mouth grazed the pulse beating wildly at the base of my throat, I tensed and Theo drew back immediately.

"Hey. Still with me?" He kept his voice low and soothing, his eyes focused intently on my face.

I fought to steady myself. "I—yes. I'm with you."

"Are you sure?" he asked softly. "You looked scared for a second there."

"How much I want you, that scares me," I admitted, dropping my eyes to the collar of his shirt. "I haven't wanted anything or anyone with this kind of intensity in a long time. Or ever, maybe. It's kind of terrifying."

Now it was Theo who sucked in a breath, but then his face blossomed into a smile that threatened to flatten me. "I see. We'll take it slow, Esther, as slow as we need to. No expectations, no pressure."

"I've never done anything like this," I warned him.

His lips coasted over my temple, warm breath tickling my skin. "Are you trying to scare me away from you? Because it won't work."

"We've already established how unscary you think I am."

A soft chuckle vibrated against my ear. "You're thinking too hard about this. Why don't you just let me kiss you some more, and we'll see where things go from there?"

There was no need for me to reply with words, because his mouth settled against mine again and I was lost. Fear, trepidation, self-doubt—they all dissipated like mist.

After some indeterminate amount of time, he wrapped his arms around my body and rotated us so I ended up straddling his lap again, all without breaking the kiss. I huffed a laugh as I settled onto him, cradling the insistent bulge behind his zipper.

He dropped his forehead to my sternum. "You are so fucking soft, it's unbelievable."

"And you are not soft at all," I teased, drawing a groan from deep in his chest as I rocked my hips against him.

His lips returned to mine like he couldn't bear to be apart for more than a moment. No matter how eager his body felt beneath mine, he stuck to those slow, tantalizing kisses that made me feel drunk on sensation.

When his fingers teased under the hem of my sweater, dancing across bare skin, I wriggled closer, pressing my breasts to his chest. He splayed one hand across my lower back and let the other rise to tangle in the dark curtain of my hair as I clung to his shoulders like I might float away if I let go.

I felt his tongue dart out to explore my collarbone and sighed at the pleasure of being worshipped like this. His voice rumbled through me when he spoke, lifting goosebumps along my arms.

"Tell me what you need, Esther. Let me give it to you."

I rested my forehead against his as I caught my breath. He hummed a little as he trailed tiny kisses across my cheekbones and winked at me after one landed at the tip of my nose. A soft sigh slipped past my lips and I shifted just enough to lay my head on his shoulder. Without removing the hand that had snuck under my sweater, Theo wrapped his arms around me and rested his cheek against the top of my head.

"You make me feel like I don't come with a whole lifetime of baggage," I mumbled into his throat.

"We all have baggage. Yours is just a bit heavier than others."

The hand against my lower back began stroking slow lines up and down my spine and, without his dark, perceptive eyes watching my face, I let the emotions slide through me. Hope, uncertainty, anticipation, and underneath it all, an undercurrent of joyful excitement that swept the breath from my lungs.

It might have scared me if I hadn't been so turned on, so eager for whatever Theo would give me. Everything about this moment felt different from how things had been for me in the past, from the soft adoration in his eyes to the frequent check-ins.

I hadn't been with a man since Steve, hadn't trusted anyone with my time or energy in that way, but with Theo, I wanted to.

I sighed and said, "I never thought I'd be able to forget about it, even temporarily, but I feel like I could get lost in you."

"Is that what you want?" he asked, the words a low rumble against my ear. "To lose yourself?"

After a beat of silence, I shook my head. "I don't think so. It's tempting—so, so tempting. But it's part of me and maybe I need to own it. I lost myself for a long time, in a different, horrible way, and I'm afraid of letting it happen again, even if the method is different."

Theo's arms tightened around me before he let go in order to tip my face up to his. "I like who you are, Esther. I won't let you get lost, not even for my own gain."

Something inside me cracked, some part of myself that had been hidden away long before Steve finally died. From that tiny fissure, hope bloomed, warm and sweet. I tried to blink back the tears that blossomed alongside it, but one escaped to roll down my cheek. Theo brushed it away with his thumb and kissed my forehead.

"You are unlike any man I've ever known," I said quietly.

"I'm going to take that as a compliment."

I laughed, feeling a sudden lightness that banished every trace of fear or sadness. "Good, because it was meant as one."

"For what it's worth," he said as he cupped the back of my head and drew me close enough to kiss again, "you're not like any woman I've ever known, either."

Makeout sessions on the couch were never part of my youth, aside from what I saw on television, but Theo had spoken the truth—he really was content to simply kiss me, and kiss me, and kiss me. His hands strayed now and then, coasting up the muscles of my back or sliding along my rib cage, but he always stopped before things progressed too far.

When I wriggled, rocking my pelvis against his, he groaned into my mouth. "Easy, easy," he whispered. "You're making this harder."

"I noticed," I replied, laughing breathlessly when he growled.

Though his fingers tickled my ribs in retribution, this time he didn't catch himself before reaching the underside of my breasts. He leaned back, watching the way my eyes fell shut when his palms brushed lightly back and forth over my nipples. They hardened into tight buds against the fabric of my bra.

"This okay?" he asked, his voice ragged at the edges, like he was desperate to see the flesh he was teasing.

My eyes opened, heavy-lidded and dazed. Before I could overthink it, I leaned back, pulled the sweater over my head, and tossed it to the cushions beside us. "Better than okay."

"Thank fuck." His gaze went hungry as he drank in the sight.

"I want you to touch me. Please," I gasped.

He chuckled against my collarbone. "I might die if I don't."

Without another word, he rose to his feet, keeping me clasped against him as a laugh bubbled out of me. I was certain we'd both tumble back down the stairs, but before I knew it, we were in the guest bedroom. Anita had transformed it into an oasis of blues and greens, lush textures and thoughtful decorative touches.

My favorite part, by far, was the large bed centered against one wall, its four posts draped with gauzy swaths of fabric. Based on Theo's expression, it was his favorite now, too.

He carried me to the bed and kept my legs wrapped around his waist as he crawled over to set me down against the mountain of pillows. As though unable to resist another taste, he dropped his head to kiss me again before drawing back to say, "Talk to me. Tell me what you're thinking."

"My mind is racing. All I know is if you don't put your hands on me right now, I'm going to explode."

A soft rush of air swept over my skin when he laughed, but I nudged him backward so I could sit up, unclasp my bra, and fling it to the floor. Theo's expression went stark, ravenous, and a shiver ran through me at being the focus of that look. When I relaxed back against the pillows again, he threw off his own shirt, then lowered himself over me and kissed his way down my neck.

"God, you're beautiful," he growled against my skin.

The sound I made when his mouth closed over one nipple might have embarrassed me, if I'd had enough presence of mind to worry about it. He sucked hard, drawing me deep into his mouth, then grazed his teeth over the tip until I arched up to meet him. When my fingers tangled in his hair, clutching him to me, he flicked his tongue across the peak until I was nearly frantic beneath him.

"Theo," I whimpered when he moved to the other side, his long fingers toying with the first, plucking and rolling. I tried to clench my thighs together against the electric sensations zinging through me, but I only succeeded in wrapping them more tightly around his waist.

"Hmm?" The sound vibrated against my skin. "Should I stop?"

"No. Fuck no, please don't stop."

As he kissed a path between my breasts, he asked, "Are you ready for more?"

My lips parted as I met his eyes. His fingers had lowered to fiddle with the button of my jeans, making his meaning perfectly clear. "Is that a real question?"

"Is that a yes?"

I laughed a little incredulously, but when he lowered his head to trail hot, wet kisses across the soft swell of my belly, my head fell back in surrender. "It's a yes. Please," I panted.

After he deftly unbuttoned my jeans and drew them down my legs, Theo kissed his way back up, nipping the sensitive skin of my inner thigh and then my hip bone as he hooked his fingers in the waistband of my purple cotton underpants.

"It's unreal just how goddamn sexy you are," he growled as he tugged them down.

I shuddered beneath him as he crawled back up my body, his lips meeting mine just as his hand cupped me, slipping between my legs as though it was simply meant to be there. Against his palm, I already knew he'd find me wet and hot and welcoming his touch like I'd been waiting my whole life for him. My thighs fell open to his questing fingers, beckoning him further.

When one sank deep, filling me, he swallowed the soft sound I made against his mouth, then lifted his head to watch my expression as he added another finger and curled them inside me. Helpless, restless bliss filled me as I rocked my hips against his palm. With his thumb, he stroked, circling in time with the thrust of his fingers, watching as my lips parted on a gasp.

"You are stunning," he murmured.

As my muscles began to tense, I met his eyes, my own wide and dazed. The only thing I said was his name, but it felt like a plea.

"Let go, Esther. I won't let you get lost, I promise. You're right here with me. Let everything else go."

The low timbre of his voice pushed me over the edge. I arched and cried out, clenching around his fingers. Patiently, he waited as the ripples faded, slowing the sweep of his thumb as he brought me back down from the peak. When every muscle of my body had relaxed into limp satisfaction, he finally drew his hand away and pressed a soft kiss to my shoulder.

"Wow. That was...wow." My eyes fell shut while I waited for my pulse to slow. "You're very good with your hands."

Theo laughed. "Wait until you see what I can do with my mouth. How do you feel? Did you lose any piece of the brilliant woman that you are?"

I opened my eyes and looked at him, the rugged stranger who'd somehow become my first lover in longer than I cared to admit. There wasn't even a hint of smugness in his earnest brown eyes, only a fierce kind of joy. Nothing he could say would have convinced me of his own enjoyment more than that particular visual.

"No," I said softly, rolling so I was nestled against him. "Not at all. I feel...found."

Chapter Fifteen

THEO

FOUND.

It was the perfect word for it—and I found her again, and again, and again. I was sure I'd pushed her to the point of exhaustion when she came hard on my tongue that last time, but after a moment's respite, she shoved me onto my back and did some finding of her own.

"Fuck," I groaned as she trailed her lips over my abs, her fingers at work on my zipper.

"That's the idea." She grinned at me. "It's my turn to play. Just lie back and relax."

Relaxing was out of the question, but I reclined on the pillows and bent my knees to give her room. Her mouth, sweeter than any of her confections as she teased and tasted, was unlike anything I'd ever experienced. I tried to control my breathing, to keep myself in check, but *play* was exactly what she did. My hands tangled in her hair, lifting it back from her beautiful face so I could watch as she explored my cock with her lips and tongue.

Sex had been many things for me over the years—stress relief, catharsis, exercise, connection.

This was different. More. Her joy and enthusiasm were contagious.

"Esther, I'm close." I tightened my fingers in her hair, but she ignored the warning and took me deeper.

I groaned when she hollowed her cheeks on a hard pull, her hand stroking the base of my cock in time with her mouth. Then she drew back, releasing me with a loud pop, and gazed up at me from under a sweep of dark lashes, her hand still moving as I spurted across my stomach, the orgasm hitting harder and lasting longer than any I could remember.

Actually fucking her might be the death of me.

Her fingers trailed along my thighs as she sat up, surveying the mess with a satisfied smile. "I didn't know how fun that could be."

I blinked at her, feeling like my brain cells had leached out as well. "Glad I could be of service."

"Stay there," she ordered.

Watching the luscious curves of her naked body as she climbed off the bed, I was relatively sure I couldn't have moved if I'd wanted to. She returned from the ensuite bathroom a moment later and gently wiped my stomach clean with a damp washcloth.

"Queen of Sweets," I mumbled when she tossed it into the hamper. "It suits you. Sweetest mouth, sweetest ass, sweetest—"

She clapped a hand over my lips. "I get the picture."

I kissed her palm and waited until she moved it, stretched out alongside me, and rested her head on my shoulder before saying, "If I call you sweetness, are you going to accuse me of catching feelings?"

"Not after your list of my sweetest attributes," she replied.

"Good," I murmured, sifting my fingers into her hair. Every so often, as the silky strands tumbled onto her bare back, she'd shiver against me and snuggle deeper into my side.

With each passing moment, my contentment trembled on the precipice of dread. Only the fact that this relationship had an end date allowed me to shove it back down—things wouldn't drag on before ending in tragedy.

This would be different. I'd make sure of it.

To distract myself from that line of thinking, I rolled toward Esther, hooked her leg over my hip, and let my hands wander over her body until she was panting with need.

"Theo," she whimpered, trying to tug my hand between her legs.

"So impatient." I nipped at the side of her breast, sucked her nipple hard, swirled my tongue around the peaked tip, then finally gave her what she wanted.

In a sense.

She might not have agreed when I spent what felt like hours edging her upward and easing her back down just to start all over again, until we were both sweaty and breathless, before finally bringing her to one final orgasm so intense, tears sprang to her eyes and spilled over onto her cheeks.

Gently, I brushed them away with my thumbs, then gathered her back into my arms. Evening had faded into night, and when she yawned against my throat, I waited as she dressed and then walked her home to the guest house.

The way she smiled up at me when we reached her front door melted something inside me. I reached up to stroke the soft curve of her cheek and she nuzzled against my palm.

"Sweet dreams, Esther," I murmured, dropping a kiss to her forehead.

"I'll see you in the morning? We have prep work to do for the tree lightning."

"As your trusty sidekick, I wouldn't miss it for the world."

She nodded, but before she turned to go inside, she tangled one hand in the front of my shirt and kissed me properly, then smirked. "Goodnight, Long John."

I waited for the sound of the lock, then winked at the door in case she was watching through the peephole. By the time I returned to the house to feed Toni her dinner, I was so tired I could barely think, but it had all been worth it just to see those sharp edges Esther was made of growing soft and warm.

While I pulled out a can of cat food, the entire afternoon replayed in my head over and over again. The expanse of silky golden skin, the soft, supple curve of hip and breast, the way she filled my palms—fuck, she'd just left and already I wanted her back. Every time I closed my eyes, I could see those midnight curls and the hot, sweet flesh hidden beneath.

And I hadn't even been inside her yet.

With a groan, I forced myself to find a distraction—any distraction. I was too restless to sleep, so I fired off a text to Billy, my business partner, even though I knew he was handling everything just fine without me. We exchanged a few messages, most of which were thinly veiled albeit good-natured insults about my micromanaging, but that only killed fifteen minutes of my evening.

The urge to go back to the guest house was almost overwhelming. Instead, I took a shower and failed spectacularly at *not* thinking about Esther's sweetly rounded thighs wrapped around my head. My own hand barely began to take the edge off my desire for her, even after she'd made me see stars barely an hour before.

I did everything I could to keep myself busy, from browsing every bookshelf in the house to scrolling mindlessly through social media. My dad had sent me a few pictures from Florida earlier in the day, presumably while I'd been occupied with learning every inch of Esther's delicious body, but when I thought about responding, my head filled with too many other questions.

First and foremost: was this the outcome my mother had been aiming for?

Jesus Christ. I scrubbed my hands over my face. Leaving home at eighteen meant my mother's involvement in my sex life had been limited to golden tidbits like *always use a condom* and *for God's sake, learn where the clitoris is.* That one had made me groan and stomp out of the house one afternoon, desperate to get the sound of that word from my mother's mouth out of my mind, but in the end, I supposed I should be grateful. I'd made it my mission to understand what the hell she was talking about and, if this afternoon was any sign, I'd learned that lesson with gusto.

By the time I checked the clock again, I had barely managed to kill another hour. I finally brushed my teeth, undressed, and threw myself down onto the bed, only to realize her scent lingered. I drew a deep breath of vanilla sweetness, cool peppermint, and the woman underneath.

I was so screwed.

I'd lived in Asheville about as long as I had in Spruce Hill, enjoyed an active social life, had a good group of friends. Now and then, I dated, but never had I felt like anything substantial was missing from my life. I ended those relationships before anyone could get too invested—I'd learned not to let things linger and drag on.

I knew even the tightest of connections could be broken.

Maybe there was an occasional pocket of emptiness in my chest that I couldn't quite place, but my life wasn't lacking.

Or it hadn't been, before Esther.

With a groan, I rolled over and buried my face in the pillows. By the time I came up for air, Toni had hopped up onto the bed and started grooming her plumed tail as though my troubles were beneath her. I glared at her until she lifted those shining amber eyes to mine.

"Why her?" I asked simply, but the cat had no response.

Even as I tried to stop that train of thought before it could build momentum, I could *feel* that empty spot in my chest taking shape, forming into a silhouette of a beautiful, lonely baker with midnight hair and moonlit eyes.

I wanted her in a way I'd never wanted anyone before, wanted to treasure and cherish her as she deserved. I'd put my foot in my mouth with questions about her husband, but it was easy enough to extrapolate after all she'd revealed. That bastard had hurt her and she'd hidden herself away from the world because of it.

I wanted to draw her back into the light and watch her blossom, even if it was only temporary.

While I was here, I'd just...ignore any thoughts of the future. Spending time with Esther would be no hardship, that was for damn sure. We'd enjoy each other's company, slake our lust, get through the holidays, and part ways. No harm done.

Since it was easier—and far more satisfying—to reflect on what had already transpired than to worry about what was yet to come, I rolled onto my back and let the events of the afternoon flow slowly through my mind. Esther, knocking at my door with cheesecake in hand. The cozy softness of her curled up at the other end of the couch. Those luscious lips, plump and sweet. Each curve and dip of her body, every silken inch of skin. The hoarse cries and restless whimpers and low moans as I stroked and tasted her.

Somewhere at the back of my mind, I knew six more weeks would never be enough.

I DIDN'T EVEN REMEMBER falling asleep, but when I awoke, the sun shone through the curtains I'd forgotten to close last night in my distraction. I groaned as I rolled out of bed, but Esther had suggested I come to the guest house for breakfast before her event preparations kicked into full swing for the tree lighting.

I wasn't about to miss whatever time I could get with her.

After a quick shower, I fed Toni, glanced out the kitchen window toward the guest house, and grabbed a jacket to combat the frigid morning air. Esther texted to let me know she was awake and to let myself in, so I rapped briefly on the door just to avoid startling her before I entered the guest house.

"Hello?" I called, hanging my coat on the hook behind the door.

She wandered out of the kitchen, dressed in leggings covered in tiny cupcakes and a wide-necked sweatshirt that fell off one shoulder. She was still adorably tousled and sleepy, cradling a mug of coffee in both hands. An unexpected wave of tenderness flooded my chest just looking at her.

"Morning," she mumbled.

"Good morning," I replied. Before I said anything else, she set the coffee down, walked straight into my arms, and buried her face in my chest. "Did you sleep well?"

"Like a rock," came her muffled response.

I chuckled against the top of her head. "Good. Can I help with breakfast?"

Reluctantly, she peeled herself away from me, though I caught her at the waist and kissed her, slow and deep. She sighed into me, just as soft and warm as she looked. When I released her, she smiled up at me.

My heart stuttered inside my chest.

"I've got it covered, but there's coffee if you want to make yourself a cup."

I followed her into the kitchen, my eyes on the smooth roll of her hips. Though I wanted nothing more than to sweep her into my arms and spend the day in bed, she'd made it clear that we had work to get done before the event this weekend. When she handed me a mug, though, I couldn't resist leaning down to nuzzle the soft skin at the base of her neck.

Esther hummed quietly, swaying against me. "Remind me why I said no sleepovers?" she asked breathlessly.

Laughing against her skin, I laid a trail of kisses to her shoulder. "Because you're not ready for that and we're taking it slow?"

"Five or six orgasms doesn't seem slow to me," she replied.

"Oh?" I lifted my head. "Does that mean you lost count, sweetness?"

She wrinkled her nose at me. "It is possible, yes. You're very talented, you know."

I opened my mouth to reply, then caught sight of a swatch of red on her neck. "Did I do that?" I asked, mildly horrified at having marked her beautiful skin.

"It's called beard burn, and yes." She lifted one hand to gently scrape her fingernails through my beard. "I found it in various other sensitive places, too, but before you apologize, it was well worth it."

"Was it?" I mused, stroking my fingers over the redness. "I could shave."

"Don't you dare," she protested. "Nothing wrong with a little reminder."

Pure heat streaked through me. I hooked one finger in the loose neckline of her sweatshirt and let my knuckle tease along her skin. She shivered under the caress.

"Maybe you should show me those other reminders, just in case they need some attention."

She wrapped her arms around my waist. For about half a second, hope sprang, then she tipped her head up to me and grinned.

"No such luck, sidekick. We've got work to do."

Chapter Sixteen

ESTHER

Seeing Theo's face fall was almost enough to convince me to drag him into my bedroom and tear his clothes off, but we did, in fact, have plenty to get done. I kissed him once more, then let go of him to pull a French toast casserole out of the oven.

"First we eat," I told him, "then we work. Then, if we get all of our work done, we get naked. Deal?"

A whoosh of breath left his lungs, but he nodded. "Given the right inducement, I can work *very* hard, Esther, and I can't think of any better reward."

His enthusiasm for life was swiftly becoming one of my favorite things about him. He ate with gusto, vocalized his appreciation every step of the way, and was willing to assist whenever possible. As my temporary sous-chef, he was in charge of putting my color-coded cupcake papers into pans, handing me ingredients, and tasting any leftovers. He even tried his hand at frosting a few of the extras, though his rosettes were a little cockeyed.

While I was demonstrating the technique again, Sofia invited us for Thanksgiving dinner via a group text.

"Shit," I whispered.

"This is exactly why we're doing this. We'll politely decline and tell her we're spending the day together. Alone. In peace."

I gestured for him to proceed, made him show me the response before he hit send, and then my phone lit up on the counter beside us while Theo's stayed silent. It was a separate text from Sofia featuring some incredibly explicit dessert suggestions and ending in a string of fire and eggplant emojis.

Theo burst out laughing while I stared down at the screen in horror. "Even before you propositioned me, you did say she was going to make assumptions," he reminded me.

"Yeah, I just...didn't realize she'd make them right away. While you're standing here. Or that she'd suggest such an off-label use of chocolate syrup."

His voice rumbled against my ear as he leaned down to say, "I'd choose your homemade frosting over chocolate syrup any day. I know just where I'd put it."

There was no hiding the shiver that worked its way through my body, not with him standing so close, so I stayed silent while he laughed softly and pressed a kiss to my temple. It took another minute for me to get my brain back into gear until it was time to break for lunch.

As we sat down at the table with sandwiches, my phone rang. Theo lifted a brow when I answered, repeated my "hello" a second time, and hung up.

"Spam?" he asked.

I wrinkled my nose. "I think my information must've ended up sold to some new list, I've been getting a lot more than usual lately."

We ate our lunches and got back to work, but midway through the afternoon, I realized I was dangerously low on several important ingredients.

"I should run to the grocery store so I can get these finished tomorrow," I said glumly. I was as excited about reward time as he was.

"No big deal, I'll come with you," he replied with a shrug. "I could use a few things at the house anyway."

With that settled, I packaged the final batch of cupcakes we'd just finished and placed them in the industrial fridge taking up most of my back hall. The wilting bouquet of lilies sat dejectedly on the windowsill, so I grabbed it to throw out on our way to the car. Theo frowned at the flowers when I walked back into the kitchen, waited until I tossed them down on the counter, then caught me around the waist and kissed me softly. When he drew back, he winked and swiped his thumb across my jaw.

"Had a bit of powdered sugar there," he murmured, popping his thumb into his mouth.

I stood there, captivated by the sight of his lips closing around his knuckle. The memory of that mouth moving over my skin hit me like a fist to the stomach, knocking the breath right out of me. Curse the man, he seemed to know exactly what I was thinking, because he smiled as he slipped his thumb from his mouth.

He leaned down until his cheek brushed mine and whispered, "Not as delicious as you."

A shudder ran through me. "We should go so we can get back here and...um. Put the groceries away."

"And then we're off the clock?"

I nodded, a little frantically. "Yes. Definitely."

Theo winked as he took a step back, offering me his arm. "Then let's get this over with, shall we?"

We donned our jackets, tossed the lilies into the trash can tucked behind the main house, and hopped into his truck. As we made the short drive to the nearest grocery store in town, my veins buzzed with nervous excitement. I didn't realize my leg was jiggling with it until Theo pulled into a parking spot and laid his hand on my knee.

"Easy there," he said playfully. "You're going to vibrate right out of your skin. Are you nervous or excited?"

I jerked in surprise. "Are you kidding me? Excited. Very excited. I know what I want, Theo, and it involves both of us naked and having orgasms. Together, this time."

He laughed, letting his fingers caress the inside of my thigh before he removed his hand to turn off the engine. "Then for Christ's sake, let's get what we need and get the hell home."

The grocery store was not nearly as vacant as I expected for a weeknight, but as Theo pointed out, there were only a few days left before Thanksgiving. Despite his comment about needing some groceries of his own, he only grabbed a basket after I shot a pointed glare his way.

Unfortunately, it appeared that he was more of a novelty in Spruce Hill these days than I was. Half a dozen people stopped him in the aisles to say hello and attempt to catch up. While he was deflecting the increasingly probing questions about his years away, I wandered away into the produce section.

I felt guilty enough for knowing any of the details of his past when he hadn't been the one to tell me. Eavesdropping on his answers felt a little too intrusive.

He managed to untangle himself from the grasp of Mrs. Hubbard, the freshman English teacher at the high school, and was winding his way through fruit displays toward me when a mocking voice said, "Why, as I live and breathe."

Theo stiffened, turned, and inclined his head with measured coldness. "Alex."

His brother sauntered slowly closer, cocky as ever, and I felt an odd wave of panic rising in my stomach. The two of them looked eerily similar side by side, but the harsh glint in Alex's eyes shocked me as much as the chill in his voice, so unlike Theo's glowing warmth.

"So, you finally deigned to come crawling back here, did you?" Alex asked. "You couldn't just leave us all in peace?"

Theo turned to the display of apples and took his time picking out a few to add to his basket. "You should probably keep your voice down, little brother. We wouldn't want the entire town to find out what a spineless asshole you are when you've worked so hard to hide that fact from everyone."

Alex sneered and opened his mouth to reply, but on instinct, I made my way to Theo's side and slipped my arm through his. For a heartbeat, Alex froze in place, his expression a picture of shock, then he forced his features in a semblance of a smile.

"Esther, nice to see you again," he said smoothly.

A faint tremor slithered up my spine and I felt Theo's arm tighten in response, but I gave a tiny smile. "Hello, Alex. Sorry to interrupt, but we have to get going. Happy holidays."

With a look of surprise that would have been comical at any other moment, Alex blinked at us, ignored Theo's smirk, and watched as we walked toward the checkout. I said nothing as I took the apples from his basket—the only thing he'd managed to grab—and added them to the conveyor belt with my own items.

Neither of us spoke as we got back into the truck, the paper bag of groceries nestled at my feet. Theo started the engine, but when he didn't pull out of the parking lot, I glanced over at him. His grip was tight on the steering wheel, his body radiating tension.

"Are you okay?" I asked softly.

"Me?" He sounded incredulous. "You're the one I'm worried about."

I frowned, trying to make sense of that. "What? Why?"

He shifted in his seat to face me and took my chin between his fingers. "When Alex spoke, you went white as a ghost. I thought you were going to pass out in there."

"I'm fine," I replied.

"Do you and Alex have some kind of history?" There was a healthy dose of hesitation in his voice and a furrow between his brows.

"Oh," I mumbled. "No. I've seen him around, obviously, but that's the extent of it. I don't think we've ever had a real conversation."

Theo was silent for a long moment. "He reminded you of Steve," he said finally.

I wanted to deny it, but he was too perceptive for his own good. "Yes. A little. It was his tone, I think."

With a soft sigh, he slid across the seat to wrap me in his arms. I nestled close, surprised to realize just how much I needed it, and he dropped a kiss to the top of my head. It was several minutes before his arms loosened.

I offered a wobbly smile. "It's fine. Really. Is it always like that with you two?"

"Our relationship is...contentious. He's holding onto a lot of bitterness from a long time ago."

For a long, quiet moment, I studied him. Without knowing more about their history, it was impossible to extrapolate from such a brief exchange, but I got the impression Alex wasn't the only one still nursing old wounds.

I wanted to ask him about it, try to help with whatever had to be going through his head right then, but he spoke before I could think of a way to inquire without him throwing up shields.

"Esther," he murmured, "I wish you'd let me help you."

"How?"

The word erupted past my lips, hiding the fact that I was about to say practically the same thing to him. He was so ready to leap into action for my wellbeing—didn't he care about his own?

For so long, all I wanted was someone to help me, to step into the hellhole that became my daily life and drag me out of there. Now that I was on the other side of it, I was no longer a damsel in distress, but the fact that Theo was so willing to offer assistance and smooth things over for me still nudged at that desperate woman I once was.

My outburst hung between us for a moment, then his palm moved slowly, slowly down to my jaw. With a gentle sweep of his thumb, he stroked my lower lip.

This time, I was sure he felt my swift intake of breath when he said, "Any way you want. Anything you need."

"I think we should get home and put these groceries away first," I replied.

So maybe our defenses would stay engaged a little longer—I couldn't make him open up to me any more than he could dig into my own past trauma without my participation.

He grinned as he slid back into the driver's seat and buckled his seatbelt. "Whatever you say, sweetness."

Chapter Seventeen

THEO

WHEN WE GOT BACK home, I hovered while Esther put away her groceries, watching for any sign that she was going to change her mind—or give in to the shuddering panic that had thankfully dissipated while I held her in the truck—and forcing myself not to think about my brother.

Fuck, I wished our reunion hadn't taken place in front of a full audience, especially one including the woman I was about to romance, but I didn't want to reflect on how it felt to see my little brother again.

Definitely didn't want to think about how much he hated me.

As far as Esther was concerned, instead of falling apart, the routine activity only seemed to strengthen her resolve. She lined my three apples up along the countertop, flashed me a saucy grin, and gestured for me to follow her.

As soon as we reached the bedroom, I swept her off her feet with an arm behind her knees and tossed her onto the bed. Her laughter floated around us as I crawled over her. This room was quintessentially Esther, comfortable and cozy and feminine, decorated in a mixture of soft grays and rosy pinks. The curtains boasted stripes of both colors, shot with silver strands that glittered in the light of the setting sun.

"I wish I'd woken up beside you today," she murmured when I kissed my way along her jaw.

"You made the no sleepover rule," I said against her throat. "But if you'd like to rescind that one, I think it can be arranged."

It didn't take long for her to grow impatient with slow, teasing kisses that gave way to nipping little bites across her incredibly soft skin. She struggled into a sitting position and threw off her sweatshirt and bra, baring her torso. Before I could move to feast on that bounty, she shoved me playfully away and ordered me to strip.

As I rose to my feet and started pulling off my shirt and jeans, her eyes followed every movement. I paused once I was standing there in just my boxers, but she just waved imperiously for me to continue. With my gaze locked on her face, I shoved the waistband over my hips and stepped out of them. I couldn't decide what was more erotic, the sight of her lying there waiting for me or the dazed, hungry expression she wore.

"Esther," I said softly, waiting for her eyes to meet mine. "You're calling the shots."

She nodded, scrambled off the bed, and pulled off her leggings, tossing them onto the dresser in the corner. When she turned back to face me, I could see the rapid rise and fall of her chest with each breath, the faint flush under her skin. Though she opened her mouth, she snapped it shut again and held out one hand.

I took it, drew her body against mine, and kissed her until she started shifting restlessly against me, trying to get closer.

"You're an impatient little thing," I growled against her lips, then I dropped my hands to the perfect globes of her ass and pulled her hips tightly to mine, grinding against her. "Is this what you want?"

Her head fell back on a quiet gasp. "Oh, yes."

Without releasing my hold, I walked us backward until she tumbled down onto the bed. I kneaded her hips gently, my eyes locked on those dark curls at the apex of her thighs. Before I said anything, she spread her legs just enough to reveal a flash of hidden pink flesh and I groaned.

"Do you have any idea how bad I want to be inside you?"

"Then what are you waiting for?" she demanded.

I bent down and nipped the inside of one thigh until she opened further, then kissed my way across the softness of her stomach as I cupped one hand between her legs. She gasped when I slid a finger inside, moaned when I added a second, then bucked against my hand when I curled them and pressed the heel of my palm against her clit.

"So. Fucking. Perfect."

"Theo, please," she whispered, but her hips lifted helplessly as I began to tease her in earnest.

I captured one nipple between my teeth before soothing it with my tongue, using every drop of knowledge I'd gleaned about her body the night before to draw her closer and closer to release. By the time I switched my attention to her other breast, she was panting, writhing beneath me, her muscles quivering as the pressure built.

Just before she crested, I shifted up to kiss her sweet mouth, swallowing her cry as she shattered. My fingers slowed, soothing and teasing, as she caught her breath. No matter how many times I'd gotten her off last night, it was still a beautiful revelation, watching her let go. I couldn't imagine ever getting tired of seeing it.

"Theo," she groaned, dropping her head back as I dragged my lips along her throat, "please tell me you have condoms."

"Esther," I replied between kisses, "I have condoms."

She tangled her fingers in my hair. "Then you should grab one and acquaint me with your Long John, hmm?"

I snorted a laugh against her neck and rolled away to grab the string of foil packets I'd shoved into my back pocket earlier.

As I rolled one on, Esther turned onto her side to watch me. She looked sultry, sexy, like a goddess awaiting her due. I was more than ready to worship her, to spend the entire night at her service. When I settled back onto the bed beside her, I smoothed one hand over her hip, relishing the way her flesh filled my palm.

"I want to know what you like, what you don't like, okay?" I murmured, peppering her face with kisses.

"Okay. It's just been a long time, and it...wasn't great even then."

I cupped her cheek in my hand and kissed her lips. "We'll discover together, then. Just tell me what you're feeling while we do."

This time, her nod was more confident, then she shifted onto her back and tugged me over her. I dropped my head to nuzzle the sensitive spot below her ear, braced myself on one elbow so I could stroke my fingers between her legs again until she whimpered in frustration, then positioned myself at her entrance. With her pale eyes locked on mine, I pressed in, an inch at a time, watching her lips part on a soft, sweet sigh when I was finally fully seated inside her.

"Good?" I murmured against her lips.

She wrapped her legs around my hips and whispered, "Very good."

Understatement of the century. All of that sweetness I'd enjoyed the night before was now concentrated into the blissfully sleek heat of her. I froze for a moment when she tightened around me, stifling a groan of pure need.

Though a small voice in my head urged me to speed up, I ignored it, moving slowly as I acquainted myself further with her body. I paid attention to each sound she made, each gasp, each lift of her hips to meet mine, and adjusted accordingly. A slight change in angle drew a low moan from her throat and I hid a satisfied grin against her skin.

Of course, that angle was fucking amazing, and I was determined to give more than I took. "Ready to try something else? I think you'll like it."

She mumbled her assent almost incoherently when I thrust deep once more before reluctantly withdrawing. I guided her onto her side so she was spooned in front of me, draped her top leg over my hip, and eased into her from behind.

"Oh, *Theo,*" she breathed, arching so the lush roundness of her ass nestled snugly against me.

I grinned against her shoulder. "Good?"

"Beyond good," she replied.

Cupping her breast in my palm, I teased her nipple, rolling and pinching, drawing those sweet sounds from her throat as I moved slow and deep inside her. I let my teeth graze the spot where her neck met her shoulder, then soothed it with my tongue and slipped my hand down between her legs.

With a low purr of pleasure, she spread her legs as far as she could in this position and I took full advantage, keeping my thrusts slow to ensure she came again before I did. Based on the way she squirmed, she was getting close.

"That's it," I murmured in her ear, the low words making her shiver. "I want to feel you letting go. Go on."

On a guttural cry, she did, her hips rocking hard against mine as every muscle clenched around me, squeezing like a vise. I trailed kisses over her shoulder and the side of her neck, leaving my fingers in place to brush over her sensitized skin as I increased my pace and started thrusting in earnest.

"So good," I whispered. "You feel so good around me. I could spend all night inside you."

A soft whimper escaped her as she dropped her head back against my chest. "More. Please," she whispered.

"More of this?" I asked, circling the tip of my finger around her clit, then I shifted to grip her thigh and thrust hard. "Or this?"

"That," she gasped, clamping her hand over mine to keep it there, pressing my fingers deeper into her soft flesh.

I laughed hoarsely against her skin and did as she commanded. Her muscles still rippled around me from that last orgasm, driving me closer and closer to the edge. Both of us were panting, moaning softly, until I couldn't tell whose breath was whose.

When Esther's grip loosened, I cupped my hand between her legs and stroked twice until she arched again and let out a trembling moan as another orgasm rocketed through her. I buried myself deep and came hard, muffling my own groan against her shoulder.

For a long moment, we stayed linked together like that, then her body shuddered in front of me.

"Hey, hey, don't cry," I whispered frantically, horrified.

She rolled her head to look at me and I realized she wasn't crying at all—she was laughing. That elusive dimple was out in full force, her rosy lips curved into a glorious smile, green eyes aglow. I stared at her, fascinated, until she twined her fingers with mine and lifted our joined hands to press a kiss to my knuckles.

"That was incredible," she said dreamily.

Her laughter was contagious; even before I pulled out of her, I started chuckling into the silky mass of her hair.

"*You* are incredible," I corrected.

As I withdrew, she lifted her leg off of me and curled into a little ball of contentment. I kissed her shoulder one last time before rising to throw away the condom, then I curved my body around hers and blanketed her with my arm.

While my pulse slowed and my skin cooled, I was overcome by one thought: I would be happy to stay right here for the rest of my life.

Chapter Eighteen

ESTHER

S EX WITH THEO WAS at once overwhelming and comforting, like I'd finally found a place where I could set myself free and still come back together again afterward. Somehow, he managed to be the perfect combination of demanding and endlessly accommodating.

And his stamina—well. No complaints there.

Though he teased me for once again losing count of the orgasms he doled out like candy on Halloween, it was impossible to keep track of the pleasure. He made me feel not like I'd been living under a rock, but like I was free to explore, and explore we did. Positions I'd only read about in romance novels were presented for my choosing, and even if we tried more than I'd ever dreamed possible, he paid close attention to my response to each and every one.

When we rolled out of bed to eat a slapdash dinner, he pulled on his jeans but stayed shirtless, which I appreciated immensely. The dark hair on his chest did nothing to hide the muscles underneath, sculpted and bronzed and, as I'd learned, definitely not just for show.

Once I tied the belt of a satin robe around my waist, I ran my hands over his skin for the sheer joy of the contrasting textures, all wiry curls and warm skin. I sighed with pleasure and he laughed softly.

"Come on, you. We need some food if we're going to keep this up," he teased, clasping my hands and kissing them in turn.

I smirked up at him. "Right. Food. Let's go."

Dinner was only the briefest of interludes, then Theo put his renewed energy to good use until we collapsed into a heap of exhaustion. With his fingers sifting through my hair, I realized I was hovering at the edge of sleep.

"Will you stay?" I mumbled into his bare skin.

"As long as I won't be punished for breaking your rules."

I huffed a laugh. "Rules, shmools. Sleepovers are hereby allowed by royal decree."

"Good," he said, kissing the top of my head as he pulled the blanket over us. "Now get some sleep."

I awoke at some point during the night, disoriented by the feeling of his big, warm body beside me. When I shifted, he tugged me into his arms, brushed his lips over my hair, and ran a reassuring hand up and down my back until I drifted off again.

Pale sunlight streamed through the windows, shimmering off the curtains, when I woke up in the morning. Theo's arms were still wrapped around me, clutching me to his chest like a favorite teddy bear. I stretched as much as I could, but I froze when I inadvertently rubbed against his impressive erection.

Theo made a sleepy sound in my ear. "Again, you insatiable woman?"

I lifted my head to look at the greatly depleted supply of condoms, finding only one left on the bedside table. "Just thought we might as well finish this off with a bang," I joked, causing him to snort a laugh against my hair. "You'll have to restock after that. I'm sure the town will be very excited about your purchase."

"Oh, Christ," he muttered. "I'll drive into the next town. Wear a disguise. Bribe a teenager outside of the gas station to run in for me."

Laughing at his horrified tone, I leaned over and grabbed the last packet. We both watched as I reached down to stroke him first, admiring the way that velvet hardness leapt against my hand. While my fingertips grazed the underside of his crown, I leaned over to nip his jaw.

"I'll make it worth your while," I promised, then rolled the condom slowly down his cock. I shoved him onto his back and straddled his hips. "Do we have a deal?"

Theo groaned quietly. "God, yes. I'm at your mercy."

This was new, this powerful woman who'd been hidden somewhere deep inside me, the kind of woman who took charge, who played an equal role in the bedroom.

And it was glorious.

I held his gaze as I sank slowly downward, watching his eyes darken to a rich coffee brown as I drew him deeper. When he was fully sheathed within me, I paused, tilting my head back at the sheer pleasure of it. His hands were tight on my hips and, fuck, I'd never criticize those curves again, not as long as I could remember the feel of his clinging fingers holding me right there, tight against him.

"Esther," he said hoarsely, but that was all.

When I lifted up again on my knees, dragging along his length, he groaned again and dropped his head back onto the pillows.

I ran my palms up his stomach, over his chest, across his shoulders. The muscles rippled under my hands, his expression stark and intense as I kept every rise and fall to the same slow, infuriating pace. It was only when I bit my lip to hide a smile that he realized I was doing it on purpose, goading him into action.

"You little minx," he growled.

Sitting up suddenly, he wrapped his arms around my lower back to keep me from toppling off of him and resumed the same sensual torture he'd been inflicting on my breasts the night before. I gasped at the heat of his mouth, the pulse of sensation as he tugged at my nipple, the way he pressed upward into me, not faster but harder.

I didn't notice he had moved one arm until his thumb brushed between us, circling my clit with measured precision. Within seconds, I shattered, my back bowing over the steely band of his forearm. For a second, he stilled, letting the waves of release sweep through me as I caught my breath, then he rolled us over and grinned down at me.

I laughed breathlessly, but it morphed into a moan when he drew my knee up past his hip and thrust deep.

"Oh, god. Yes. There."

The words slipped past my lips, barely coherent, but he heard them and growled against my throat. "You like that, do you?" he asked, nuzzling his nose along my jaw. "You feel so fucking perfect around me."

Whether it was the new angle, the words, or the husky roughness of his voice in my ear, it didn't take long before I was barreling toward another orgasm, whimpering and writhing underneath him. He rose up onto his knees, braced his hands on either side of my shoulders, and watched my face with a concentration that normally would have made me self-conscious.

From Theo, it felt like a caress, like a gift—his eagerness to see my pleasure was as baffling as it was beautiful.

When the climax burst through me with shuddering intensity, he thrust hard one final time and followed me over the edge. From my haze of pleasure, I watched him reluctantly pull out to throw away the condom, then he was drawing me into his arms, his heart beating wildly under my ear as our skin cooled.

I must have dozed off again, because when I blinked my eyes open, the room seemed brighter than before. Theo's fingers threaded lightly through my hair, lifting the strands off my back before letting them fall again.

Everything about him was so different from Steve, it was like I'd entered a new reality altogether. Considerate, sweet, dedicated to my pleasure in a way I'd never experienced—I let the beauty of it wash over my body, languid and peaceful.

If not for the dwindling hours between now and the tree lighting this weekend, I would have gladly stayed right there all day long.

As I rolled onto my back, I groaned quietly at the pleasant ache suffusing my limbs. "I don't think I can move," I grumbled, causing Theo to laugh and tickle my ribs.

"Unfortunately, I'll need to run home to feed Queen Toni her breakfast," he said as he sat up and swung his legs over the side of the bed. He glanced back at me over his shoulder and grinned. "And put together my disguise for condom shopping, I suppose. What do you need to get done today and how can I help?"

I flung one arm across my eyes as I thought through my to-do list. "As much as I appreciate the offer, I'll probably get more done without you here to distract me," I said, hoping the truth wouldn't offend him.

Theo circled the bed and dropped a kiss to the center of my chest. "Then I'll go stock up and stay out of your way for a while. Can I pick up dinner for you, maybe? I can't imagine you feel like cooking after baking all day long."

"That would be heavenly." I plopped my arm back onto the bed to smile up at him.

"Text me what you want and whatever allergy instructions I need to give them," he said as he leaned down to kiss me for real.

A rush of affection washed over me as I nodded, caught him in a more lingering kiss goodbye, and watched him dress to return home. He ordered me to stay in bed rather than walking him out, so I lay there, listening to his footsteps and the sound of the door closing behind him.

This is temporary, I told myself, but my body didn't care about that. Every nerve ending inside me was still dancing, buzzing with pleasure. I could lie here all day, floating through the memory of every incredible moment with Theo.

No, you can't.

I had preparations to get through and I'd be damned if I lost sight of everything I'd worked for just because a man with magic hands came into my life. I rolled out of bed, trudged to the shower, and reminded myself—again—that this fling had an expiration date.

Unfortunately, while my mind understood it, the rest of my body seemed content to remain in blissful ignorance of that fact.

Chapter Nineteen

THEO

IF I HADN'T ALREADY been remembering all the reasons I hated small town life, finding a place to buy condoms without drawing attention to myself would have done it. I even considered convincing Ollie to get them for me, but that would've led to a conversation I wasn't ready to have.

Not that Esther was a *secret*. She was a treasure, but I wasn't ready to share that, not even with my best friend.

In the end, I drove for forty-five minutes before deciding a drugstore at the outskirts of Rochester would be anonymous enough. I made it in and out of the store without running into anyone I knew, though the kid behind the counter smirked when he scanned three value-sized boxes of condoms and put them in a paper bag for me. My goal was to not have to come back anytime soon.

Without flinching, I stared back at the young cashier, daring him to comment, but he simply handed me the bag and my receipt with a quiet, "Have fun."

Oh, I would.

I grabbed lunch, stopped at the hardware store for a few things since I had nothing better to do just yet, and returned home to putter for a few hours before dinner. I left the condoms on the kitchen table, caught up on some work emails and payroll, and—in true creeper style—glanced repeatedly out the kitchen window toward the guest house. Each time I picked up my phone to text Esther, I forced myself to set it back down. The last thing she needed was me interrupting her while she was working.

After fixing a squeaky plank on the basement stairs and watching a documentary about whale decomposition that made me cringe so hard I worried my face might get stuck that way, I jumped when a text from Esther appeared.

I read through her food choices and instructions, recognizing it as the same dish she'd ordered when we were at The Mermaid with Sofia and Oliver, asked what time she'd be done with her baking, then ran upstairs to shower and change into something less grungy. When I called to place our order, the server who answered the phone passed me straight to the chef herself.

Maybe I was projecting, but the woman sounded equal parts competent on the food allergy front and ecstatic about Esther being part of a dinner for two.

By the time I picked up our dinners—reconfirming that all of the allergy protocols had been followed, because I didn't want to risk fucking it up and harming Esther—I was filled with the kind of nervous energy I associated with first dates. It was ridiculous, given that I'd spent most of the night inside her and the rest wrapped around her, but my pulse was hammering by the time I knocked on the guest house door.

She opened it quickly, still wearing a purple apron with *The Nutless Wonder* emblazoned across the front. Her smile was a little shy but so wide it immediately soothed my nerves.

"Hi," she said softly, stepping back to let me in.

"Hi," I repeated as I paused to kiss her lightly on the lips. Traces of telltale sweetness lingered, and I winked at her before admonishing, "Someone's been sampling the goods."

Eyes wide with feigned innocence, she blinked up at me. "I'm responsible for quality control. My sidekick was away on a very important mission."

I laughed and set the takeout bag on the table. "Was your day productive?"

"Very," she replied, untying the apron to hang it on a hook in the kitchen. "And was your mission successful?"

I snorted. "I drove almost to Rochester, for fuck's sake. Next time I'll just order them online. I'm pretty sure the kid at the cash register thought I was about to host an orgy."

Esther smirked at me. "Just how many did you buy?"

"Three of the biggest boxes I could find. You *are* insatiable, after all."

Amusement lit her features, but she only hummed in response to the accusation. I took that to mean she agreed my purchase was worth the trip. While she pulled plates from the cupboard, I unpacked our food.

It wasn't until we were seated at the table that she realized I had ordered the same pasta dish she'd gotten, since I didn't want to inadvertently consume something that might trigger a reaction. When I explained my reasoning, she blinked back a sudden sheen of tears.

"Hey, it's okay," I said quickly, reaching for her hand across the table. "That's nothing to cry about, is it?"

She shook her head and took a moment to compose herself before saying, "No, it's just really sweet of you."

When she cleared her throat and turned the conversation to the upcoming event that weekend, I didn't protest. A low simmer of anger toward her selfish asshole of a husband had taken up residence in my gut, but I had no desire to bring forth another wave of tears. I tamped down those feelings and focused instead on the animated way she talked about the food truck, even though she confessed to being nervous in crowds.

Just as we were clearing the table, her phone chirped with a notification. Esther blinked in surprise before her eyebrows drew down.

"That's my business email," she explained, reaching for the phone. "Hopefully it's not some issue for this weekend."

I dried my hands on a towel while she checked it, but when her frown deepened, I joined her at the counter. She turned the phone toward me and I saw that it was a photo—a cupcake lying on pavement, smashed by the sledgehammer still embedded in the rubble of frosting and crumbs.

"What the hell?" I muttered, zooming in on the image. Around the cupcake were shards of what looked like peanut shells. "Is this some kind of joke?"

One glance at Esther's face convinced me that she didn't think so. Her cheeks were pale, her eyes a little too wide, her mouth tight. I pulled her into my arms without a second thought.

"Hey, it's okay," I murmured into her hair.

She nodded against my chest, but her body trembled ever so slightly under my hands. For another minute, I soothed her, keeping up a steady stream of reassurances as I rubbed my hands up and down her spine. When I drew back, I tipped her chin up so that she met my eyes.

"Has this happened before?"

With an unsteady breath, she shook her head. "No, nothing like this. I told you I got a few weird calls in the last couple days, though, always from private numbers. At first it was just hang-ups, so I figured it was just someone dialing the wrong number."

"At first?"

"Today I answered one and it was like...heavy breathing. Like obviously someone was on the line, but they didn't hang up right away. Later on, I had a voicemail that was the same."

A jolt of adrenaline shot through me, though whether it was brought on by the quaver in her voice or the fury I felt over someone screwing with her, I couldn't quite say. My arms tightened around her as I tried to settle myself down and think logically. She hadn't given me many details about her husband, but I got the impression flying off the handle would scare the shit out of her.

No matter what, I was determined never to give her reason to fear me.

"Do you still have the voicemail?" I asked, stroking one hand along her back.

"Yes."

"Good. Don't delete the photo. We might be able to trace them. It's probably just someone messing around," I said as calmly as I could manage.

"Okay," she mumbled.

I pressed my lips to her forehead, more a promise than a kiss. "And let me know if anything else like that happens, okay?"

Esther nodded and took half a step back, her shoulders squaring as her resolve strengthened. "I will. I'm sure you're right. Just a stupid prank."

"Why don't we sit and you can give me the rundown on how this weekend will go?" I suggested.

She let me guide her to the living room and tuck her onto my lap in one corner of the loveseat. As she described the tree lighting event, I teased her about her organizational skills—the timeline she relayed from memory was impressively exact, right down to the minute.

"I see why my mother loves you," I told her, kissing her temple.

"Because I'm practically perfect in every way?"

"I was thinking more like she was dazzled by your color-coded spreadsheets, but yes, that too."

"Ah, yes. My spreadsheets are one of my best traits," she mused.

I laughed, but when her fingers started trailing over my chest, leaving a tantalizing path of heat in their wake, I leaned close to her ear and said, "I can think of a few others I'd rank higher."

"Oh? I'd like to hear all about them, but I believe you mentioned something about orgies?"

OUR PREVIOUS DISCUSSIONS ABOUT Thanksgiving had generally revolved around avoiding having to sit through dinner with any of our friends, but at some ungodly hour of the night—or maybe in the early morning—after we both awoke in a warm, sleepy haze and Esther rode me to a dreamlike orgasm before collapsing onto my chest, we decided we'd celebrate our own way.

"What's your favorite Thanksgiving dish?" I asked, my voice low even though we were at no risk of disturbing anyone from her bed.

She nestled closer, her lips tickling my skin when she replied, "Sweet potatoes."

"With marshmallows?"

"No, definitely not. I make them with brown sugar and pineapple. What about you?"

"Stuffing, definitely. And rolls."

"A carb man," she mused. "I dig it."

"Turkey?"

She wrinkled her nose. "I don't eat a lot of meat. The texture weirds me out."

"Right. Sidesgiving, then."

While we debated the merits of pumpkin versus apple pie, Esther drew swirling designs across my chest and I glided my fingertips up and down her spine. I thought about how long she'd been alone, how readily she reacted to the faintest touch, how deeply she'd buried this part of her.

"You're very quiet," she whispered.

"I know you like keeping to yourself, but you must have been lonely."

For a moment, she stayed silent, and I was afraid I'd crossed a line. Then she pressed her lips to my jaw and nodded in the darkness.

"I didn't think so until I met you."

My heart tripped on those words and my arm tightened involuntarily around her. "I don't like the thought of you being sad."

"Not sad," she corrected, "just...I don't know. Missing companionship, at times. I like my life, Theo. I'm happy with the choices I've made, proud of what I've done. Just very, very occasionally, I consider what it might be like to have someone to share it with. Then I come to my senses."

The last bit was light, teasing, but I felt the truth underneath it.

"I'm not sad," she reiterated, her fingers digging gently into my chest.

"I believe you."

She was quiet for a moment, then said, "I'll be okay when you go home, Theo."

"I know you will. But I want you to get your fill while I'm here, okay? Soak up as much as you need from me. Will you do that?"

She huffed a laugh against my skin. "Use you to fill my quota of physical affection?"

"Yes."

Before answering, she snuggled closer into me and propped herself up to look down at my face. I'd never tire of seeing those luminous eyes shining through the darkness, of their warmth and curiosity glowing in her beautiful face.

"Do you feel like I'm using you?" she asked quietly. "In a bad way?"

I squeezed her hip with one hand and cupped her cheek with the other. "Not in the least."

She studied my features for a long time, though I doubted she could see very much, then she dropped her head to kiss my lips—softly, sweetly—before snuggling back down. I tugged the covers up over her bare shoulders and tucked them around us both.

"Good," she whispered.

"Better than good," I murmured into her hair. "Now get some sleep."

Chapter Twenty

ESTHER

THEO WAS EXTREMELY GOOD at many things, not the least of which was the ability to take my mind off both the stress of event preparation and the bizarre messages I'd received. Given the immense relief of living on my own after Steve died, I didn't like the thought of some stupid jokes making me afraid to be by myself.

Still, Theo's warm, steady presence was a balm for my soul. And if I was able to lose myself in his arms, well, it served as a welcome distraction from all the rest.

By the time we huddled over the table with toasted waffles on Thanksgiving morning, my entire body was still humming. A tiny flutter of nervous energy had taken up residence in my stomach, though, like my subconscious couldn't bear to let such joy go unchecked.

"Hey," Theo said softly, in that tone I'd come to associate with him seeing the occasional flare of panic in my eyes. "Doing okay?"

I puffed out my cheeks. "I'm freaking out a little."

"Too many orgasms?"

A loud, startled laugh leapt from my throat and I slapped a hand over my mouth in embarrassment. He grinned, squeezing my other hand on the table between us. The nerves dissipated under the warmth of his expression.

"Is this your superpower? Calming me down when I start to freak out?"

He winked. "It might be. Seems like a good skill to have. Are you worried about the phone calls? The event this weekend? Or is this about us?"

"All of the above, maybe? Like I said, it's been a long time, and I don't just mean the sex," I joked weakly.

I'd already recognized Theo was as perceptive as his mother, but it was different with him. Where she tended toward quiet observation, tracking patterns or trends before coming to a conclusion, he seemed to catch every individual nuance of tone or expression. Somehow, that hadn't stopped me from offering up gems that were sure to attract his attention.

His head tilted curiously as he studied me. "How long had it been, exactly?"

Oh, god. I could feel my cheeks heating, but if I deflected the question now, I was absolutely sure it would come up again, probably when I had less willpower. "Six years."

Shock flooded his handsome face. "Jesus. When did Steve die?"

I shrugged a little, dropping my gaze to the syrup on my empty plate, and said, "Four years ago."

"So for two years of your marriage..."

"There were very few things that seemed to be in my control at the time. I couldn't bear to lose any more of myself."

"And he accepted that?" Theo's eyebrows nearly reached his hairline.

"I told him in explicit detail what I would do to him if he didn't."

He squeezed my hand. "I'm sorry. I didn't mean to bring it up again. Now that I know you better, I just can't imagine anyone treating you that way."

What he meant was he couldn't imagine *me* putting up with that. I could barely imagine it, now that I was out of the situation, but it wasn't something I explained to anyone other than my therapist.

With Theo, though, I wanted him to understand.

"The first year we were married was...I don't know, normal. He was attentive, charming. It wasn't a grand passion or whirlwind romance, but it was fine. Comfortable. During that second year, things changed. He started with the backhanded compliments and subtle digs, and sex became something I tolerated so he'd leave me alone and go to sleep. I felt worse and worse about it until I snapped."

"And your parents refused to help you." His expression was grim. "Were they the only ones you went to during all of that?"

"Yes, and before you say it, I know Sofia or your mom would have tried to help. Looking back, I wish I'd gone to one of them, and if he hadn't died, I probably would have. Eventually. I had no money of my own because he encouraged me not to find a job after college. And through it all, he made comments, vague enough for him to deny if I called him on it, but convincing enough to scare me out of involving anyone I cared about."

He was silent for a beat, then said, "Sometimes I wish that rumor was true."

"That I killed him?"

"Esther," he murmured, waiting until I looked back at him to go on. "I was taught that unless it's an enthusiastic yes, it's a definite no, and I can't imagine disrespecting that premise the way he did. I'm sorry for what you've been through. You didn't deserve any of that. "

I sighed and shook my head, forcing the memories away. "I know. I know it now, anyway."

Theo looked like he wanted to yank me onto his lap and protect me from the world. If I was honest with myself, part of me wanted that, too. What was it about this family that they were able to not only see all the walls I'd put up, but also to burst through them like wrecking balls? I narrowed my eyes at the man across from me, attempting to hold onto a glare.

"Don't even try it," he warned, his lips tipping up at the corners. "I didn't force you to tell me a damn thing, so no rules were broken. And sometimes it feels better to talk about it."

I humphed softly, but he was right. My therapist had been an amazing help over the years, but she was the only one I'd spoken to in any kind of detail. In the early days after Steve died, Sofia would try to encourage me to talk about it, but my continued resistance had resulted in her abandoning those attempts.

I wondered what would have happened if I'd taken her up on it.

"Right. So, I'm familiar with your incredibly precise timeline, but what else do we need to do for this weekend?" Theo asked, drawing me back to the present.

"Oh!" I said excitedly. "I have something for you, hang on."

He waited at the table, clearly amused, while I ran to the bedroom closet and grabbed the item. I presented it to him with an elaborate flourish, then bobbed impatiently while he unwrapped the tissue paper around it.

"I thought you said no gifts," he teased.

I scowled at him. "No Christmas gifts. This is different."

When he held up the purple t-shirt, he grinned. "Oh, Esther. My very own Nutless Wonder shirt? This is incredible."

"Check out the back."

He turned it over and howled with laughter when he saw *Long John* written across the shoulders. "When on earth did you have this made?"

"As soon as you offered to be my sidekick," I answered, delighted with his response. "There's a little print shop on Main Street that makes my stuff, and they said they'd be able to get it done in time. Can't have a sidekick without a uniform, can I?"

Carefully, Theo draped the shirt over the back of my chair, then caught me around the waist and pulled me down onto his lap. Punctuating each word with a kiss along my jawline, he said, "You. Are. Amazing."

This continued until his big hand came up to cup my breast, then I tutted and scooted off his lap. "No, no, no, we have plenty to do today, Long John. I hope you're ready to level up on your cake decorating skills tomorrow, because after Thanksgiving is over, you're up."

He grinned, his expression turning to an invitation I couldn't possibly miss. "I have a feeling I'll be up long before dinner, Esther."

Throughout the day, I took him up on his offer to soak up as much physical affection as I could. After starting my favorite stuffing recipe in the crockpot, we trudged over to the main house, which boasted cable television instead of just streaming services, in order to curl up on the couch and watch the dog show—my favorite part of Thanksgiving Day.

"That one looks like an actual mop," Theo muttered.

"Hush, he's a little darling."

"A darling little mop, maybe."

I scowled up at him but didn't move from my spot, nestled under his arm with my own draped across his middle. It was warm and incredibly comfortable, and he hadn't stopped drawing curlicues across the small of my back from the time I settled there.

Learning the volumes that could be spoken with just a touch became my new favorite lesson.

Unfortunately, the soothing nature of his fingertips meant I fell asleep before a springer spaniel named Lord Grantham won Best in Show, then I woke up to Theo watching a home improvement special with the volume turned down.

"Sorry," I mumbled, pressing my face into his ribs against the bright glare of daylight.

"There's only one situation where I'd begrudge you falling asleep on me, and I will do my best to avoid that ever happening."

I huffed a laugh and glanced at my watch. "We should get dinner started."

"Yeah."

His lips moved over the crown of my head and it suddenly struck me that maybe Theo, too, needed his fill of affection from this arrangement. I'd noticed how touchy-feely his family was—not with me, probably because my expression was the human equivalent of a neon *KEEP AWAY* sign, but with each other. It was as natural to them as breathing, this tendency to hug or brush fingers or squeeze a shoulder as they went about their business.

For the first time in a long time, I wanted that.

"You're looking very serious," Theo said, trailing his lips along my ear.

I shivered at the caress before leaning in with my chin propped on his shoulder. "I like this."

One dark brow lifted as he asked, "What do you like, Esther?"

Those words, that low rumble of his voice reverberating from his chest into mine, held me frozen for several beats, staring into his warm gaze.

"Being with you."

The admission was so quiet, he probably wouldn't have heard me if we weren't so very close to one another, but I watched it hit him, watched the softness that came over his expression before he tipped his face down to kiss me.

I was in over my head. I knew it, he knew it, even the cat in the corner of the room probably knew it as she stared at us with golden eyes full of feline judgment.

It was just...I couldn't bring myself to worry about it.

For right now, everything I needed was right in front of me, and I was going to reach out with both hands and hold on for as long as it lasted.

Chapter Twenty-One

THEO

SIDESGIVING WAS AN UNPRECEDENTED success.

Since the meal included only our favorite items, there was no need to gorge on things we didn't like just to be polite, leaving room for all the things we loved. Esther's sweet potato dish was to die for, the stuffing came out perfect, and the blissful look on her face when she bit into one of my homemade dinner rolls had my body clenching with desire.

It was the best Thanksgiving dinner I'd ever had. Sharing it with Esther was certainly the deciding factor.

Once we'd finished the meal, cleaned up, and finally enjoyed the apple pie that had been a joint effort when we came back to the guest house after the dog show, we collapsed onto Esther's bed to recover from eating so much. We lay there, side by side, only our fingers entwined.

Long after the sun had set, Esther rolled toward me without saying a word. I mirrored her movement, turning into her arms as they wrapped around me, finding her lips in the darkness. A hint of cinnamon lingered on her tongue, and I spent what felt like centuries exploring that sweetness before her hands tugged at my tee.

We moved together in silence, like it was all part of a hazy fantasy instead of real life. Even my name on her lips when she came was barely more than a breath, a magic spell weaving its way around us both.

I drifted off there in her arms, my head on her breast as I slid into sleep, where soft swirls of vanilla and peppermint soaked deep into my soul, twining there like ivy.

For the first time I could remember, I wanted to stay right where I was instead of walking away, consequences be damned.

I awoke to the weak morning sunlight gilding Esther's skin under my cheek. The only sign she was awake was the soft scrape of her nails along my scalp. Turning my head, I pressed a kiss to her golden skin and then met her gaze, warm and sleepy.

"Good morning, sweetness."

"Morning."

Her fingers stayed in my hair as I trailed my lips across her torso, pausing only for the briefest moment when she arched upward as I licked her nipples into tight peaks before moving down her ribs, trailing kisses over the soft swell of her stomach. The dreamy haze persisted even when I settled my mouth between her legs, teasing until her breathless cries and tugging fingers pulled me up over her body.

Some amount of time later—an hour, a day, a lifetime—Esther declared it was time to get to work.

After a quick breakfast of coffee and leftover apple pie, during which her sated expression never faded, I ran back to the house to feed Toni. When I returned, Esther was already setting out everything we needed.

Fortunately for both of us, I was much better at sprinkling candy cane shards and placing mini vegan marshmallows than I was at actually frosting cupcakes. I made Esther describe each flavor so I could recognize them on sight, but she went a step further and set aside one of each of the offerings for the tree lighting for me to sample throughout the day.

Delicious as everything was, I was grateful she chose limited menus for events like this. My blood sugar couldn't handle the dozens of options she offered on custom orders.

Watching her work was fascinating. She got this look of intense concentration on her face as she added artistic touches and printed labels on decorative cardstock. When she pulled out a bright pink folder to hold a stack of printouts, I raised a brow.

"What's that for?"

Esther's teeth were caught on her lower lip as she sorted and paperclipped them into some kind of order. "Ingredient lists and allergy protocols. Most of my customers have already spoken to me about that stuff in the past, so they trust that I know what I'm doing, but sometimes I get people visiting from out of town or who have newly diagnosed allergies and are still navigating. It helps to have something they can look over so they can make a decision."

I paused in my garnishing to smile at her. "Have I told you that you're amazing?"

With a snort, she said, "Only six or seven times this week."

That feeling spilled through my veins again, the tender rush of affection for this woman who'd been through so much and still had so much to give to others. I thought back to the night I'd called her bait for my parents' trap, but that wasn't it at all.

She was a promise, a treasure at the end of a long quest. My heart clenched painfully in my chest.

This treasure is not for you.

I almost argued with that quiet voice in my head, but what was there to say? No attachments, no pain—that was how I lived. Esther had given no indication she wanted anything more than what we'd agreed to, but she'd made it clear her life was here in Spruce Hill.

Apparently, I'd been frozen in place long enough for her to notice. "You okay?" she asked. "I can finish those up if you have other things to do."

"No, I'm good. I'm almost done," I assured her, smiling until her concerned expression softened.

We made it through the remainder of the preparations, loaded them into the refrigerator in her back hall, and took a break to eat sandwiches on the loveseat. When we finished,

Esther curled against my side and I toyed with a lock of hair that had slipped from her braid.

As my fingertips brushed over the back of her neck, she snuggled closer and sighed contentedly. "That feels good."

"I could spend all day exploring your skin," I murmured.

"Mmm. I'll write you in for tomorrow, then," she replied, peering up to grin at me. "We do have most of the day before the event."

I laughed and kissed the tip of her nose. "I can think of a few activities to kill time."

She rose to her feet and held out a hand, saying, "Then by all means, let's get some practice in before tomorrow."

I caught her fingers in mine, kissed the inside of her wrist, and followed her to the bedroom.

SATURDAY PASSED IN MUCH the same fashion, a mixture of preparations for the evening's event and abandoning our duties to explore one another—and it seemed like every exploration led to some new discovery, whether it was a position Esther didn't even realize she enjoyed or a quiet moment that burrowed deep under my skin, settling dangerously close to my heart.

We crawled out of bed for a shower and a makeshift dinner, changed into our matching Nutless Wonder tees, and loaded the food truck with all of the night's offerings. Once we were back inside, I kept my boots on and gestured toward the house.

"I'll feed the queen before we go. Anything else I need to bring tonight?"

Esther moved to the kitchen to take a peek at her checklist. "Just a coat for when we go watch the lighting, I think."

Before I left, I came up behind her, wrapped my arms around her middle, and kissed the side of her neck. She hummed and leaned back against me, folding her arms over mine. We stayed that way until she finally glanced over her shoulder with a smirk.

"Yeah, yeah, I'm going," I muttered. "Tomorrow, though, you're mine. No interruptions, no baking, no work intruding."

The radiance of her smile warmed me to my core as she turned in my arms and rested her chin against my chest to beam up at me. "That's the best offer I've had all year," she teased, then shooed me out the door.

Toni ignored me completely as I prepared her dinner, though she allowed me to give her a few quick pets before swishing her tail in my face. For a moment, guilt tugged at me for leaving her alone so much these last few days, but whenever we came to the house, she stayed several yards away from wherever we were sitting.

Still, I decided to see if Esther was open to spending some nights in my bed, even if hers had become my new favorite hideaway.

I grabbed my coat and made my way back to the guest house, waiting in the clear, cold night while Esther locked the door behind us. We hopped up into the food truck and headed toward town.

Though the event didn't officially start for another hour, there were already people milling about in Town Park when we arrived. Esther carefully maneuvered the truck along the service road, following the orange-vested volunteer's directions to our assigned spot. The sight of kids chasing each other around the playground at the edge of the grass threw me straight back to my childhood. I jerked myself from the memories when Esther turned off the engine and followed my line of sight.

Together, we watched for another minute, then she quietly asked, "Do you want kids?" At my startled look, she flushed. "Not with me. I meant in general. Someday."

"Maybe someday," I hedged. "You?"

For a long moment, she was silent. I started to think she wasn't going to answer when she gave a tiny shrug and unbuckled her seatbelt. "Maybe."

The way she said it made me think there was a lot more to her feelings on the subject, but she hopped out of the driver's seat to open the back of the truck and started sorting through the carefully organized desserts on tonight's menu. I followed more slowly, giving her a few extra seconds of privacy, if that was what she needed. The temptation to simply fold her back into my arms was strong, but I forced myself to resist.

We got everything set up, including a cash box and Esther's iPad for credit card purchases. The evening was chilly, and though it hadn't snowed yet, the promise of it hung in the air. When Esther paused to inhale deeply, I offered a fond smile instead of teasing her about it.

She wrinkled her nose at me and busied herself with making sure the chalkboard menu on the outside of the truck's serving window was updated and smudge-free.

The residents of Spruce Hill took their townwide festivities very seriously; before long, the park was teeming with people. Strings of lights delineated the row of food trucks and vendors before opening wide to the green in front of a huge eastern white pine. There were a few carnival-type games set up down the lane and Christmas music played from speakers dotting the area.

"This is much cooler than I remember from when I was a kid," I said after she handed a small box of cupcakes to a family of four.

She batted her lashes at me. "Does that mean you're going to win me a teddy bear before the night is through?"

I glanced over at the games, then flexed my biceps dramatically for her. "Hell yes it does," I vowed, winking when she laughed.

"Purple is an excellent color on you, by the way."

"Not as good as it is on you. In fact, after careful consideration, I know what dessert I'm going to choose at the end of the night," I murmured into her ear.

"Oh, do you?" she asked. Her eyes shone like discs of pure moonlight as she blinked up at me with wide-eyed innocence.

Behind the counter, hidden from view, I cupped my hand over the curve of her ass and kneaded lightly. "Oh, yes, Esther, I do."

Chapter Twenty-Two

ESTHER

Before I could respond to Theo—or shoo him away—a group of customers appeared and he removed his hand to help me serve them. We had a line at the window from that moment until a tiny lull half an hour in, then a steady stream that kept us too busy for either conversation or covert groping.

Of course, quite a few of our customers lingered to express their delight at seeing Theo back in town. Fortunately for him, the people lining up behind the gossip mongers prevented anyone from asking too many questions.

Theo was unfailingly polite, but as he deflected another round of well-intentioned probing, I began to feel bad about putting him in this position.

"You don't have to do this," I said when we had another moment to breathe between orders. "I can handle things here if you want to leave."

He drew up to his full height and scowled down at me. "Esther, I take my role as sidekick seriously. A few busybodies aren't going to scare me away, trust me. Besides, I'm sure you've dealt with far worse."

That much was true.

In the early days of the business, even before I bought the truck, every delivery required an extra ten minutes to parry with inquisitive customers who wanted to express their condolences and dig for juicy details. The rumor that I'd killed my husband was actually one of the best things that could have happened at the time—a few bland smiles, a cryptic answer here and there, and people started to shy away from prying.

Just the memory of it made me huff out a quiet laugh, but Theo heard it and waited until we had a break to ask what was so funny.

"Just thinking about how ready everyone was to believe I killed my husband. Am I really that scary?"

He threw back his head and laughed. "You seemed put out when I told you I didn't think you were a murderer, remember?"

"I could be," I grumbled, "under the right circumstances."

"Esther, you are a delight," he said as he dropped a quick kiss to my lips.

I started to reply, but a chorus of coos came from the window and I flushed hot when it turned out to be the entire crew from our dinner at The Mermaid. Ollie and Julian had their heads tipped together and hands clasped to their chests like we were the cutest thing they'd ever seen, while Melody, Theresa, and Sofia grinned like the Cheshire Cat. Only Chase looked embarrassed to have caught us in a private moment, mouthing, "Sorry," at us before his wife elbowed him in the ribs.

"For the love of Christ," Theo muttered, adopting an impressive scowl until I pinched his hip and nudged him out of the way.

"Hey, guys. Everyone having fun?" I asked.

After a round of answers encouraging us to check out the adult beverage tent before the end of the night and a friendly wager between Theo and Oliver regarding the ring toss, the group of them ordered half a dozen cupcakes and a few brownies, thanks to Theo's sales pitch. We promised to come find them before the tree lighting and they mosied away with a bevy of knowing smiles and pointed looks.

I grinned at Theo's exaggerated sigh of relief once they were gone. "You know you love them. It's good to have friends."

He waited patiently while I directed my attention to a family of twin preschoolers with peanut allergies, then when I turned back, he quietly said, "You're right, it is."

The implication that they were my friends too was not lost on me, but an announcement saying the tree would be lit in ten minutes came over the loudspeakers, so we got the truck closed up and threw on our coats. Theo took my hand in his so we wouldn't get separated in the crowd as we set off toward the green.

With his height advantage, it was much easier to find our friends than it would have been for me on my own. When I told him as much, he squeezed my hand and bent his head to whisper, "They don't call me Long John for nothing, you know."

Once we were positioned on the far side of the park, huddled together for warmth, the middle school chorus started their holiday repertoire with enthusiasm that waned steadily from song to song. Oliver teased Sofia about her chorus years, Melody and Theresa sang along under their breath, and Theo wrapped me in his arms like he could single-handedly ward off the chill.

He succeeded.

I leaned into him, ignoring Sofia's raised eyebrows, though I couldn't hold back a smile. These people had been my friends before Steve came into my life, and even after all the times I pushed them away, here they were, ready and willing to welcome me back.

Maybe Theo had served as a bridge, but hopefully things could continue like this even after he left.

The wave of sadness that crashed over me nearly took my breath away. Theo leaned down to rub his cheek against mine as though he'd felt the change, even if I told myself he was probably just being his usual affectionate self. In any case, the chorus finished off their final song and merged back into the mass of bodies standing around the tree.

"Here we go," Theo murmured into my ear.

A hush fell over the crowd, then the dark pine tree erupted into thousands of twinkling lights and a cheer went up from everyone in the park. Theo's arms tightened around me as fireworks went off somewhere beyond the tree. A toddler perched on his father's shoulders beside us began to wail at the loud booms and pops.

I sighed and relaxed into Theo's embrace, staring up at the display. Events like this were the kind of thing Sofia had dragged me to in college, the kind of thing that made me feel like I was part of something bigger, that made Spruce Hill feel like home.

Now, surrounded by friendship and kindness, I finally felt that way again.

Steve had put a lot of stock in public appearances, but only when it would benefit him in some way. There would never have been friendly banter about carnival games or trips to the booze tent, only subtle digs at what I was wearing or who I smiled at or how I'd disappointed him at some ritzy function or another.

As if summoned by those unhappy memories, the crowd on the other side of the tree shifted and I caught sight of Tyler, standing alone and scowling in our direction. My body stiffened enough that Theo bent down and asked, "What's wrong?"

"Nothing," I replied swiftly.

"It's not nothing. I felt you go solid." He rubbed his hands up and down my arms like he could brush the tension away.

"I saw Tyler over there," I said, keeping my voice low.

Theo followed my gaze, but even in the light of the enormous tree and the colorful flashes overhead, Tyler had disappeared from view.

"Tell me if you see him again," he murmured in my ear. "I'll take care of it."

I wasn't sure exactly how he intended to do that, but I didn't want a brawl on my conscience—Tyler would probably fight dirty and might hurt Theo—so I just nodded.

When the fireworks came to a close and the high school chorus took the stage in front of the enormous tree for their performance, Theo and I slipped away to check out some of the vendors. While he said hello to a few acquaintances, I chatted with the gluten-free baker whose goods I often kept in stock during the busy season. I left so she could help a customer, and a familiar voice called my name.

"Drew, hi!" I replied, smiling as I turned to greet the young man who was one of my regulars. He worked in the event center where I sometimes parked the truck during lunch hours.

"How have you been?" he asked.

As usual, he looked at me with something like hero worship, which always made me vaguely uneasy. Not long after Steve's death, Drew had asked me out to dinner. Though he'd accepted my refusal easily enough, I always got the impression he was waiting for me to tell him I was finally ready to date again.

"Really good, thanks. I hope you had a nice Thanksgiving?"

He nodded and started to respond, but his gaze caught on something over my shoulder and instead he said, "I gotta run, Esther. I'm sure I'll see you again soon."

A second later, Theo returned to my side, wrapped his arm around my waist, and said, "Now, show me which teddy bear to win for you, milady."

Not only did he win the bear, he also funded the ring toss efforts of at least four or five little kids who showed up to the counter beside him. By the time we headed back toward the truck, his wallet was significantly emptier but my heart was full enough to burst.

At the end of the night, we'd sold out of almost everything. As soon as the truck was officially closed up and off-duty, I presented Theo with a couple brownies I'd hidden away for us to share. His caramel eyes melted when he saw them.

"I realize you made your dessert intentions fairly clear, but I also know I'm usually starving by the end of these things, so I figured we deserved a treat."

"Esther," he said in a reverent tone, "you are an absolute goddess."

I laughed, handed him a brownie on a napkin, and lifted my own in toast. "To the best sidekick I've ever had."

"To both of us," he corrected, then wolfed down the brownie in three big bites.

Once we finished eating and brushed the crumbs from our laps, I drove us home through the dark night, guided by the lamp posts along Main Street and houses adorned with their own colorful light displays. I wasn't sure if Theo had just been teasing, but when he followed me inside instead of returning to his parents' house, he proved that he'd been completely serious about his intentions.

There was more than one benefit to having a sidekick.

Chapter Twenty-Three

THEO

WE SLEPT IN LATE the next morning, late enough that when I snuck out of Esther's bed to go home and give the cat her breakfast, Toni sliced open my forearm. I swore—colorfully and at great length—as I cleaned the wound, then glared at the feline before returning to the guest house and the soft, sleepy woman under the covers. She was just beginning to stir, but she noticed the scratch immediately.

"You know, we can stay at the house instead," she told me as she inspected it. "She's probably lonely."

I laughed, but Esther's willingness to venture out of her little bubble of safety here warmed me through and through. "If you're sure, we can head over there later. I don't want you to be uncomfortable, but I wondered if you were open to the idea."

"As I recall, your bed was quite lovely," she teased.

Propping myself on one elbow to gaze down at her, I gave a solemn nod. "And your body spread across it was even lovelier."

We lingered in Esther's bed until lunchtime, showered together, then returned to the house to try to soothe the ginger beast's loneliness. Esther cooed over her as soon as we walked in, which resulted in losing half an hour to the queen's demands for attention. When the cat finally decided she was done with affection, she retreated to her favorite sunny windowsill.

Finally free, I tugged a giggling Esther upstairs and reminded her of my plans for the day. As I planted a line of kisses across her belly, I said, "Today. You. Are. Mine."

Very wisely, she did not disagree.

By the time the sun started to set outside the window, we were sprawled across the bed in a boneless tangle. The color scheme in here was a perfect backdrop for the sated woman beside me, calm and soothing, changing her eyes from silver to topaz to icy green in the span of a moment. My fingers swirled idly along her spine, drawing goosebumps and an occasional ticklish shiver, but she just nestled closer until her head rested right over my heart.

Throughout my entire life, I'd always been a light sleeper. I remembered creeping into my parents' room after hearing the first low rumble of thunder or an odd whistle of the wind or the bang of a car door closing. As an adult, I still woke often during the night, though fortunately I'd long since learned how to get myself back to sleep.

With Esther? I slept like a log.

She often shifted away from me during the night, which I attributed to both valuing her own space and overheating when we were wrapped around one another, but even her movements didn't wake me. As a result, when I blinked myself awake in the morning light the next day, I felt like I'd just gone under anesthesia or experienced a time jump. Esther was still fast asleep at my side, her hands tucked under her chin.

For several long minutes, I debated whether I should stay there until she woke up or go make us some breakfast. There was nothing more enticing than her sleepy smile when she reached for me, sometimes just to snuggle until her brain kicked into gear, sometimes to guide me into her for a slow, lazy round of lovemaking. Still, the last few days had taken their toll on her, especially being "on" in public the other night, and I wanted to be sure she got enough rest to fully recover.

With the decision made, I eased out of bed, tugged the curtains more tightly closed, and crept downstairs.

I fed Toni, who graced me with a swish of her tail instead of a flash of claws, and had just started scouring the cupboards when an insistent buzz came from somewhere behind me. For a second, I was convinced there was a bee in the kitchen, until I remembered Esther had tossed her phone onto the table when Toni demanded love the day before.

I intended to just hit the decline button and tell her about it when she woke up, but when I saw *private number* flashing across the screen, I remembered her comment about the prank calls. Instead of declining, I answered it, hoping that the sound of my deep voice instead of Esther's would scare the caller straight.

"Hello?" When no one spoke, I snapped, "Who the hell is this and why are you calling?"

The sound of heavy breathing came through the line and a surge of fury rose in me. There was no response to my questions, and after another few seconds, the caller hung up.

I swore under my breath, pulled out my own phone, and texted Oliver. One of our high school friends, Rose Hanson, was a detective on Spruce Hill's tiny police squad. I remembered Ollie mentioning her years ago, telling me she'd become the department's tech expert.

Fortunately, Oliver wasn't bumming around the way I was; he was already at work at the bank he managed in town. His reply came quickly, and though I could tell he was curious, he didn't ask any questions about why I wanted Rose's number. I thanked him, promised I'd update him after I had more information, and called her.

"Detective Hanson," she said when she answered the phone.

"Rose, hey. It's Theo Silver. I hope you remember me, or else this is going to get super awkward."

She laughed, the same deep, booming laugh I'd always loved to hear in the middle of the cafeteria at school. "Theo, I don't think a single person in this town has forgotten you. As much as I'd like to pretend this is you calling to apologize for knocking out my first loose tooth on the playground when we were six, I'm going to assume it's not a social call. What's up?"

"Oh, right. Well, I am sorry about that, actually. I'm calling for Esther Malek, though. She's been getting some creepy phone calls, and a vaguely threatening email came through recently. I wondered if there's anything you can do to help us figure out who's behind it."

"I can try," she said, sounding a little skeptical, "but no promises. Can you bring the phone by the station today?"

I assured her we would make time for it, like our busy schedule didn't consist solely of meals and sex, and thanked her profusely. Feeling better about the whole prank call situation, I returned to the pantry to triple check the ingredients list on a box of pancake mix. I set it aside to start a pot of coffee, then pulled out the rest of what I needed and started whisking.

As though summoned by the aroma of fresh coffee, Esther came plodding into the kitchen in bare feet and a fuzzy pink bathrobe she'd brought with her. I paused to appreciate the view.

"You look like you should be wearing bunny slippers right now," I said as I left my batter on the counter to run my hands over the plush fabric of the robe.

"I like to be cozy," she said primly, but she buried her face in my chest. "Good morning."

I kissed the top of her head and gestured to the ingredients I'd lined up along the countertop. "I checked everything, but I wanted to make sure it's all safe. And, obviously, I hope you like pancakes."

From our previous meals together, I'd gotten the distinct impression that Steve "The Asshole" Pautler had never lifted a finger in the kitchen, nor ever really taken her allergies into consideration. She blinked rapidly at the line of items, like she was swallowing back tears, then inspected each box and container.

"All good, and I love pancakes," she whispered.

"Hey," I said softly, pulling her back into my arms. "It's okay."

Esther nodded against my shoulder. "It's more than okay, it's great. Thank you. Not just for the pancakes, but for being great."

"You deserve great."

"I'm just not used to it," she admitted. "Steve was...well. Not great."

With one finger, I tipped her chin up and kissed her gently. She was still sleepy and sweet, practically melting against me. I didn't let her go until I was positive she'd stopped thinking about the son of a bitch she'd married.

"Why don't you sit and have some coffee while I make these?" I suggested.

I watched from the corner of my eye as she poured a mug of coffee, stirred in cream and sugar, and trudged toward the table. It was only when her eyes landed on the phone that I remembered I needed to tell her about the call.

To my great relief, she seemed annoyed but not concerned. When I explained about Rose, one side of her mouth curved upward.

"Detective Hanson was the first one to show up when Steve died," she said.

I thought I'd learned my lesson as far as talking about him, but given that opening, I had to ask. "How did he actually die?"

"Aneurysm."

She said it simply, like she'd explained it a dozen times, and maybe she had. Knowing Spruce Hill, I wouldn't be surprised.

"And the rumor that you killed him, where the hell did that come in?"

Now her lips tipped up in earnest, though she appeared to be fighting the smile. "I might have gotten tired of being interrogated by townsfolk," she hedged.

My jaw dropped. "You sneaky little minx. You encouraged the rumor, didn't you?" When her pink-clad shoulders lifted and fell with dainty nonchalance, I snorted out a laugh. "Oh, Oliver would pay good money for that little detail, you know. What do you say we go halfsies?"

She laughed, cradling her coffee mug between her hands. "It's a deal."

As we settled in to eat breakfast together, I wondered why this felt so good, so *right*. I might have ended all my relationships well before we moved in together, but it wasn't like I'd never spent the night with a woman I was dating. Hell, Annabelle and I had spent a week together in the Florida Keys a couple years ago, a month before I reminded her I wasn't looking to get married and she dumped my ass. I'd made that clear to every partner right from the beginning, because I wouldn't risk fucking up someone else's life the way I once had.

Still, I couldn't quite pinpoint why such mundane things seemed so natural when it came to Esther, as though they were simply meant to be.

I must have been staring blankly down at my empty plate for longer than intended, because when I glanced up, Esther was watching me with those silky black brows drawn almost together over her pale eyes.

"Everything okay?" she asked, her tone light despite the concern written across her features.

"Yes, totally fine. This is just...really nice. I like being around you." The words sounded stupid as soon as they left my mouth, but her expression eased.

"It is nice," she agreed. "You're pretty handy to have around, you know."

For at least a short while, I would bask in the blessedly normal joy of having breakfast with the beautiful woman sitting across from me. Real life could remain tucked into a little box to be dealt with some other time.

Chapter Twenty-Four

ESTHER

I TRIED TO QUELL the jitters brought on by walking into the tiny Spruce Hill police station and *almost* succeeded, thanks to Theo's warm hand wrapped around mine. He seemed more worried about the prank calls than I was, which in turn increased my own anxiety.

Rose Hanson, however, put my mind at ease just as quickly. She was matter-of-fact, sharp as a tack, and beautifully competent. "Hey, Theo. Hand it over and go fetch me a Coke from the break room fridge, would you? Want anything, Esther?"

Laughing, I shook my head and sat down in the chair across from Rose's computer. Before I was even fully seated, her attention toggled between the phone and her computer screen. Theo returned a few minutes later, slid the can across the desk to

Rose's waiting hand, and lowered himself into the chair beside me.

"The email came from the same phone as the calls," she said eventually.

I frowned. "Is that good or bad?"

Rose waved her hand from side to side. "Both. It means the number blocker they used for the phone calls doesn't matter, because we've got the source from the email. They didn't block that, either because they didn't know how or because they didn't realize it would show up like that. The bad news is that it's a prepaid cell phone like you can get at most convenience stores, so it'll be harder to track down who bought it."

"Harder, but not impossible?" Theo asked.

"Are you doubting my skills?"

He held up both hands. "Of course not."

Rose glared at him for a second before typing a few more things into her computer, then she passed the phone back to me. "I want to know if you get anything else, okay? I'll keep working on this in the meantime and will let you know if I find any answers."

We both thanked her before heading back out into the cold. Flurries were in the forecast, though it was always a toss-up whether any snow would stick to the ground at this time of year. I leaned into Theo when he wrapped his arm around my waist.

"You're like a furnace," I told him, snuggling close.

He waggled his eyebrows dramatically. "I'll warm you up any time, sweetness."

Just before we pulled into the driveway, Theo's phone started playing an oldies song. I burst out laughing as his cheeks grew pink, but he winked at me before answering the call.

"Oliver, sir, how can I help you?"

The conversation ended quickly. I knew it involved some kind of invitation, even hearing only one side of it, and was formulating my excuse when Theo ended the call. He must have seen in my face that I wasn't ready for another outing, because he leaned over and pressed a reassuring kiss to my lips before he spoke.

"They asked if we'd come to dinner at their apartment tonight. Julian's cooking. We don't have to go, Esther," he said gently.

"Please don't take this to mean I want to get rid of you, because I don't, but I think you should go on your own. You guys have been friends for a long time, and just because I'm an unrepentant introvert who can't handle so many outings in a short time doesn't mean you should suffer for it."

Theo huffed a little at that. "Yes, because spending my evenings with you is such a hardship."

I set my hand on his knee and said, "I'll still be there when you get home, Theo. We can't live in each other's pockets for the next however many weeks, anyway. While I'm absolutely willing to be your excuse to not see people you don't want to spend time with, I thought Ollie and Julian were the two you'd want to see more of before you go home."

"You're right," he conceded with a sigh. "I'll tell them I'll be there. What are the chances of coming home to find you naked in my bed?"

Laughing, I shook my head. "Slim to none, but you can swing by the guest house and offer your best pickup line. If it's good enough, I'll come home with you."

He cupped one hand around the back of my neck and leaned in to kiss me, the kind of deep, thorough exploration I'd come to expect from him. When he finally drew back, he grinned at me.

"I suppose we've got all afternoon, huh?"

B Y THE TIME HE left for dinner with Oliver and Julian, I felt like every inch of his body was imprinted on mine. He leaned down to kiss me goodbye and I barely had the energy to respond.

"How am I supposed to make pleasant conversation when all I can picture is you all sexy and naked here alone?" he growled against my throat.

"Sexy? I have become a puddle of womanly goo," I complained.

Theo laughed. "The sexiest puddle I've ever seen. Text me if you need me to come back and service you again."

Determined not to let him have the last laugh, I shot him a mournful expression. "Your stamina is something to behold. I guess you must get it from your father."

His face froze in a mask of horror as he pulled away. "Why would you know that?"

"I walked in on your parents here once, before I moved in. They were banging on your mother's desk, it was over there," I said, pointing to the corner where my dresser now stood. "I didn't see much but if your mom's commentary was an indication..."

Theo groaned and dropped back onto the bed, burying his face against my belly. When he shook his head back and forth, mumbling a stream of what I took to be simply the word *no* over and over again, his hair tickled my skin and I tried valiantly not to knee him in the face as I contorted. Apparently, he realized what was happening, shot me a devilish grin, and set about tickling me in earnest.

I shrieked and shoved at him. "You have to go! They're waiting for you!"

With one final nip to my hip bone, he stood up again. "That was a low blow, Malek," he said grumpily. "I don't want to think about my parents having sex. Ever. I scrubbed every flat surface in the house when I first got here, you know."

A laugh burst from my lips, but he was still shaking his head despondently. It took another three minutes to shoo him out of the guest house before silence finally fell around me once more.

For a while, I stayed there in my puddly state, listening to the quiet that had been my companion for so many years.

It felt different now.

Instead of the peace I usually drew from the silence here, it now seemed oppressive and unsettling. I rolled my head on the pillow to check that my phone was still on the nightstand, then curled up on my side and closed my eyes.

If I was honest with myself, *everything* felt different now that Theo had come hurtling into my tidy little world.

What would happen when he was gone again?

The question brought on a curious ache in my midsection, right below the spot where he'd pressed his face moments ago. I could scold myself for the next few weeks, remind myself that I knew all along this was a limited interlude, but by this point I was fully aware it wouldn't stop the feelings from growing.

Even if it shattered me into a thousand pieces, this would still be far from the worst mistake I'd made. Trusting Steve Pautler was solidly in first place, as far as mistakes went. On the contrary, this thing with Theo had brought me back to life after a long hibernation.

I'd already gathered all the broken pieces of myself and glued them back together; I could do it again if I had to.

"For fuck's sake," I muttered aloud, flopping onto my back. I was certainly not going to spend an evening by myself wallowing in the misery of Theo's eventual departure.

Once I finally regained enough energy to move, I ran a bubble bath, poured a glass of wine, lit a few candles, and put my e-reader in a zip-top bag. I had plenty of reading to catch up on during my slow season, along with a Netflix queue I'd probably never manage to get all the way through even if I never worked another day in my life.

A night on my own should've been a welcome break from having someone else around all the time lately.

After my bath, I put on my comfiest pajamas, threw together some dinner, and settled myself under a blanket on the loveseat to watch a rom-com I had been saving for just such an occasion. I'd been enjoying life as a single woman for years. A handsome, talented lover wasn't going to change that.

And if the occasional texts Theo sent throughout the evening to check in made my insides flutter a little ridiculously, I blamed it on the wine.

Chapter Twenty-Five

THEO

DINNER WAS DELICIOUS, THE company was wonderful, and I spent almost the entire evening counting down the minutes until I could return to Esther's side. If Oliver's wry smile was anything to go by, I didn't do a very good job of pretending otherwise.

"If I didn't know better, my friend, I would think you were falling for her," he said, leaning back in his chair.

I groaned as I swallowed the last bite of the steak Julian had grilled to perfection. "Don't say that."

Julian slanted a look in Oliver's direction. "Stop nagging him, Ollie."

My oldest friend in the world stared straight into my eyes. "I love you, man, but you're playing with fire here. Are you sure you're going to be able to walk away from her?"

"I don't know," I said quietly, wishing I could reassure both of us here and now. "Everything feels different."

"Serious, you mean?"

"Serious, life-changing, fulfilling in a way I've never experienced. What the hell am I going to do?" I asked him.

Oliver smirked before responding. "You've got a few weeks left to figure that out, man, and you know we'll help in any way we can. I just don't want you getting burned. Or Esther, for that matter. She's been through a lot."

"I know. I don't want to hurt her."

"Then don't," Oliver replied, shrugging like it was that simple.

"Ollie, I don't do—"

He cut in. "Relationships? Commitment? Love?"

"Yes," I ground out.

"Remind me why that is?" He propped his chin on his hand, staring at me like he had all the time in the world to psychoanalyze my love life.

"Bad shit happens when I get too involved, Oliver."

He shook his head firmly, but his expression shifted to something dangerously close to pity. "Bad shit happened one time, man. It had nothing to do with your feelings for her or lack thereof, and everything to do with a single moment leading to an accident. Even that was not on you, Theo."

He was wrong. If I'd ended that relationship when I realized my feelings had fizzled, Michelle wouldn't have been there that night at all.

She definitely wouldn't have been arranging some secret lovers' rendezvous for us.

I closed my eyes for a second and turned my thoughts away from that night, away from the lesson I'd learned, and focused on the present.

"Esther's whole world caved in on her," I said quietly, "even before that bastard died. How do I make sure she's okay when I leave? Fuck, I hate the thought of never seeing her again."

None of us could answer that, but after a moment of silence, Julian spoke up. "Is there any chance of you changing your mind about leaving Spruce Hill in the rearview mirror?"

"I...don't know. A week ago, I would've said absolutely not. Now? I don't know."

Oliver studied me for a beat, then said, "It was a long time ago, you know. Nobody blamed you."

"I know at least one person who blamed me," I replied, my voice low.

"Man, that is definitely not true. Not for the accident, anyway."

"Just for everything that followed. Look, it doesn't matter. I have a life, a business, and none of it is here. Esther has all those things too, firmly planted in Spruce Hill."

"Have you talked to her to see if she'd consider leaving?" Ollie asked gently.

"No. Even if it lasted past the next month, I'm not asking her to follow me back home, to start all fucking over again, when we all know I'm not capable of offering anything long-term. She built this life for herself out of the ashes. I'm not messing that up for her."

Julian set his hand on Ollie's knee, shaking his head slightly when Oliver opened his mouth to reply, and said, "We're here for you, no matter what. You have another month left, right? Just promise Ollie that you'll be open to seeing where life leads, and I'll keep him from nagging you."

I snorted a laugh. "Deal."

Conversation turned to other mutual friends and classmates, but they knew I was anxious to get home and finally shooed me out the door when I declined the offer of dessert. After I shrugged on my coat, Ollie reached out and set both hands on my shoulders.

"It's great to have you back, man, even if it's temporary."

Though I rolled my eyes, I threw one arm around him and pounded on his back. "Yeah, yeah, cut the sentimental shit before I embarrass myself. Thanks for dinner, both of you. This was really nice."

Julian grinned over Ollie's shoulder. "Next time, we'll plan it so Esther will join us."

"Definitely," I replied, but an odd weight settled in my chest. Whether it was for enjoying myself without her or guilt over the fact that I was still planning to walk away from her, I wasn't sure.

I bid them both goodnight, forcing myself not to jog to the truck when I knew they were watching me from the front door, then raised a hand in farewell when I slid behind the wheel.

Knowing Oliver was happy with the love of his life was a balm to the current chaos inside me.

Big, fat snowflakes had started to fall during the evening, giving the impression that all of Spruce Hill was tucked inside a snow globe. I hadn't missed any part of New York winters, but knowing how Esther liked the cold, I felt that same giddy, child-like excitement I remembered from my youth upon seeing the first snow of the season.

I parked in the driveway and studied the guest house for a long moment before getting out of the truck. With the snow drifting lazily from the sky, it looked like a gingerbread house, warm and inviting, with soft light glowing through the windows.

I bit back a grin as I wondered what I might find when I went inside—would she be bundled up in something cozy or enticingly sexy?

When I reached the door, though, I noticed a package sitting in front of it. The top of the box was covered in snow, hiding it from view until I got close. There were no footprints around it, so it must have been there for a while. I tucked it under my arm and rapped my knuckles on the door.

Esther threw it open quickly, but she ignored me to poke her head out past my shoulder and grin up at the sky. Her delight was contagious, and I was content to look over her attire as she expressed her appreciation.

Cozy was the verdict—fuzzy fleece pants and an oversized hoodie.

"It's snowing!" she cried, dancing in place.

"That it is. Maybe we'll get enough accumulation for a snowball fight tomorrow," I teased. When her gaze landed on the box under my arm, I held it out to her. "This was outside the door."

She frowned a little as she took it over to the table. "That's weird," she mused as she grabbed a pair of scissors to slice through the tape. "The mail came earlier and I wasn't expecting any deliveries."

"Christmas gift?" I suggested.

"Your mother is the only person who's given me a Christmas gift in the past two years, and this doesn't even have a return address—"

She broke off as she opened it, yanking her hands away from the package.

Adrenaline ripped through me like a tidal wave. I stepped between her and the box, expecting a decapitated animal or a hissing snake, but reality was even worse.

It was filled to the brim with peanuts and, bizarrely, a few scattered white lilies.

For a second, I could only stare, wondering who the hell would've left this on her doorstep.

"What the fuck?" I breathed as I slammed the cardboard flaps closed again.

Esther's name and address were printed on the box as though for shipping, but there was no postage on it. Someone must have hand delivered it. She was still standing, frozen, a few feet away from me, her normally golden complexion now an ashy shade of gray.

"Esther, look at me," I said gently, waiting until she lifted her eyes to meet mine. "I'm going to get this out of here, then I'm going to call Rose. Do you need to wash your hands? I'll scrub off the table when I come back in. Should I change my clothes? Shower? Tell me what we need to do to keep you safe."

My ignorance broke her out of her trance. "Normally, washing our hands and the table would be enough."

"But this isn't normal," I replied.

"No. I guess to be safe, yes, we should both change. I don't know who did this, but if they went this far, the whole box could be coated in residue. If it got on our skin and then into my eyes or mouth, it could cause a reaction. It's happened to me before."

I nodded. "Okay. Go wash your hands and get changed. I'm going to take care of this and run into the house to change my clothes. Do you want me to have Rose meet us here or at my place?"

She blinked, still looking a little numb. "Here is fine, I guess."

"Why lilies?" I wondered aloud, glancing back at the box.

"I got those flowers," she whispered. "The day I brought you dessert. It was a bouquet of lilies."

"Right. Okay. I'll be back as quick as I can."

I waited until she nodded, her expression blank, before I moved. However badly I wanted to wrap her up in my arms, I didn't want to risk causing some kind of reaction after handling the package. Instead, I yanked a long string of paper towels from the roll by the sink and used them to lift the box while she started washing her hands with dish soap. I took it into the garage, wrapped it in a clear trash bag, and ran into the house to clean myself up before touching my phone to call Rose.

Impatience vibrated through my veins as I retraced my steps through the house, wiping down the surfaces I'd touched before I could wash my hands. I did the same to Esther's front door, inside and out, then scrubbed down the table while she stood in the doorway, fidgeting nervously with the hem of the fresh sweater she'd pulled on.

"I don't understand," she whispered when I tossed the last paper towel into the trash can.

I washed my hands again, then finally yanked her into my arms. She clung so tightly that I could barely draw a deep breath, but I wouldn't let go for anything in the world. We stayed like that until the doorbell rang, heralding the arrival of the police.

Rose stood at the door beside Spruce Hill's chief of police, a jolly middle-aged man named Roberts. When he asked Rose to take Esther's statement while I showed him the box, I got the impression they'd planned it that way ahead of time.

A swift rush of appreciation swept over me; this was one benefit to living in such a small town. People might be all up in each other's business, but they also took care of one another.

I squeezed Esther's hand on my way out the door and led Chief Roberts to the garage.

"Tell me what's going on, son," he said kindly. We had our own history, one stretching back to my Little League days and encompassing some of the darkest moments of my life.

"I had dinner with Oliver Jimenez and Julian this evening," I told him, though I'd already given Rose most of the details over the phone. "When I got back, the box was in front of Esther's door. I brought it in, figured it was a gift from her parents or something she ordered online."

He slanted me a look. "Have you met her parents?"

"No," I admitted.

"Let's just say they're on the opposite end of the spectrum from yours. What happened next?"

"Esther took it over to the table and opened it. Based on the way she jumped away from it, I thought there was a snake inside. Once I saw what it was, I closed it up, brought it out here, and then scrubbed the hell out of myself and everything the box had touched. She mentioned there could be peanut residue on the outside." I gestured to the workbench where I'd left the plastic-wrapped box.

Roberts nodded. "I'll take it with me, see if we can lift any prints. Your folks happen to have security cameras on the premises?"

"No, but I'll pick some up in the morning."

"Maybe get Esther a doorbell camera, too. I'll check with the neighbors, see if anyone else has one that might've caught someone walking up the driveway. Rose said there were no footprints in the snow when you got home?" he asked as I closed up the garage behind us.

"No, there weren't. I didn't notice exactly when the snow started, but I left here to go to Ollie's house around five."

"That'll narrow down the window of opportunity quite a bit, then, since it started snowing just after six," he mused.

I followed him to the end of the driveway, blinking away the flakes that landed on my eyelashes, and watched him peer up and down the street. It wasn't even very late, but the neighborhood was still and silent, cloaked in darkness and swirling snow.

Roberts looked at me and casually said, "The two of you have been holed up at home together a lot lately, is that right?"

"That's right," I replied, waiting for him to issue the same kind of warning Oliver had, but he just nodded as though he'd already known the answer.

"Anything else I should be aware of?"

I blew out a breath, watching it crystallize in the night air. "She probably told Rose, but there were flowers on her doorstep about a week back, a bouquet of lilies. We met friends at Botticelli's and had a run-in with one of Steve's old friends the night before. Esther brushed it off like it was a gift from one of her customers, but there are lilies in that box."

"Lilies," he repeated, looking pensive. "You know the friend's name?"

"First name Tyler, that's all I caught. Real smarmy little prick."

Roberts gave a humorless laugh. "Right, I know Tyler Engels. I'll have a word, see if it seems like he's hung up on Esther. Seen him around aside from that?"

"At the tree lighting, but he didn't make an approach. I appreciate you looking into things, Chief."

"Just doing my job, son. I'll get this back to the station and keep you apprised of anything we find out. You let me know if anything else happens. Hanson's already working on those calls Esther was getting. Be nice to tie this all up in a pretty little bow ahead of Christmas, wouldn't it?"

Rose came out of the guest house just as we reached the door. Esther looked slightly more composed than she had when I left her side, thankfully. I joined her in the doorway and wrapped an arm around her waist.

"I won't shake your hands now that I've touched this, but you two take care. We'll get to the bottom of this, don't you worry," Roberts assured us.

We bid them both farewell and stood there together until the police cruiser pulled out of the driveway, taking the box with them. There was no doubt in my mind that it was connected to the calls and the email, though I still wasn't sure whether any of it was meant as a real threat or if it was all some sick prank pulled by someone who didn't know just how dangerous it was.

I turned Esther in my arms, resting my chin on the top of her head. Toni would be waiting for her supper, but if Esther wanted us to spend the night here instead of at the house, I was willing to give her anything she needed right now.

When I said as much, she shook her head, brushing her nose back and forth against my sternum.

"No, we can go to the house. You were given a challenge to fulfill, Long John. Let's hear it," she mumbled.

For a second, I couldn't remember what she was talking about—this afternoon felt like another lifetime—then I snorted. "Right, right, best pickup line. Let's see. Baby, if you were words on a page, you'd be fine print," I said, complete with a leer.

Her shoulders shook with laughter and my own felt lighter as a result. "Okay, Romeo, let's go back to your place."

I waited while she grabbed an overnight bag she'd apparently thrown together in my absence, then I kissed her knuckles and led her out into the snow.

Chapter Twenty-Six

ESTHER

I NSTEAD OF GOING STRAIGHT to bed or even cuddling up on the sofa in the family room to watch a movie, Theo led me into the formal living room and nudged me into an overstuffed chair near the fireplace. I watched as he started the gas fire and then spread a plush blanket on the carpet in front of it. Toni followed us in, twitching her tail with disinterest, but as soon as the blanket hit the floor, she claimed a corner for herself.

Theo sat on the other side and held out a hand. When I joined him on the floor, he grabbed another blanket from a basket near the couch and wrapped it around our shoulders to form a little cocoon of warmth.

Tucked against his side, with the fire dancing and the snowflakes swirling outside the windows, I could almost believe that nothing bad would ever touch me again.

Except it almost had.

"Why would someone do that?" I asked dully. "Why is someone doing any of it? My only enemy in this town died four years ago."

Theo's muscles went tense against my side, then he blew out a long breath as he forcibly relaxed them. "I don't know. Rose and the chief will get it all sorted out. And believe me, if it's some asshole thinking this is funny, I'll make sure he understands otherwise."

For some reason, my eyes filled with tears. I tried to brush them away without being obvious about it, but Theo noticed.

Of course he noticed—after all, he was Anita's son.

He shifted his body and pulled me onto his lap, tucking me snugly against his chest. Without saying a word, he rubbed one hand reassuringly up and down my back while the other threaded into my hair to cup the back of my head.

The tears trickled slowly, soundlessly soaking into his shirt. I tried to remember the last time someone had jumped to my defense as he did, but nothing came to mind.

He was unlike anyone I'd ever known.

I was annoyed by the package, embarrassed at having to explain to Rose why something so basic was really such a dangerous prank, and frustrated at myself for tearing up over a simple act of kindness from the man I was sleeping with.

To shove those feelings aside, I sniffled once and mumbled, "How was your evening?"

A startled laugh burst from his lips. "I assume you mean the part I spent at Oliver's house? It was really nice, actually, aside from being so eager to get home. He and Julian are perfect for each other."

"They are, aren't they? I remember Sofia celebrating for days when Ollie finally asked him out. She takes full credit for getting them together."

Theo's chuckle reverberated under my ear as his fingers began massaging the base of my skull. I hummed in pleasure when the tight muscles eased under his hands. Gently, his lips trailed along my hairline, then he shifted a bit beneath me.

"I thought this would be really sweet and romantic, cuddling in front of the fireplace, but I think maybe I'm too old to be sitting on the floor," he said with an exaggerated groan.

I laughed and climbed off him, then held out a hand to help him up. "Come on, old man. Let's go to bed."

"Now that is the best offer I've had all day."

Since Toni was still curled up in her corner of the blanket, we left it there for her, though she glared from one golden eye when Theo turned off the fireplace. We crept upstairs as though we weren't alone in the house, climbed into bed almost fully dressed, and lay together there in the dark for a long time without speaking or sleeping.

When the words finally slipped out, they came as unexpectedly as the tears had downstairs. In a hushed tone, I told him about my first playdate without my mother in attendance, how it had been drilled and drilled into my head that I wasn't to eat anything she hadn't packed in my unicorn lunchbox.

"My kindergarten best friend and I were building Play Doh castles at their dining room table, not knowing her older brothers ate peanuts there the night before, and when I cried because it was time to go, I rubbed that residue into my eyes and swelled up like a boxer who'd just lost the fight. On school picture day two days later, I still looked like I'd been punched in the face. The skin under my eyes was still all puffy and bruised. My mom took one look at the proofs and hid them in the back of a closet."

"Jesus," he whispered.

"After that, the invitations dwindled, not that my mother would have allowed me to accept any of them, anyway. Nobody wanted to be responsible for a mistake like that."

Theo held me as I spoke in fits and starts, more stories about allergic reactions and teasing and isolation, about my own husband moving in to kiss me before I caught a whiff of candy bar on his breath. It was worse than if he'd come home smelling of another woman's perfume, a disregard not only of my feelings, but my safety.

"He was an asshole." The growled words settled over me like a weighted blanket.

"The relief after convincing him to keep his hands off me was incredible, because I could finally stop worrying he'd inadvertently send me into anaphylaxis with his carelessness."

My breath hitched, causing Theo's arms to tighten around me.

As they poured out into the darkness, all those memories and anxieties, the pressure that had taken root in my chest the minute I opened that box finally began to ease. My body melted into his, boneless and weightless, as he stroked my hair and waited for the words to trickle to a halt.

When nothing else came out, his lips found my forehead in the darkness. "Tomorrow morning, I want you to show me how to use the EpiPen, just in case."

I nodded, my hair whispering over the fabric of his t-shirt. Sometimes it seemed so hard to know if I was overreacting—that had been such a common refrain during my marriage, and the years of therapy had never quite removed the doubt from my mind when it came to certain things.

Hearing Theo's unveiled anger over the package, his commitment to keeping me safe, untangled another tiny knot in my chest I hadn't realized was there.

Whatever happened down the road, he was here now. I'd let him keep pulling me back into the light, out of my solitary existence, so I could regain the strength I'd need when he was gone.

There were always lessons to be learned, weren't there?

My thoughts slowed from a whirl to a lazy review of all I'd learned from Theo, and without intending to, I slipped off to sleep.

Chapter Twenty-Seven

THEO

FOR THE FIRST TIME in our short acquaintance, sleeping together meant exactly that. When I awoke, it was with a crick in my neck and Esther still tucked against me, her head on my chest and waves of silky black tresses everywhere, including one stuck to my lower lip. I managed to dislodge it without waking her, then shifted carefully against the pillows to stretch the side of my neck.

Those late night confessions had been cathartic for her, I knew, but each one had landed like a blow to my soul. She was truly remarkable, this woman in my arms, and I felt like practically everyone in her life had failed her time and again.

How could I join that line of tragedies in her life, knowing what I did?

Logically, I understood that what happened between us wasn't just up to me. Emotionally, the urge to shield her, to love and cherish and protect her, was nearly overwhelming in its intensity. She could take care of herself, but I didn't want her to *have* to.

Hard to take care of someone from twelve hours away.

That tiny voice in my head taunted me, leering and vicious in its honesty. What was I even thinking? Would I ask her to uproot her life and move to North Carolina with me? Or was I really considering moving back to the hometown I'd forsworn almost twenty years ago?

No answers came from the silent house, not that I expected any. Since the moment I left Spruce Hill, I'd told myself nothing would force me back here, and yet here I was. If a spoiled ginger cat had convinced me to return during my parents' absence, was it so outrageous to think that a woman like Esther would be such a lure?

Maybe it was time to lay the past to rest.

I was grateful she was still asleep during this little crisis of faith. Her stance on baiting my mother's trap had been perfectly clear right from the start—she wouldn't stand for it.

Surely my mother would have known that, too.

Not for the first time since my arrival, I wondered what sequence of events my mother had foreseen when she orchestrated this. Maybe she'd expected nothing more than a fling, something to soothe Esther's spirit and brighten my return.

As soon as the thought occurred to me, I rejected it. My mom was just as fiercely independent as the woman in my arms, just as sharp and intelligent. Even if she thought it might work, she would *never* put Esther in a position like that, even if I was meant as a gift for Esther rather than the other way around. While my mother might presume to toy with my life, she wouldn't toy with Esther's.

Back to square one.

Esther began to stir, waking up slowly, sweetly. I set aside the endless stream of questions parading through my mind and let myself enjoy the simple pleasure of holding her in my arms, of being the first thing she saw when she blinked her eyes open, pale green in the morning light that snuck through from behind the curtains.

"Hi," she murmured, her lashes dropping to shield her eyes from the sun as she burrowed closer to me.

"Hi," I echoed with a smile.

It struck me then and there that *this*, this beautiful, private moment with her, was the true temptation. Of all the things that might bring me back to Spruce Hill after so many years away—my parents, my best friends, my history—this was like a hook between my ribs, pulling me inexorably closer to my roots. I didn't want to give it up.

I didn't want to give *her* up.

Of course, there was a hell of a lot more to it than just deciding such a thing, so I kept my mouth shut and enjoyed the way she stretched like a cat, her shirt riding up to reveal a golden swath of skin just above one hip. I managed to wait three beats before rolling so we were facing one another and sneaking my hand up to that spot, not in any seductive capacity but simply to appreciate the warm silk of her skin.

When I was finally sure she was awake, I gave her hip a squeeze and asked, "What do you have going on today?"

"I have a small order to get ready for a company Christmas party on Thursday, and then I need to make up a bigger order for the high school's winter formal this weekend. I think that's it until the Carolcade the weekend after."

"Do you have any objections to me installing a doorbell camera on the guest house? Roberts suggested it and I think it's a good idea." I tried to keep my tone light, unconcerned, but she tensed under my palm.

"No, no objections, if you think it's necessary," she replied.

I did, though I wasn't about to scare her more than I had to. The thought of someone watching the house, waiting until I left her alone, then creeping up to her door with something that could kill her—fuck, it made me want to burn the world down in her honor. Instead, I kissed her temple and ran my hand down to cup her ass through the fuzzy pants she had on.

"What time do you need to get started?" I asked, trailing my mouth down her cheekbone to nip at her bottom lip.

She laughed. "Not just yet, Romeo. We've got at least an hour or two. Think you can get done whatever it is you wanted to do before then?"

I moved my hand to the crevice behind her knee and hooked her leg over my hip, kissing a path toward her collarbone. Even as I explored the tiny hollows there, the delicate bones that carried so much on her sweet shoulders, I debated what I treasured more: her low, husky laughter or her helpless, throaty purr.

Reversing the path, I kissed my way back up to her lips and murmured, "I guess that'll just have to do."

Chapter Twenty-Eight

ESTHER

THOUGH HE HID IT well, Theo was worried.

I saw it as clearly as the lust that darkened his eyes from caramel to espresso. Still, I accepted the diversion he offered, because when I stopped to think about it, I was worried, too.

My concern, though, was less about the box of peanuts or the silly phone calls. It was more focused on the fact that something inside of me wanted to throw caution to the wind and keep riding the wave of our weeks together with reckless abandon, regardless of the inevitable crash at the end.

I told him at the start that I didn't want to lose myself, but now? An unmistakable part of me wanted to ignore every warning from the logical side of my brain and let it happen.

While I updated my accounting spreadsheet from the tree lighting and confirmed a couple of New Year's Eve party orders, Theo left to track down the cameras he planned to install. The guest house felt quiet, almost somber, in his absence, so I turned on the radio station that played non-stop Christmas music starting the day after Thanksgiving and got to work.

At Theo's insistence, I'd bolted the door when he left. I was busy mixing batter and dancing around the kitchen when the doorbell rang, scaring the daylights out of me. A startled shriek slipped past my lips before I could contain it and my heart launched into double time before I forced myself to go to the door.

I didn't know what I was expecting to see through the peephole, but on the other side was Sofia, bundled up in a puffy pink jacket.

"Hey," I gasped as I swung the door open. "You scared the hell out of me."

Her eyes flew wide. "Oh, shoot, I'm so sorry! I should've called first, I was just out to grab a couple things and wanted to check on you. Theo told Ollie what happened last night. Are you okay?"

"Come on in. I'm fine, I promise," I said as I stepped back to let her through the door. "Just a stupid prank, that's all."

"Theo doesn't seem to think so, from what Ollie said," she countered, studying my face like she could see straight into my soul.

I sighed and turned back toward the kitchen, just in case she really *could* read my thoughts about him. "Do you want some coffee or something?"

Sofia shook her head. "Is Theo a sore subject for some reason? If he hurt you, I'll kick his ass."

"Sore? Not at all."

Aside from Anita, Sofia was one of the few other people who always saw through my bullshit and never hesitated to call me on it. For a long moment, I felt her gaze on my face, reading every nuance of my expression. When I finally glanced up, her own had gone soft and a bit sappy.

"Oh, Es," she sighed.

A laugh that morphed into a sob burst from my throat. "I am such an idiot."

"Don't say that. Who knows what the future holds? You deserve happiness, honey."

"The future holds me falling head over goddamn heels for a man who lives hundreds of miles away and has avoided this town since he was eighteen years old. What could go wrong?"

Sofia came over and wrapped her arms around me, her coat compressing against my body like a marshmallow. "Has he told you why he stayed away?"

From anyone else, I might've assumed this was fishing for gossip, but not Sofia. She and Oliver loved Theo like a brother and, though I knew she was curious, the way she'd always respected my privacy convinced me she would do the same for Theo.

"No, we haven't talked about it. I'm not sure it makes any difference. He has a business down there, a life. The last thing I want is for him to resent me for trapping him back in the town he couldn't wait to get away from."

"Have you ever considered that maybe you're worth it?" she asked quietly.

The question hung in the air between us, heavy enough to suck the air from my lungs, but I was saved from having to answer when Theo knocked lightly at the front door and poked his head in.

"Hey, Sof," he said brightly, then his gaze landed on me and grew soft, tender. "Hey, Esther. I'm back, but I'll be out here setting everything up for a bit."

That look seeped through my limbs with the kind of languor I'd come to associate with Theo. All my protests, all my defenses, melted away under the warmth of it. Knowing Sofia's focus flitted between us, ready to pounce, I just nodded in acknowledgment. Theo waited until her face was turned back toward me to wink and slip back outside.

"Jeesh," she breathed when the door was closed behind him. With one hand, she fanned herself. "That was...intense."

"Tell me about it," I muttered.

She laughed. "I need to get going, but really, Es, please let me know if you need anything, even if it's a break from that stud out there. I've really missed you, honey."

Hot shame crept along the back of my neck as I pulled her into another squishy hug. "I've missed you, too. Whatever happens with Theo, I promise I won't go radio silent again, okay?"

"That's all I ask. You know how to reach me. We'll see you two at the Carolcade?"

"Yes, we'll be there," I promised. "And maybe...maybe we can have dinner sometime soon. You and Chase, me and Theo?"

Her face lit with delight, sending another pang of guilt through my chest. "I'd love that."

In true Sofia fashion, it took another five minutes to get her out the door, but once she was gone, the quiet felt suffocating even with the music still on. Unfortunately, I had cupcakes ready to go into the oven, so there was no escaping it just yet. I turned off the radio, slid the pans in, and wondered if everything Sofia said was right.

I didn't reach any conclusions.

When Theo returned a while later, his triumphant expression dimmed when he saw me sitting at the table in silence, my unfocused gaze on the window over the kitchen sink.

"Hey, you okay?" he asked as he shoved his gloves into his pockets and hung his coat on the rack.

Don't do it. Do not do this. Just answer the question.

I opened and closed my mouth two or three times before finally blurting out, "Why did you leave Spruce Hill?"

His face went blank for a beat, then he sighed heavily and sat down beside me, scooting his chair close enough for our knees to touch. "Does it matter?" he asked gently. There was no belligerence in his tone, nothing defensive, just a quiet sort of resignation.

"I think it might," I admitted.

Without knowing what it was that sent him away, I couldn't let myself consider whether he might ever change his mind about returning. I half expected him to shut down the conversation, which would be an answer in itself, but instead he nodded.

"When we were kids," he began, "Alex and I were close. We were only one grade apart in school, so for most of our lives, we were more like twins than anything. I met Oliver in kindergarten, but even that didn't cause a rift between us. It was always the three of us running around together. Brothers, but also friends."

He paused, so I reached over to lace my fingers through his. I had only Sofia's vague speculation to go on, leaving me virtually clueless here. From his expression, though, I gathered the truth was more painful than I'd imagined.

After a deep breath, he continued. "In high school, Alex started to drift, I guess. Started to resent me, or at least that's how it felt. I was first string in soccer, older, half a foot taller already. During my senior year, I went out with a girl from his class, Michelle McNulty. He was barely speaking to me at that point, so I had no clue he was into her. If he'd told me, I never would've asked her out in the first place."

"Bro code," I said, drawing a wry smile from his lips.

"Bro code, yeah. In any case, I didn't know, and we dated for the last six months of my senior year, but with me heading to college, we decided we weren't going to try to stay together beyond that summer. My feelings just weren't strong enough to try to keep it going long-distance, so I figured we'd end it on good terms. I thought she felt the same."

I blinked in surprise. My assumption was totally wrong—I thought he'd been so in love, her death had scared him away from serious relationships.

"On the night of our prom, I invited Alex to come to the afterparty. I hoped it might bridge the gap between us before I graduated, you know? Someone's parents owned a summer house on the lake and offered to let us use it. The cottage was out past the public beach, near the lighthouse."

Theo rubbed his forehead with his free hand, looking like just reliving this tale was sapping his energy. I squeezed his fingers and shifted my chair so my thigh pressed tightly against his, lending him strength.

"There was a kid at the party whose brother worked at the lighthouse, giving tours or something for the Historical Society. He borrowed the keys and suggested we go see if it was really haunted. The schools do field trips there, so we'd all been inside before, but Michelle—"

When his voice broke, my heart jumped into my throat.

"I guess I was wrong that she felt the same way about breaking up. Most of the other kids were drunk and didn't want to go up all the stairs inside, but she dragged me up to the top floor, kept talking about how romantic the view was. I should've put my foot down, I just didn't think. She'd been drinking, but she wasn't smashed or anything. When we got up there, she was all over me, trying to kiss me, begging me not to dump her."

"Theo," I whispered.

"I told her it was over. Fuck—I wasn't very nice about it, but I was blindsided by her throwing herself at me like that. Alex was coming up the stairs and heard me tell her I didn't care if she didn't agree, we were through. He started yelling at me, telling me I didn't deserve her, that I ruined everything."

I closed my eyes for a beat, shaking my head. "That's not true."

"We'd tussled as kids, but my mom always shut it down quickly, so I didn't expect him to start throwing punches. I took a right hook to the jaw, fell back and hit my head against the wall so hard I had a concussion. I got up and grabbed him so he couldn't hit me again, but Michelle tried to shove past the two of us. She made it down a handful of stairs before she tripped over her dress."

Ice filtered through my veins. "Oh, no."

With a sharp nod, he forced himself to continue. "She went over the railing. She was dead the minute she hit the ground, right in front of a dozen of our drunk classmates."

"Jesus, Theo. I'm sorry. I'm so sorry," I said, turning in the chair to wrap my arms around him.

When he buried his face against my neck, I tangled my fingers in his hair, anchoring him against me. Though he wasn't crying, a harsh breath shuddered from his lungs. After several long moments, he squeezed me tight and put his hands on my hips to set me back a few inches in order to finish the story.

"It was an accident. A horrific accident. It wasn't Alex's fault, but I just—I couldn't look at him. And he blamed me. Rightfully so."

"It wasn't your fault, either."

"He didn't feel that way, and neither did I. I should've ended things the minute I realized my feelings had changed. If I'd been clear about it, she wouldn't have tried to change my mind. We never would've gone up there."

"You can't know that for sure," I said firmly, but he shook his head.

"Even when the paramedics forced me into the ambulance, Alex was screaming at me that I always ruined everything for him."

I scowled, forcing his face up toward mine. "It was an accident."

"Yeah." He drew a breath. "You know what it's like, hearing the whispers, seeing the looks people give you. Nobody was up there with us, so you can imagine what the rumors said. He pushed her to get back at me, I pushed her because she was cheating on me with him, we made a blood pact not to let a girl get between us and both pushed her."

"Jesus, what is wrong with people?"

"I was supposed to start college here, but I couldn't bear to be so close. I applied down at UNC and left that summer."

My heart shattered for him. The soccer star, the eldest son of a local legend like Anita Vasquez-Silver, exiled himself because of a freak accident that cost a young girl her life. It was no wonder people didn't talk about it in any detail—none of them even knew the real story.

This wasn't juicy small town gossip, though. This was a true tragedy.

"I'm sorry, Theo." The words were weak and insignificant, but they were all I had. "I shouldn't have asked."

Theo pulled me down onto his lap, pressing his face to the top of my head. "You deserved the truth. I'm sorry I didn't give it sooner."

The truth doesn't always set you free.

With a history like that, one thing was certain—I could never, ever expect him to stay here.

Chapter Twenty-Nine

THEO

LETTING ESTHER INTO MY sordid past hadn't been on my radar, not after the drama she'd endured, but once it was done—and when she didn't recoil from me in horror—it felt like the heavy burden of carrying that around had been lightened.

The doorbell cameras, motion lights, and two security cameras pointing toward the driveway and backyard helped, too.

Though I offered my sidekick assistance for her upcoming orders, I really just ended up keeping her company while she worked. Occasionally, while waiting for the timer to go off, she'd move past me and brush her fingertips along my jaw, a silent show of support and affection.

When that finally boosted my mood enough to recover from explaining my past, I tugged her into my arms and slow-danced around the kitchen to the continuous Christmas music she liked to play.

With her, *everything* felt lighter.

Still, there were times when I knew she needed space, so as the week crept by, I retreated to my parents' house and invented things to do. I built a shelf for the garage out of planks I found in the basement, read through a couple books I found on the side table in the family room, and sketched out some landscape designs I'd been thinking about.

Through it all, I tried to figure out what would need to happen if I decided to move back to Spruce Hill.

It still felt like a nebulous prospect. However amazing things were with Esther, I knew better than to assume she wanted something long-term. There were times when she still seemed almost skittish, like she was in too deep already and starting to flounder as she tried to recover her footing.

I wasn't sure how to bring up the possibility of something more without scaring her off.

By the time the week ended, leaving another crazy few days of preparations for the next food truck booking at the Carolcade, our little bubble burst on its own. We'd just finished cleaning up after dinner when my phone started ringing from the kitchen counter. I'd updated my parents on the bare minimum of what had happened, mostly because they'd find out about the cameras as soon as they returned, but I thought I'd convinced them it was nothing to worry about.

Frowning, I grabbed the phone. Billy's name flashed across the screen, igniting a sick sort of dread in my gut. I shot Esther an apologetic smile and said, "It's my business partner, I need to take this."

She waved me off as she disappeared into the family room, probably to curl up on the couch where we planned to watch a movie. Hopefully Billy's curt, concise manner would keep the phone call short.

"Billy boy, what's happening?"

"Hey, boss," he began. Given that we were equal partners, he only called me that when he knew I wouldn't like what he was going to say. My stomach clenched as he continued, "We have a situation down here."

I rubbed at my forehead, leaning back against the kitchen counter. "Tell me."

"Remember that zillionaire, Orlando Wylie? Guy's got a mansion that rivals the Biltmore and gardens to match."

"I remember," I said slowly. "He hired Brooks to redo the gardens, didn't he?"

Billy gave a low hum, then said, "Brooks just shattered his hip falling off a ladder. Out of commission for months, and his partner retired last year to move to Mexico. Guess his team can't manage without him and tried to push off the job until summer, so Wylie fired them on the spot for breach of contract. He wants us to take the job."

"Shit," I breathed. That job was not only a goldmine, but an absolute dream for a landscape architect. "We'd have to do a little shuffling with other jobs, maybe hire a few more guys."

"Yeah. Problem is that Wylie wants us both there to meet with him before he'll sign a contract, and he wants the meeting to happen this week. Apparently zillionaires are used to getting what they want."

Shit. I could drive down and back, which would mean at least three full days away from Esther, if not more. I knew she didn't need my help with the baking—hell, she didn't really need my help on the truck, either, but given the potential threat inherent in what had been happening, I didn't want to leave her alone at a crowded event.

"Okay. I'm going to check out flights. See if he can fit us in for Wednesday, maybe. Keep me posted," I said, blowing out a breath.

Billy agreed and ended the call, leaving me staring blindly down at the phone. This was a huge opportunity for our company, for me, but I felt curiously blank. I forced my brain back into action, pulling up an airline site to see if I could get down there and back without spending a small fortune two weeks before Christmas.

Esther was curled up in her favorite spot on the couch when I walked in a few minutes later. She gave me a soft smile and asked, "Trouble on the homefront?"

I laughed, sat down with my back against the arm of the couch, and tugged her until she sprawled along the length of my body. Once she'd settled comfortably against me, I stroked my hand along her spine.

"I have to go home for a couple days to meet with a client. There are some direct flights, I'm just waiting for Billy to set up the meeting before I pull the trigger on booking. I'll fly back right after, so I'll be back before the Carolcade."

Tilting her head up to look at me, Esther said, "I'll take care of Toni while you're gone. And don't worry about the Carolcade. I can manage it on my own if I have to."

My arms tightened around her as I dropped a kiss to her lips. "I know you can, but I said I'd help and I want to be there."

She didn't respond, just snuggled into my arms and nodded. We started the movie, something sappy and Christmas-themed, and half an hour later I got a text from Billy.

Can't meet us till Fri at 2 pm. Can you get here?

I groaned aloud and shot back, *I'll make it happen. Thanks man.*

Send me flight details, I'll pick you up.

Esther's fingers tangled in my shirt, just over my ribs. "What's up?" she asked, sounding like she'd almost dozed off already.

"The meeting is Friday afternoon," I said, reluctant to even speak the words aloud, but the woman on top of me just shrugged one shoulder as she pressed her lips to the center of my chest.

"It'll be fine, Theo."

With one hand threaded into her hair, I used the other to book the only flight option with seats remaining. I'd have to leave Thursday afternoon, and without knowing how long the meeting would run, I bought a ticket home for Saturday morning. After forwarding the information to Billy, I set my phone on the coffee table and pulled a blanket off the back of the couch to drape over both of us.

I knew she was right, but I was still anxious about being away from her. As the main character of the movie finally kissed her love interest under artistic swirls of snow, I tried to dissect the uneasiness that roiled in my stomach. It felt simultaneously like I was overreacting *and* not taking it seriously enough.

Was I worried for her safety? Was I concerned about letting her down? Or was I simply afraid that putting distance between us would damage what we'd been building?

Maybe it would remind her that she was perfectly fine on her own, that she didn't need anything more than an incredibly hot, intense affair. Maybe I would be reminded that I'd built my life and my business from scratch down in Asheville and that walking away from it was as stupid as it sounded.

Or, my heart whispered, *maybe you'll realize you can't live without her.*

I tamped down every maybe and what if, brought my focus back to Esther's warm, soft body sinking into mine, and watched the big city girl on the television screen fall in love with the small town doctor who'd won her heart.

If only real life were that simple.

Chapter Thirty

ESTHER

THEO WAS A BUNDLE of nerves in the days that followed. I couldn't quite parse whether he was worried about this client meeting, afraid of flying, or just that reluctant to be apart again, but I was too busy to reflect on it in any great depth. Event prep was soon underway and if letting Theo pour his nervous energy into rolling out allergy-friendly Christmas cookies was all I could do to keep his mind off things, so be it.

Despite my offer to drive him to the airport, he saw the chaos of my kitchen on Thursday morning and steadfastly refused.

"You have work to do," he insisted, "and this way I can haul ass back here when I fly home Saturday morning to help you get the truck loaded."

"Theo, listen to me. If your flight is delayed or you need to stay longer, I swear to you that I will be *fine*. You can repay me in orgasms after you get home if you're feeling guilty, but I can manage the Carolcade alone if I have to. Do what you need to do. It will all be fine."

He looked unconvinced, but after I set out the final batch of cookies to cool, I took his hand and led him to the bedroom to get his mind off his imminent departure. This time felt different somehow, like he was desperate to memorize every inch of me, to make sure I memorized the feel of him, the heat and the strength and the reverence of his touch.

When he finally needed to leave for the airport, I kissed him goodbye, told him to text me when he landed, and calmly accepted the way he fussed over me, reminding me to lock the doors and check the cameras and keep my phone with me at all times. Finally, I shoved him out the door, blew one last kiss, and made sure he heard me throwing the deadbolt.

Once he was gone, my tiny, cozy house felt cavernously empty.

I kept myself busy until Theo's text came through several hours later, but I was determined not to turn clingy just because he was away. Instead, I thanked him for letting me know, wished him sweet dreams, and tucked my phone back into my pocket.

We hadn't slept apart since that very first night, so after feeding Toni her dinner and spending half an hour placating her with pets on the couch, I crawled into my own bed and stared up at the ceiling for a long time before finally falling asleep.

Though I'd expected Friday to crawl by in his absence, I was so busy decorating cookies and finishing up more batches of the most popular cupcake flavors from the tree lighting ceremony that the hours flew past. I took a mid-morning break to spend time with Toni, who was sweet as pie around me, so I sent Theo a photo of the fluffy ginger cat curled up on my chest with her head tucked under my chin.

What I would give to trade places with that rotten feline right now, he replied.

I scratched her cheeks and texted back, *Starting to think you cut your arm on something else that day you said she clawed you. Look at this sweetheart, she wouldn't hurt a fly.*

When his response appeared, I laughed aloud and startled her into leaping off of me. *Pretty sure my mom invoked a demon and faked the shelter's adoption paperwork.*

Without the cat to keep me there, I threw my coat back on to return to the guest house, still grinning when I stepped outside. The grin fell away when I ran smack-dab into Alex, standing in the driveway.

"Shit!" I gasped. My phone slipped out of my hand and into the few inches of snow that had accumulated on the concrete that morning.

"I'm sorry," he said quickly, crouching down to grab the phone. "I didn't mean to scare you. I heard Theo was away and came to take care of the driveway for you. It's supposed to keep snowing through tonight, so I'll swing back later and again tomorrow morning."

I glanced behind him and saw his truck with a red plow attached. My heart still threatened to beat straight out of my chest, but I managed a tight smile. "Right. That'd be great, thank you."

Before that moment, I'd thought of Alex as a smoother, slimmer version of Theo. He'd always been quick with a charming smile, but today he looked as flustered as I felt, nervously running a hand through his hair. I wasn't thinking about the accident from his youth or the fact that he and Theo still hated each other when I spoke again.

"Alex, are you okay?"

His gaze shot to my face like that simple question was the last thing he'd expected to hear. "Yeah, I'm fine."

"If you say so."

A rueful grin tugged at his lips. "Careful, though, the driveway is icy underneath the snow."

I nodded, started toward the guest house, and immediately slipped. Alex caught me under the elbow before I could go down and I found myself staring straight into his eyes.

Theo's might have ghosts lingering at the edges, but Alex looked downright haunted. My heart broke for him, for both of them.

"Let me help you to the door. I'll salt after I clear the snow," he said, his grip firm but gentle on my arm.

"Very chivalrous of you. I've had my share of spills on icy pavement over the years."

"Not on my watch," he assured me.

We fell silent in the remaining few yards to my door, but when I glanced up to thank him, he was biting his lip like he wanted to say something.

"What is it?"

For a moment, he hesitated, then he said, "I just don't want to see you hurt. I know that's stupid, it's just...Theo is quick to run away. He's hurt my parents enough already, and if he breaks your heart, it'll hurt them even more. They think the world of you."

I stared at him blankly while my brain processed all of that. "I appreciate your concern, but I'll be okay, Alex. I know he's leaving."

"He told you why he went away, didn't he?" he asked, reading my expression as accurately as his other family members could. When I nodded, he scrubbed a hand over his face. "I know it was my fault. All of it, start to finish, it was on me, not him. But he didn't have to abandon them like that. They're not getting any younger."

"This feels like a conversation the two of you should be having," I said gently.

A harsh laugh broke from him. "He won't even speak to me, Esther. It's fine. I don't expect his forgiveness. I never meant to hurt anyone, though. You don't need to be afraid of me."

Startled, I repeated, "Afraid of you? I'm not afraid of you."

"Esther, every time I'm near you, you flinch. I thought for a long time it was because you knew about what happened back then. If that wasn't why, then what is it about me that you hate?"

This seemed like a bizarre conversation to be having as we stood outside in the falling snow, but he looked truly upset about the fact I hadn't warmed up to him in the years I'd been living outside of his parents' home. I drew a deep breath as I thought back to all of our past interactions.

"You're charming," I said simply.

He blinked at me with eyes so like Theo's and yet so different. "Charming."

I wasn't about to bare my soul to him, even if he looked like a lost puppy at the moment, so I just nodded. With his dark brows drawn down, he studied me, then his expression cleared.

"Like Steve," he said.

"God, you Silvers," I muttered under my breath. "You're all so freaking perceptive."

To my surprise, Alex laughed, and the resemblance between the brothers was clearer than ever. "So it wasn't personal."

"No. It was never personal," I confirmed.

A shy smile lifted his lips as he took a step back. "Okay. That's good. Go on inside, get out of the cold. I'll take care of the driveway, make sure you can get out tomorrow for the Carolcade. And Esther?"

"Yes, Alex?"

His smile widened ever so slightly. "Thank you."

I gave a tiny wave before hurrying back into the guest house and locking the door behind me. Briefly, I wondered what the chances were that Theo and his brother would have a heart to heart before he left town again. Alex wasn't at all what I'd thought him to be; it seemed like maybe he wasn't what Theo thought, either.

Before long, I was caught up in baking and frosting, dancing around the kitchen and printing out labels. I hadn't even realized that dinner time had rolled around until a text from Theo appeared, letting me know that the meeting went well and the contract was signed. With no one there to hear me, I cheered aloud, congratulated him, and told him to go out and celebrate tonight.

My own celebration was more mundane, involving a plate of cookies and a glass of wine while I curled up to watch another holiday rom-com, but I was truly happy for Theo. And if there was the faintest twinge of sadness at the edges of my conscious-ness, I steadfastly ignored that. It was *good* that his business was thriving, *good* that he was finding success.

At least if he was dreading his return to North Carolina as much as I was, he'd have something to keep him busy when he got back.

As Alex predicted, the snow continued straight through the night and well into Saturday. Normally, I'd rejoice in the magic of the first real accumulation of the year. I could hear kids yelling down the street, throwing snowballs and building snowmen. The hill behind the middle school would be teeming with sleds while parents sipped at hot drinks in travel mugs.

Instead, I stared down at my phone, wondering what to say. Theo's flight home had been canceled due to the weather and he was trying desperately to find a new one.

In the end, I just texted back that it was fine, the driveway was plowed, and I'd manage on my own tonight at the Carolcade. I didn't tell him it was Alex who'd returned multiple times since our run-in yesterday to clear the driveway, and I definitely didn't mention that Alex had shoveled a wide path from my doorstep leading straight to the truck.

Or that I'd offered him a cup of coffee as a thank you. Alex had turned it down anyway, but he *had* accepted a cutout cookie in payment.

"You know, I'm seeing this woman," he said, his expression a little dreamy. "Her son was just diagnosed with some food allergies. Could I put her in touch with you? She's having a hard time figuring out how to handle holidays with her family. I don't think they get it."

"Of course," I said with a smile. I grabbed one of my business cards from a drawer and handed it to him, along with a small box of cookies for the little boy. "Tell her to email me and we'll chat."

Alex offered a broad grin and a quick salute as he took the cookies. I was starting to think his charm was just a mask to cover up the softness underneath. Even if they didn't talk about it or have all the details, practically everyone in Spruce Hill must have known about the accident; it couldn't have been easy for him to stay in town after that.

But, a little voice in my head whispered, *he's not the one who ran away.*

"Do not get in the middle of whatever happens between brothers," I said aloud as I got dressed in layers for the evening. "It's none of your business."

It was bitterly cold, but the snow had started to taper off. I threw on a long-sleeved pink thermal under my purple Nutless Wonder shirt, then a cardigan, then my heavy coat. The temperature inside the truck tended to fluctuate and rushing around to serve a line of customers always caused me to overheat. Layers to shed or add as needed were vital for winter events.

Despite my reassurances to the contrary, having Theo to help in the truck had made a huge difference in my stress levels, but I'd managed to survive without him every other time.

I could do it again. I'd have to get used to doing *everything* without him again.

It was only when I was easing the truck along the narrow plowed pathway in the park that I realized I'd left my phone at home. For a panicked moment, I tried to remember if I had my purse—and in it, my EpiPen—but once I parked the truck in my assigned spot, I found those on the floor behind my seat and sagged with relief. Everyone else on the planet had a cell phone handy in case I actually needed one, after all.

Okay. Game on.

In that strange stillness after a snowstorm, I set up everything for the evening, double-checked the menu board, and slipped over to the hot cider booth to grab myself a cup before the crowds started to fill in.

The tree lighting was my favorite holiday event, mostly because I was a sucker for pretty Christmas lights. I had a whole box of strings at home to put up along the mantle and around the doorways, but with Theo's presence to distract me this year, I hadn't done it yet.

Still, the Carolcade was fun. It was like a mix between a concert and a sing-along, and the benefit to being there with the food truck was that the groups traipsed up and down the rows of vendors as they sang. I didn't even have to brave the crowd in order to enjoy the music.

The truck had a steady stream of customers, most of whom I was able to greet by name. Drew came by during a slow moment, bought a cupcake, made a little small talk, and wandered off as soon as other customers showed up. I'd been worried that in Theo's absence, he might decide to ask me out again, but he offered nothing more than his usual overly friendly smile.

The rest of the night passed in something of a blur, which was good for business but less awesome for my energy levels. By the time Sofia and Chase appeared at my window, I was dragging.

"Hey, honey! Do you need a hand?" she asked, looking concerned.

I forced a bright smile and shook my head. "No, I'll be closing up soon. What can I get for you guys?"

Chase, a quiet lumberjack type who looked at his gorgeous wife with hearts in his eyes, smiled shyly up at me. "I heard those Christmas cookies were to die for. Got any left?"

"You're lucky I set aside a friends and family stash," I whispered as I reached under the counter for the box I had packed up earlier. "You have to share with Ollie and Julian though, if they're here."

Sofia groaned in mock disappointment, but a grin lit her rosy cheeks. "Yes, ma'am!"

Despite my insistence that I didn't need help—and that I was *not* lonely or pining for Theo, which Sofia asked about in a low voice when Chase turned to greet a coworker—the two of them hung around the truck until it was time to close up. Oliver and Julian had dropped by at least three times, as well, and I started to wonder if Theo had asked them to check in on me.

I was just packing up at the end of the night when I heard a chorus of exclamations. When I peered around the corner of the truck, I found Theo being passed around for hugs like he'd been gone for a century instead of days.

After his years away, I couldn't really blame them for celebrating his return.

His gaze landed on me and his eyes went soft. The rest of his friends—our friends—stepped away and left him to stride toward me as though pulled by an invisible thread.

"Hey," he murmured, cupping my face between his hands. That warmth he always radiated seeped into my cold cheeks. "I'm so sorry I missed it. Did everything go okay?"

Unable to speak around the strange surge of emotion clogging my throat, I nodded. Theo bent down slowly, like he was savoring the sight of me, until his lips met mine. I shivered at the butterfly-light caress, drawing closer when his hands settled on my hips. By the time he drew back to smile at me, I'd forgotten he even asked a question.

"I missed you," he said, apparently forgetting as well.

"You're right on time for cleanup," I replied. The words came out as wispy as the puff of my breath in the cold night air.

Theo's smile only widened. "Good. Get into the truck, your hands are frozen. I'll take care of everything that's left."

Though I considered protesting, I *was* freezing and the prospect of a few quiet minutes in front of the heating vents sounded too good to pass up. There wasn't much left to do, anyway, and Theo finished it in record time before launching himself into the passenger seat with an exaggerated shiver.

"Where's your truck?" I asked.

"I walked over from the house so I could ride home with you. Didn't you get my texts?"

I grimaced. "I forgot my phone at home."

Theo groaned as he slapped a hand to his forehead. "Fuck, now I'll have to watch you reading all the sappy shit I texted you all evening."

"Sappy, huh?" I asked, grinning over at him.

At that moment, he looked beyond happy to be there, beaming across the space between us. His cheeks were as pink as Sofia's had been, his dark eyes gleaming with pleasure. I let it flow over me like warm honey until his comment sunk in.

"You walked two miles in a foot of snow?"

His grin turned boyish. "Uphill. Both ways."

I snorted a laugh. When we pulled into the plowed driveway at home, his continuous smile from the drive finally slipped a little, but I refused to bring Alex into this moment with us. Fortunately, Theo didn't voice the question in his eyes.

Before we unloaded what was left in the back, Theo pulled me into his arms and kissed me, bracing his arm behind me against the side of the truck to keep my body away from the cold metal. I knew how badly I'd missed him, but I hadn't realized just how intensely my body had, as well. It felt like I was blooming against him, like the warmth flooding my veins was filled with heat-seeking missiles tugging me straight into him.

Laughing, I pressed my hands against his chest. "It's too cold out here for this, Long John. Let's get the leftovers put away and then you have me all to yourself."

"Fine, fine. But I intend to take full advantage of that," he warned, his voice low against my ear.

Envisioning all that was likely to be involved in that particular promise, I didn't even notice the car that pulled into the driveway until my parents stepped out of it.

Chapter Thirty-One

THEO

I SAW ESTHER'S EXPRESSION go slack, her golden skin paling even in the fluorescence of the new motion lights I'd installed along the driveway. When I spun around, I expected to find an assailant, an attacker, a man in a ski mask with a crowbar.

What I didn't expect to see was a middle-aged couple wielding crumpled up pieces of paper in their waving fists.

At first, I couldn't even understand the words they were yelling, I only knew it was directed at Esther. I shifted on instinct, shielding her from them with my own body, but I should've known Esther wouldn't let that fly. She pushed forward to stand beside me.

"What is the meaning of this?" the older woman shrieked. From the look of her, she could only be Esther's mother. She was slender as a reed, devoid of any curves that I could see, but she had the same shining black hair and high cheekbones as her daughter.

The man, half a foot shorter than me and apparently the source of Esther's pale green eyes, glared at her with such fury that Esther actually jerked back at my side.

"Haven't you done enough with your ridiculous truck? How could you do this to your mother?"

"Hold it right there," I said, raising my palm to stop them from advancing on her. "What exactly are you talking about?"

Her father shoved the paper into my hand and I smoothed it out. Esther peered around my shoulder at the image printed there. It was a nude couple having sex, the woman's bare breasts thrust upward as she straddled the man's lap. I knew immediately that it was fake, but Esther's face was superimposed on the woman's body. It was quite convincingly done, actually.

Esther's gasp of horror gutted me, but my gaze caught on the note at the bottom, which read, *Trash, just like you.*

"Where did you get this?" I demanded.

"They came through the mail slot at our home," her father replied stiffly. "Both pictures."

At his gesture, Esther's mother handed me the other one, which was a different pose but similarly edited. I knew more about Esther's body than my own, but to someone who didn't, I could see how they'd be fooled.

This one said, *Reap what you sow.*

Since her father was right in front of me now, I looked straight into his eyes as I tore the two printouts down the middle and said coldly, "I don't know who did this, but they're fake. That's not your daughter, it's sure as hell not me, and I'd like to know why your first inclination was to come here and start blaming her for someone else's behavior, especially when it seems clear to me that *you* are the target of these notes at the bottom."

The older man sputtered for a moment, his gaze shifting between the two of us. "I'm not the one with a crude joke on my business cards. What did she expect with a business name like that?"

My patience, already down to a swiftly unraveling thread, snapped when I felt Esther stiffen beside me. I opened my mouth to tell him where he could go with *that* judgmental, victim-blaming bullshit, but Esther stepped forward to stare her father down.

"I want you to get the hell out of here," she told them both. "And do *not* come back. As far as I'm concerned, I have no parents. You ensured that the minute you sent me back to an abuser when I came to you for help. I'm sure if you pretend whoever sent these doesn't exist, you'll be able to move on as happily as you did when you refused to help me."

Internally, I cheered for her, though I hadn't realized just how deeply messed up her relationship with her parents was. Knowing she'd gone to them during the misery of her marriage and been sent away was one thing, but seeing their disdain in person?

It made my blood boil.

Both of her parents fell silent, staring at Esther like they barely recognized her. Though her mother opened her mouth to speak, she snapped it closed again, looking mildly contrite. After a quick glance at my scowl, the two of them turned around and got back into their car.

Esther stayed perfectly still as the headlights blinded us before they pulled out of the driveway.

I shoved the torn pictures into my pocket. "Let's go inside," I murmured. At her nod, I started toward the guest house, but she shook her head.

"Your bed. Now, please," she whispered.

Suddenly, she looked more fragile than I'd ever seen her, like she might crumble under my hands. I locked up the guest house before wrapping my arm around her waist to guide her to the side door. A fine tremor had started working its way through her body, some mixture of adrenaline and cold. Even so, she stopped to pet Toni when we walked into the kitchen.

"Why don't you get into bed?" I suggested. "I'll be right up after I give her some dinner."

Esther nodded again, altogether too pliant. I watched her until she disappeared up the stairs, fed the cat, then smoothed out the pictures I'd torn without even thinking that they were more evidence to turn over to the police. Once they were flattened and reassembled, I snapped photos on my phone and emailed them to Rose with a quick note about what went down. Then I shoved the ripped pages into the cupboard over the fridge where Esther wouldn't stumble across them.

By the time I got upstairs, she was curled up in the fetal position under my blankets. I stripped down and slid in to join her. She moved toward me like a magnet until she was in my arms at last. It might've been barely forty-eight hours, but it was like I'd been going through withdrawal without her near me.

"Doing okay?" I asked softly.

With a shuddering sigh, she nodded. "That wasn't the homecoming I planned to give you."

"Fortunately for you, I'm a simple man. This is all I need."

It was true. I felt like I'd been missing a limb, like I was finally complete again now that I had her in my arms. The trembling had stopped, though her cheeks still felt colder than the rest of her against the warm skin of my shoulder. I would happily hold her like this all night if that was what she needed.

After a few minutes, though, she tipped her face up to mine. "This isn't some kid playing thoughtless pranks," she said quietly.

"No," I agreed.

Though I knew most teens these days could probably manage that kind of photo editing from their phones, this felt distinctly more targeted than the previous acts. Whoever was behind this went to a lot of trouble to not only create the images, but to hand deliver them to Esther's parents in the next town over. The other pranks had been generic bullying moves, even if the box of peanuts was more inherently dangerous.

"Your parents don't approve of the food truck, obviously."

She scoffed. "Understatement. They don't approve of any part of my life. Not only did I not follow their chosen path, my marriage was a failure, owning a food truck isn't a respectable career to begin with, and I chose a business name that they find crude. I'm an all-around disappointment."

"No," I said, rolling us so I could cup her chin in one hand. I kissed the tip of her still-cold nose and added, "You, Esther Malek, are the epitome of success. You not only survived a marriage that would've crushed most people, you managed to build an entire life for yourself after that. You have a job that helps countless kids to never have to feel the kind of isolation you did when you were young. Your business is thriving because of how amazing you are."

A single tear rolled down her cheek. I caught it with my thumb, then smoothed her hair back from her face. It was true, every word of it, but I managed to choke down the others that came to the tip of my tongue, the ones that said I was well on my way to falling in love with her.

Esther cleared her throat, like maybe there were words she had to swallow, too. "I'd guess there are other people who hate the truck. All this could be some weird attempt to shame me into closing it down or changing the name."

I chewed on that for a minute. "Has anyone else ever complained?"

"No, not to me. Dolores Brody down the street bitched to your mother about the truck being parked in the driveway last year, but you know your mom. She quoted the town's by-laws that allow it verbatim and suggested Mrs. Brody read up on such things before 'spewing vitriol,' I believe were Anita's exact words."

Grinning, I said, "Oh, man, I would've paid to see that. Mrs. Brody is the worst. She was always the one who ratted us out when we ran through her lawn as kids."

"Still, there might be others, I guess." She sighed softly. "I can't see Mrs. Brody scouring the internet for nude photos, nevermind having the skill to put my face on them. If she owns a computer, it's probably from the late nineties."

I couldn't help it. I burst out laughing, trying to imagine the little old lady down the street sitting in front of a boxy computer monitor as she hatched her evil plan. After a second, Esther joined in, giggling helplessly against my chest. While we laughed, the tension ebbed slowly from our bodies, leaving us both languid by the time the giggles ceased.

"God, I'm happy to be back," I said without thinking.

Esther froze for an instant, then relaxed again, her lips tickling my ribs when she murmured, "I'm happy you're back, too."

That wasn't exactly a declaration, not something I could ascribe any deep meaning to, but it felt *good*. I let it buoy and bolster me, both my own feelings on the subject and hers, too.

If I had anything to say about it, we wouldn't need to be apart again anytime soon.

Chapter Thirty-Two

ESTHER

WHEN I AWOKE ON Sunday morning, I felt strangely detached, almost disconnected from reality. A showdown with my parents had definitely not been on my mental bingo card of strange occurrences this holiday season.

Of course, a few weeks ago, sleeping with Anita's eldest son hadn't been on the list, either.

We spent the day in a bubble of contentment, aside from the brief intermission when Theo went outside to talk to Chief Roberts about the photos. Given the realistic impression those pictures gave of my naked body, even if it wasn't *actually* mine, I was grateful to be allowed to skip that particular conversation.

The week started off blissfully uneventful, as well. Christmas was only ten days away and we received our first invitation to a holiday family dinner from Sofia on Monday evening. She was sweet and completely unsurprised when we declined, especially because she'd heard about my parents showing up at the house.

That night, another four inches of snow fell over the town like a blanket of pristine white.

After breakfast, Theo went into the mudroom and returned with a pair of brand new snow pants in my exact size. He tossed them to me with a mischievous grin, saying, "Time for that snowball fight. Winner picks tonight's movie."

"You're on," I taunted as I pulled them on.

It had been a very, very long time since I'd last worn snow pants, but the swishing sound the fabric made as I walked over to where Theo knelt before a bin of hats and gloves was like an echo of childhood.

"Your little mittens are adorable, but they're not going to cut it. Try these on," he said, passing me a pair of stiff gray gloves.

I let him help me like a toddler getting ready to go sledding, trying to remember the last time someone zipped my coat or tucked my hair under a warm hat. He must've seen it in my face, because once I was bundled up, he kissed the tip of my nose and offered a tender smile.

"You look precious," he said.

"Well, enjoy it while it lasts. I doubt you'll find me so precious when I'm pelting your ass with snowballs."

His laughter rang out in the small entryway, bright and joyous, and I watched him get decked out in similar fashion. When he was ready, we clomped across the newfallen snow on the driveway and headed for the back of the yard, behind the guest house. There were drifts up to my knees, but Theo caught me every time I stumbled.

As I slanted a suspicious glance in his direction, he grinned and said, "I'm not going to annihilate you until the fight has officially begun, my sweet."

I snorted. "I'm not the one who's been going soft down south for years. We'll just see who annihilates who."

Despite my bravado, I was fairly certain he'd be kicking my ass. I had spent too much time admiring the sleek muscles of his arms and back to doubt he could best me in a physical battle. As a child, I'd actually hated snowball fights—my older sister liked to end them quickly by nailing me in the face with hard-packed snow—but I trusted Theo to be careful with me.

Unlike the rest of the world, he'd never been anything *but* careful with me.

We squared off from opposite sides of the yard. When he shouted, "Go!" I ran for the sparse trees at the back of the property, figuring I'd need some cover to help me. Theo didn't run at all, just dropped to his knees and started building ammunition.

Half an hour in, I was laughing so hard that my snowballs were ridiculously subpar, even if my aim was better than I expected. At least, it seemed like it, until I tried to nail him in the stomach and ended up hitting him right in the balls.

With a dramatic groan, he clutched his groin and fell onto his side in a snowbank. "Esther," he moaned, peeking from one eyelid to see my reaction. "How could you do this to me?"

Chastened but highly suspicious, I edged closer to him, my gaze locked on his hands. "Poor dear. Do you surrender?"

"Of course. Come help me up, you little monster."

It was a trap. I knew it, but I still couldn't resist. Slowly, I approached, watching in case he made a move to suddenly chuck a snowball at me. By the time I was only two feet away, his hands were still cupped around his purportedly injured anatomy, so I decided I was probably safe enough. With a pathetic moan, he held out one hand for me to help him to his feet.

I clasped it and immediately recognized my mistake.

He yanked me forward so I landed perpendicularly across his stomach. Though I yelped, his thick jacket and the snow beneath us cushioned my fall. Now that I was immobilized by his arms, one across my back and the other behind my knees, he flopped onto his back.

"I can't believe you fell for that," he said, still breathless from my landing.

"You fight dirty."

One of his hands stroked over my ass, padded though it was by the snow pants. "Dirty sounds good right about now, doesn't it?"

I propped myself up on my elbows and said, "I thought you were mortally wounded. Now you want to get frisky? You've got balls of solid rock, Long John."

We stumbled to our feet, pink-cheeked with the cold, and trudged through the snow to reach the driveway. The whole way, Theo whispered naughty promises into my ear, but when we clambered over the plowed pile of snow at the edge of the concrete, he stopped so suddenly I tripped over him and would have landed face first on the driveway if he hadn't managed to catch my elbow at the last second. I hissed an expletive before peeking around him to see what he was looking at.

Alex was slipping something under the front door of the guest house.

I started to smile at him, but Theo lunged forward, grabbing his brother by the front of his coat. "What the hell are you doing here?"

"Jesus, Theo, I was just leaving something for Esther," Alex said as he shoved his brother off him.

Theo reared back. "It was you?" he bit out. "You're behind all these fucking pranks?"

"What?"

"Theo, no," I said, grabbing his arm. "It's not him. Alex wouldn't do that."

"You two are friends now?" He glanced at me, his expression shifting so quickly I couldn't get a grasp on it. "Jesus, have you been friends all along?"

I opened my mouth—to say what, I had no idea—but Alex beat me to it. "Yes, we're friends. It's a recent development."

I flinched, but he wasn't wrong.

Though I expected Theo to yank his arm free and go after Alex again, he went utterly still instead. "You always thought I'd stolen Michelle from you. You decided you could return the favor to get back at me?"

Now I was the one who jerked as if he'd slapped me. He shrugged off my hand, his gaze traveling between us, growing colder than the air biting at my cheeks. In that terrible moment, I barely recognized him.

"What are you saying?" I whispered.

He only shook his head and turned away, like he couldn't bear to look at me, and I was suddenly transported back to the soulless condo I'd shared with my husband, to a life of alternating silence and screaming rage.

God, I felt like I was going to be sick.

I stumbled away from Theo's side, my boots sliding across an unsalted patch of ice at the edge of the driveway. Alex stepped forward to help me, but I gave a tiny shake of my head, so he dropped his hand to his side.

"I have to go," I said numbly as I hurried toward the guest house.

Memories bombarded me, nuances of expression and tone that had ruled my entire life for those years with Steve, drowning out the sound of Theo calling my name.

Behind me, Alex said, "What the fuck is wrong with you?"

"Are you trying to save her from me?" Theo's hoarse demand cracked through the night like a whip. "To take her from me?"

Too much. It was all too much.

I needed to escape, to burn away the suffocating emotions clawing their way up my throat. Between the clunky boots and all the layers of snow gear, I couldn't move fast enough.

"She's a human being, you asshole, not some contest to win. You think the second you turned your back, I swooped in to seduce her? For fuck's sake, man. Even if you think that little of *me,* I can't believe you'd think that of her," Alex continued, his voice vibrating with rage on my behalf.

Even that was more than I could bear.

I'd left a backpack of clothes at the main house, along with my spare EpiPen, but I sure as hell wasn't going back in there with Theo right now. God, I couldn't even stand to look back toward the two of them, squaring off at the edge of the driveway.

It took me impossibly long to tear off my gloves and fumble through my pocket for my key, but I finally got the door open, went inside, and slammed it behind me.

There on the floor lay a red envelope with my name written in scrolling silver marker. I picked it up and slid my finger under the flap, more for something to do with my hands than because I was desperate to know what was inside.

It was one of those photo collage cards from Alex's girlfriend, Isabelle, featuring pictures of herself and her toddler, plus one of Alex with his arms wrapped around them both. On the back, she'd added a handwritten note, thanking me again for answering her allergy questions via email.

A choked laugh tore from my throat. All this drama over a silly Christmas card.

I set it aside, peeled off my layers of soaked outerwear, and flung them all to the floor. The curtains were blessedly closed, so I didn't have to risk looking out at the two men who were probably still standing outside arguing. I started the electric teakettle on my countertop and then dropped down into a chair, covering my face with my hands.

Forty-eight hours. Theo had been gone for two days, and he thought I'd cheated on him with his brother during that time? I hadn't even moved that fast with Theo. Or did he think we'd been conspiring against him all along, whispering behind his back? I would've laughed if I hadn't been so close to tears.

I heard a truck engine start and then slowly fade to silence, presumably as Alex got the hell away from his brother's Jekyll and Hyde act. A few seconds later, there was a soft knock at the door. I let my hands fall but didn't stand.

"Esther, I'm sorry. I'm so fucking sorry," Theo called.

To his credit, he sounded so utterly ashamed of himself that I almost wavered and opened the door for him. Then another surge of nausea swept over me as I remembered him turning his face away, like he couldn't bear to look at me. I fled to the bedroom where I could no longer hear his apologies and sat at the edge of the bed, but memories of him haunted me until I wanted to weep.

My chest felt hollow, like my heart had been carved from my body and the gaping hole filled with sawdust. I stared down at my hands, clenched together in my lap, and waited until the kettle started whistling to force myself to stand.

When I returned to the kitchen, I put a bag of herbal tea in a mug, poured the water to steep, and finally went over to the front door. Through the peephole, I saw Theo's profile, his head hanging down in abject misery.

If I spoke to him right now, I would hurt him. I wanted to lash out, to cause him the same pain that streaked through me, twisting my insides into knots. I would say something cruel, because I was still horrified that he would think so little of me when I'd already started tipping over the edge into the dangerous territory of loving him.

I pressed my fist to my mouth to stifle a sob as I backed slowly away from the door, away from the sight of him.

Who was I kidding? I was already in love with Theo Silver.

Chapter Thirty-Three

THEO

I T WAS LIKE A scene from a horror movie, replaying over and over in my mind. Alex's indignant fury on Esther's behalf, the look in her beautiful moonlight eyes as her trust in me shattered into a thousand pieces.

What the hell was wrong with me?

I knew the answer. I had plenty of time to think about it, because Esther refused to speak to me in the days that followed. It all boiled down to a single night, the span of a few hours in the midst of my thirty-eight years.

It was fear.

Fear that someone else would be hurt because of me, that I wouldn't be able to give her what she needed and tragedy would ensue. Fear that I might lose someone else I cared about.

I'd fucked this up royally. For twenty years, I let Michelle's death keep me from living my life to the fullest, and now I'd hurt Esther in my own idiotic belief that I could somehow keep her from harm.

Though I tried not to bombard her, I texted and called at least once each day—to apologize again, to beg her forgiveness, to seek any sign that she didn't utterly despise me now.

She never answered.

The roiling anxiety in my stomach grew with each passing hour of radio silence. Even Toni seemed to be glaring in silent judgment over my idiocy.

On Wednesday morning, Esther finally replied to my text, but it did nothing to assuage my guilt nor to reassure me that I hadn't caused irreparable damage to our relationship. In fact, I was fairly certain the two word response only amplified those feelings.

I'm fine.

An icy fist clenched around my heart. *What can I do to fix this?* I texted back, desperate. The little dots bounced, then disappeared. Even after waiting half an hour, they never showed up again.

I wanted to lay my head down and weep, but that wouldn't solve anything. Instead, I went to the corkboard in the kitchen, found my brother's phone number, and called him. There were other relationships left to repair, and if I couldn't make things right with Esther just yet, I could at least bury the hatchet with my brother.

If my future was here, I wanted to move forward with a clean slate.

"Hello?" he said, sounding distracted.

I realized that he didn't have my phone number in his contacts and felt immediately like a jerk. "Alex, it's me."

His voice turned wary as he replied, "What do you want?"

The clock on the kitchen wall ticked loudly in the silence as I pondered that. I wanted to rewind it, go back to Sunday's snowball fight, stop myself from becoming the kind of asshole who inadvertently wounded the woman he loved.

Loved.

The word hit me like a hammer striking an anvil, echoing into my chest.

"I wondered if we could talk." My voice was hoarse from disuse these last few days. It seemed fitting that I would sound as terrible as I felt.

My brother was silent for so long I glanced down at my phone screen to see if he'd hung up on me. Just before I asked if he was still there, he said, "Okay. When and where?"

We settled on meeting at a coffee shop at the edge of town in an hour. I checked my texts again to see if Esther had replied, but there was nothing more. Since I'd been operating in lovelorn dumbass mode for three days now, I ran upstairs to shower, threw on clean clothes, and headed out to the cafe.

Alex was already seated at a table with a tall coffee cup in front of him like a shield. His cool gaze raked over my face, but he must've decided to take pity on me because his expression softened slightly.

"Go get yourself some coffee, you look like hell."

By the time I returned to the table, my brother seemed significantly more relaxed, tipping back his chair so it balanced on two legs—I could practically hear Mom's voice scolding him for it as she had throughout our entire childhood. Apparently my misery was disarming, but I'd take whatever advantage I could get if I was going to grovel.

Somehow, Esther had gotten past her comparisons between Steve and my brother. If she could find the good in him, I would try my hardest to do the same.

The apology I'd been rehearsing evaporated as soon as I opened my mouth. "How've you been?" I asked, wincing at the inanity of the question.

Alex puffed out his cheeks. "Good, actually. Really good. But I can't imagine we're here for small talk, Theo. Is Esther still pissed?"

"She's not speaking to me," I said miserably. "Well, she finally replied to a text today with two words, but that's the first I've heard since she slammed the door on Sunday."

"Tell me one thing, man. What difference does it make if she stops speaking to you now or in a few weeks when you leave town again without a backward glance?"

I flinched, squeezing my eyes shut for a moment. "I deserved that."

Alex sat forward, bracing his arms on the table. "Yes, you did. Hasn't she been through enough? What the hell have you been thinking, getting involved with her?"

"As you so wisely pointed out, she's a human being who sure as hell knows her own mind," I replied, then I hesitated. Maybe patching up my disaster of a relationship with my brother wouldn't fix anything with Esther, but it felt like the necessary next step. I swallowed hard and said, "I'm in love with her."

"Shit, man," Alex muttered.

"You're telling me," I replied weakly. "While I was home last week, I talked to my partner about buying out my half of the business."

His eyes widened. "You're moving back here?"

I gave a humorless laugh. "I haven't talked to Esther about any of it yet. If she can't forgive me, then...I don't know. I just can't imagine the rest of my life without her."

For a long moment, my brother was silent, studying my face like it was the first time he'd seen me. Hell, it practically was—my parents had sent me photos and updates over the years, so I was sure they'd done the same for him, but he'd just been a kid when I left. A sad, broken kid, suffering for a single moment in time that had changed the course of so many lives.

I studied him in return. Of the two of us, he looked like an exact replica of our father.

It hit me in one breathless rush that I'd missed out on seeing my little brother turn into the man sitting before me. At the time, I hadn't believed I could do anything *but* get as far away from Spruce Hill as possible. Looking back, I realized my path had been the easier route.

Alex had recovered, rebuilt himself despite everyone in town knowing about the worst moments of his life.

I must have stared for too long, because he finally lifted a brow and said, "What? Something on my face?"

"You grew up." It was a simple statement, but it was true.

Alex scoffed. "You're the one who became an old man," he replied, his eyes sparking with that familiar mischief I remembered so clearly from our youth.

"I'm sorry I left." The words were quiet, but I saw their immediate impact on him.

"You know you're not the one who needs to apologize," he countered. "Can you ever forgive me?"

I closed my eyes. Some of the memories had dimmed, but I could still see his face in the flashing lights from the ambulance, his expression of abject horror, the tears streaming down his face. I could hear him screaming at me, fighting to get to Michelle, begging God to take him instead.

When I opened my eyes again, I saw all of it reflected in his own dark gaze. "We were just kids," I said. "It was an accident. Nothing that happened was your fault."

"A kid who started throwing punches at the top of the fucking lighthouse in the middle of the night. It might have been an accident, but I was the one who caused it," he replied, so matter-of-fact that I knew he hadn't ever forgiven himself.

"I never meant to hurt you," I croaked. "I didn't know. If I'd ended it sooner, if I'd just—"

His brows tugged downward. "Wait. You've been blaming yourself this whole time? I thought you left because you hated me after that."

"Jesus, Alex, of course not. It was my fault."

For a moment, he simply stared at me, looking utterly appalled. "Explain."

"We'd agreed to break up when I left for school that summer, but I guess I misunderstood her feelings on the subject. She brought me up there to try to convince me to stay with her. If I'd ended things sooner, she'd still be alive."

"Fuck me," he whispered. "That's why you're so afraid. Why you're fucking things up with Esther. It's like a subconscious defense mechanism."

I blinked at him, wondering how the hell my baby brother had turned into the man sitting in front of me. "How do you know all that after five minutes of conversation?"

"My girlfriend is a social worker. I've been in counseling since just after the accident, but Isabelle and I talk a lot about processing things in a healthier way. I came with a lot of baggage, as you can imagine, but I owe it to her to deal with my shit, you know?"

"That's why you tried to talk this time instead of punching me in the face?" I joked, but my voice broke.

He shook his head at me, a tiny smile tugging at his lips. "I should have talked to you before prom night, and I should never have gone with you to the party. Third-wheeling with my big brother and the girl I was obsessed with? No way."

"I wish you'd told me you were into her. I wish I'd realized how much you hated me back then."

At that, Alex shook his head. "I never hated you, Theo. I should have done a lot of things differently before that night, and during, but none of it was on you. I loved you. Still do, you asshole."

Christ, if anyone had told me I'd start blubbering in the corner of a coffee shop with my brother during this trip, I wouldn't have believed it. I covered my face as the tears fell. When Alex moved into the chair beside me and wrapped his arm around my shoulders, I didn't protest, just leaned my head against his. He didn't speak as he offered the kind of unconditional support that I'd denied him ever since that night.

"I'm so sorry," I told him again, the words muffled by my hands.

"I'll forgive you for everything if you sort this shit out with Esther," he said dryly, but he squeezed my shoulder. "Seriously, Theo. She deserves to know what you're feeling. It's her future, too."

I wiped my cheeks and looked up at the ceiling to try to quell any more tears. "You're right. I know you're right. I'm just so fucking afraid that she doesn't feel the same."

With a laugh, Alex said, "Dude, she hasn't dated since that bastard died. I've never heard so much as a whisper that she's had even a one-night stand. She's barely seen her friends, for fuck's sake. If she's been putting up with your stupid ass day in and day out for weeks now, I think that's a pretty good sign."

"When did my baby brother get so wise?"

"Probably since I started dating Isabelle. You'll like her, man. She has a two-year-old son who's just the coolest kid I've ever met. Before her, I was just, I don't know, surviving. Coasting along. I didn't think I deserved to find real happiness."

I flinched. Eighteen years later and he was still paying penance for an accident. "And you found it with her?"

His smile widened. "Yeah, I did. Dominic has food allergies. That's why I put her in touch with Esther. They emailed back and forth a bit, and Isabelle wanted me to drop off a Christmas card for her."

"I am the world's biggest asshole," I muttered.

"Maybe, but you're a lovable asshole. Tell her everything, Theo. The truth, all of it. Let her make a decision based on that. If she thinks you're still planning to leave, then I can't say I'd blame her for not wanting to put up with your bullshit just to see you walk away."

I turned and hugged him tight to my chest, releasing him only when he thumped my back twice to get me to let go. "I love you, even when you're pointing out what a dick I am. If Esther forgives me, maybe we can all have dinner sometime, the five of us."

Alex's smile lit up like the Christmas tree in Town Park. "Yeah, man, that'd be great. Good luck with Esther."

I thanked him, hugged him again, and took my coffee with me as I stepped out into the cold. If Alex could forgive me even after eighteen years of pain, hopefully Esther could, too. Throughout the short drive home, I started to think maybe my luck would turn again, that she would gladly open the door to let me throw myself at her feet and beg her forgiveness.

But my luck had apparently run out, because when I got back to the house, Esther's car was gone.

Chapter Thirty-Four

ESTHER

THREE DAYS OF SWITCHING from nighttime pajamas to daytime pajamas and a steady diet of coffee, Christmas cookies, and popcorn had started to wear thin. When I heard Theo's truck leave on Wednesday, I threw myself into a lightning fast shower, pulled on real clothes, and hightailed it out of there.

I wasn't sure where I was even going. Barely consuming any real nutrients meant my fridge was still fairly well-stocked, so the grocery store was out. I'd ordered gifts for my sister's two kids online, and my presents for Anita and Lou had been wrapped and perched on the mantle since before they even left town.

Maybe I'd pick something up for Sofia and Chase.

For the first hour, I drove aimlessly, weaving through Spruce Hill, until I found myself at the *Welcome to Oakville* sign. My hometown was truly tiny, more a hamlet than its own township. Where Spruce Hill had grown and flourished over the years, Oakville had maintained a minuscule row of stores on Main Street and a single fall apple festival that attracted tourists for day trips before they moved to greener pastures along Lake Ontario or the Finger Lakes.

I hadn't been back to Oakville since the day my parents sent me away.

Though I didn't intend to stop, I pulled into an open parking spot in front of a bookshop. There I sat, staring out the slowly fogging windshield toward the display windows. Everything was decorated for the holidays, draped in garlands and big red bows, a wreath on almost every door. This stretch of shops looked like it belonged on a Christmas card.

The emptiness I'd been all too happy to cultivate started to fold in on itself, bringing back the ache in my chest as I imagined myself and Theo in each of the couples strolling down the street, bundled in scarves and hats, laughing and pausing to kiss under a sprig of mistletoe hung in a doorway.

Maybe because of the proximity, maybe as a side effect of heartbreak, I started to wonder if my parents had ever been one of those couples. I could easily picture Anita and Lou like that, young and in love, but thoughts of my parents invaded my mind.

They had loved me, no matter how hard my sister tried to convince me otherwise during my childhood. My mom wouldn't have been moved to do all of that baking if she hadn't cared about me, but somewhere along the way, once I was old enough to look out for myself, things changed. My choices stopped mirroring their view of what my future looked like.

Was I destined to be a disappointment to everyone in my life, or was I just a scapegoat for things that didn't even concern me?

I dashed away the tear that rolled down my cheek and was just about to start the engine again when someone tapped on my window. A breathless shriek escaped my lips before I blinked the smiling face into focus and rolled down the window.

"Alex, hey," I said with forced gaiety.

His smile fell as he studied my face. "Are you okay? I didn't mean to bother you, we were just picking something up from the store and I saw you sitting here. I wanted to introduce you to Isabelle and Dominic, but we can do it some other time."

"I'm fine," I replied, swiping at my eyes one last time. "I'd love to meet them."

Alex took a step back as I put the window up and opened the car door. I recognized Isabelle and her son from the photo card, but she was even more breathtakingly beautiful in real life. The three of them were simply glowing with happiness, and I let that glow seep into the dark edges of my own sorrow, temporarily pushing back the pain.

After a brief chat, owing to both the cold and someone's impending nap time, all three of them embraced me, even Dominic. I tried not to wish Alex was his brother when he gave me a quick hug, but then he murmured in my ear, "Please talk to him."

I looked at him in surprise. "You're the last person I thought would become his champion."

"We talked this morning. He has a good heart, and he's got some things to tell you. And yes, he does stupid shit when he's scared. I always thought he was fearless, you know?"

"Fearless," I repeated, still startled to hear that the two of them had spoken.

Alex smiled gently. "Turns out the risk of losing some things is scary enough to make us all into idiots. I wouldn't be where I am if I didn't believe that everyone deserves a second chance, Esther."

With that, he squeezed my shoulder and jogged over to his little family. I watched as he swung Dominic up in the air, then bundled the little boy into his carseat. Some of the emptiness crept back into my body, so I turned away, got back into the car, and cranked up the heat.

Everyone deserves a second chance.

I didn't agree with that, strictly speaking, because Steve's countless chances only led to worse situations, but I had to concede that most people probably deserved one. After all, Theo had felt like *my* second chance, hadn't he? An opportunity to seize my fate with both hands, to let myself out of the careful little box I'd placed myself in after Steve died and I was finally free. A chance to be cherished and appreciated.

And loved, my heart chimed in.

I didn't go straight home after that, though. Instead, I drove back through Spruce Hill toward Lake Ontario. The snow prevented me from accessing the parking lot at the public beach, so I pulled onto the plowed overlook just up the hill. I hadn't dressed warmly enough to stay long, but I parked the car and got out, wrapping my arms around my body against the cold as I stared out across the water.

The view was chilly and pristine, shades of gray and blue broken only by the rocky outcropping that housed the tall stone tower of the Spruce Hill Lighthouse in the distance.

Just as I closed my eyes and cleared my mind, hoping some universal force might guide me to the right decision, my phone vibrated in my pocket. I struggled to unlock the screen with my frozen fingers, but a faint glimmer of warmth sparked when I read the text from Theo.

Would you please consider having dinner with me tomorrow night? 6 pm, my place. No pressure, no expectations. You can even throw another snowball at my nuts first.

The smile that pulled at my lips felt rusty. I stared down at the message for another minute as a rush of longing pulsed through my veins. It had only been three days, but I missed him. I missed him like I'd missed joy during my marriage, like I missed the sun on a drizzly day.

With my phone clutched in my hand, I looked back out at the choppy gray waves dancing across the lake. I'd replayed the scene from the other day a hundred times, searching for evidence that I was right to step away from him, to nip this all in the bud before I was truly drowning.

In the end, I didn't find it. I found Theo jumping to my defense at first, jumping to a stupid conclusion next, and myself, panicking.

And yet...what did that mean? That I wasn't ready for something like this? That we'd been doomed from the start?

Or maybe just that we were both human.

I remembered telling Theo he made me feel like I didn't come with so much baggage, and his response—*we all have baggage.*

That much had never been clearer than it was right then.

I looked back down at the phone. Though I'd been paying only the vaguest attention to the calendar, I knew I had an order to deliver tomorrow afternoon. After a quick calculation, I texted Theo back.

I'll be there.

I hesitated even after typing out the words, but I made myself hit send and hurried back into the car. It was almost two o'clock, so I had plenty of time, but these days of wallowing had been a mistake. I did my best thinking while I was baking, after all.

What better way to show I was open to hearing those mysterious *things* Alex said Theo had to tell me than to show up to dinner tomorrow with an offering of dessert?

Chapter Thirty-Five

THEO

I REREAD ESTHER'S TEXT a dozen times throughout the rest of the afternoon. Not long after she sent it, her car pulled into the driveway. Lovesick fool that I was, I peeked out through the curtains and watched her hurry into the guest house without a glance in my direction.

Even as I told myself it didn't mean anything, regret stabbed through me once more.

Though I probably should have planned dinner for that night, I wanted her to have time to get used to the idea—and I wanted to do something special for her, not just reheat some frozen casserole my mother had left behind. Once I knew Esther was home safe at the guest house, I made myself stop procrastinating and started scouring recipes.

When I had it narrowed down to three options, I consulted Julian, which unfortunately necessitated explaining all that had happened to Oliver. He didn't berate me like I probably deserved, just gently supported me as he always had before passing the phone back to Julian, who walked me through the difficulty of each meal, made suggestions for side dishes, and told me he and Oliver would be rooting for me.

Gratitude for my friends flooded my chest as I made my shopping list.

Without Esther as a buffer, I steeled myself before walking into the grocery store. Three days of soul-crushing silence had given me plenty of time to think about the future, and I'd come to a decision. It wasn't fair to put the responsibility for my choices onto Esther's shoulders.

She'd carried too much for too long.

This time, when people stopped me in the aisles to chat, I gave them my full attention even if only for a minute or two. When I ran into old Mrs. Brody in the freezer aisle, I took her hand in mine and apologized for always using her yard to cut through, especially now that I understood how hard she'd worked on her landscaping. I offered to do some gardening work for her in the spring to make up for it, and she pulled me into a frail embrace before patting my cheek and moseying on.

When I moved on to select some produce, the memory of those three apples from my grocery trip with Esther almost made me laugh aloud. I found myself grinning down at the bin of potatoes until I felt the weight of someone's stare. Once I'd added the potatoes to a bag and put them in my cart, I let my gaze travel across the crowded store, wondering if I'd find Tyler glaring daggers in my direction.

No one was watching me except for a young blonde guy who looked only vaguely familiar. He glanced in my direction before disappearing down the cereal aisle.

My thoughts returned to my new plan. Regardless of whether Esther wanted a future with me, I would be returning to Spruce Hill. I wasn't sure what that would look like just yet—a northern branch of Lawn Ranger? Splitting my time between here and Asheville until I was settled enough to stay here permanently? An apartment, a house in town?

Yes, it would hurt like hell if Esther wanted nothing more to do with me, but I had let my baby brother pay the price of my absence for eighteen years. It was my turn to carry some of that burden.

Our parents weren't getting any younger, no matter how active and capable they still were, and Alex...I thought about his girlfriend and her son, about the little family he'd become part of. Could I really turn my back on all of it a second time?

The answer was a resolute no.

So instead of deflecting and dodging, I chatted and smiled, accepted and returned holiday greetings, and felt the weight of eighteen years slowly melt away.

When I got home, I put away the groceries, limiting myself to a single glance out the kitchen window. Once everything was sorted, I settled down on the couch with my laptop to search for an apartment in town. Toni, who I suspected was missing Esther as much as I was, curled up against the side of my thigh.

A week before Christmas was probably not the best time to be apartment-hunting, but I'd have to work with what I had. In an ideal world, I'd get this sorted out before dinner with Esther tomorrow night. I wanted her to know I was serious about this and that my choice held no expectations of her own response.

Fortunately, my parents' popularity worked in my favor. By midnight, when I finally headed up to bed, I'd actually gotten email responses from two of my three top choices. I responded that my availability for a walk-through was wide open.

For the first time since the snowball fight, I felt like things were looking up.

Toni woke me up at first light by perching herself on the center of my chest. Mid-dream, I thought I was drowning, unable to draw breath, but even my flailing didn't dislodge her. I awoke to bright golden eyes looking down at me with casual disdain, and as soon as my brain cleared away the cobwebs of sleep, she hopped off of me and trotted toward the door.

For once, I was grateful for the early wake-up, because I found an email from one of the property owners offering to show me the apartment at lunchtime. I replied right away, thanked him, and read through my meal prep notes to figure out what I needed to get done ahead of time if I was going to be gone for an hour or two. Following Julian's instructions to a tee, I whisked up the marinade, added the potatoes to the container, and popped it back in the fridge. I'd even drafted up a timeline of when everything else needed to be started, but I'd be home in plenty of time from the apartment viewing, so I left the rest for later.

My primary requirement for an apartment was simply that I didn't want to live in anyone's pocket. The guest house was lovely, but even if Esther invited me to move in—which seemed unlikely at this exact moment, I had to admit—I didn't think I could handle being so close to my parents all the time.

And given how quickly the Spruce Hill gossip mill worked, I didn't want to be living that close to *anyone* I knew.

While the other place I'd contacted was in one of the fancier new buildings that had sprung up while I was away, this one was a single apartment located above Davies Soap Emporium, an artisan shop in town. I knew the owner, Mark, from childhood, but nobody else lived in the building and I trusted he wouldn't infringe on my privacy.

I entered the shop just before noon, announced by tinkling bells attached to the door. Mark Davies, who looked like he'd be more comfortable running a surf shop than making organic bath products, grinned broadly from behind the counter.

"Hey, man," he called as he came over to clasp my hand. "God, it's been ages. How've you been? Looks like North Carolina's been treating you well. Though I guess not well enough, if you're looking for a place back here?"

I laughed. "I'm good. Just exploring some options, you know?"

Mark had been on the soccer team with me when he was a sophomore and I was a senior, though we'd run in different circles apart from that, and he'd never been one to beat around the bush.

Tapping the side of his nose, he nodded toward the back of the shop. "Absolutely. You know you can trust me to keep my mouth shut, but it'd be great to have you back."

He led me up a staircase behind the storeroom, explaining recent renovations he'd made to the shop and the apartment, pointing out the designated parking spots visible through a back window at the top of the stairs. Through it all, he didn't ask any questions or even mention Esther.

The apartment boasted a single bedroom and tons of natural light streaming through the windows. It had a decent kitchen, came with appliances, and, in the only comment to indicate Mark was aware of anything going on between me and Esther, he informed me he was more than happy to rent it out on a month-to-month basis while I found my feet.

On our way out, I asked him whether any of his products contained nuts. He didn't hide his swift grin, but he assured me everything was completely vegan and nut-free, so I bought an artistically arranged little basket of products for Esther.

We'd agreed on not exchanging Christmas gifts, but I decided an "I'm sorry I'm such a fucking idiot" gift didn't count.

I left the shop with a copy of the rental agreement, a receipt for my deposit check, and an invitation to have dinner with Mark and his wife at some point in the future. That was another thing I'd forgotten about Spruce Hill—the fact that my history here contained more good than bad, when it came right down to it.

Hopefully, the future would contain more good than bad, too.

Chapter Thirty-Six

Esther

I HAD EVERYTHING READY to go for my order delivery before lunchtime, which left me time to decorate a fancy layered lemon cake *and* flutter around nervously in anticipation of tonight. As I stared into my closet, debating what I should wear, I wondered what had come over me. I was almost as jittery over seeing Theo again as I had been about that first dinner at The Mermaid.

After settling on a pair of black pants and a flutter-sleeved sage green tunic as my date night attire, I hung them on the back of the closet door and took a long, hot shower. Afterward, I threw on a Nutless Wonder shirt and my cupcake leggings with a cardigan, braided my hair into a crown around my head, and gathered up the two boxes of cupcakes to be delivered. Though I occasionally took the truck for big deliveries, this one was small enough to transport in my car, for which I was grateful given the slushy roads and dwindling daylight.

I double checked the delivery address and programmed it into my navigation app. It was an online order, one of the first local ones to come through the website, and I didn't recognize the address. Still, the directions said it was only fifteen minutes away, so I'd be home with plenty of time to change my clothes before dinner with Theo.

My heart tripped a little with anticipation, which was stupid, because it wasn't like he'd been far away during the last few days. I had spotted him several times, though I hid behind the curtains or watched from the peephole like a weirdo. My doorbell camera caught him even more frequently, and I *might* have opened the app just to see how he was doing.

He looked as bad as I felt. Still as handsome as ever, but disheveled and weary, weighed down as he trudged from his truck to the side door of the house.

Part of me had wanted to run to him, throw myself into his arms, but instead I watched from the guest house, determined to wait until we had time to sit down and talk at dinner.

As I turned right to head east along Lake Ontario, I passed the public beach where I'd stopped the day before when Theo's text arrived. The sun was setting already in my rearview mirror, and I muttered a curse directed at the poorly lit road as I tried to determine where my next turn was. I knew Peregrine Cove wasn't far from the lighthouse, but where the hell was the entrance?

Another few minutes down the road, my phone started rerouting and reloading at the speed of a drunk snail. I pulled over, put my flashers on since I was barely out of the roadway given how badly it had been plowed, and took my phone out of the cradle on my dashboard as though that might inspire it to work faster.

Just as it seemed to be pulling up new directions, it rang in my hands and I dropped it onto the floorboards when I jumped in my seat.

"Shit, shit, shit," I muttered, trying to grab it before it stopped ringing. Maybe it was the customer, wondering where the hell I was. I answered without looking at the screen. "Hello?"

"Esther? Are you okay?" Theo asked, concern coloring his deep voice.

I blew out a breath. "I'm fine, just trying to find this delivery address. I'll be back in time for dinner, I promise."

"Where are you? The connection is terrible, I can barely hear you."

"East of town, along the lake," I replied, peering out the windshield to see if any street signs were lit by my headlights. The area around me was almost completely dark, not a house in sight.

Theo sounded a million miles away when he asked, "What's the address? Maybe I can help."

"Hang on," I said, pulling the phone away from my ear to look at the order. "Peregrine Cove. Number Seven."

Static crackled so loudly in my ear that I almost dropped the phone again. I heard Theo's voice, too, but it was too broken up for me to understand what he was saying. I lifted the phone up toward the roof of the car, turning in every direction to try to get a better signal, when a pair of headlights flashed on behind me.

Squinting at the light, I said, "Someone's here, I'll be home soon."

"Esther, don't hang up—"

Theo's voice cut off as the call dropped before I even hit the red button to end it, and I felt the first quiver of uneasiness in my stomach. What if it was Tyler, luring me out here for some kind of revenge?

The face that appeared at my side sent relief flooding through me.

I smiled as I lowered the window and said, "Drew, hi. What are you doing out here? I'm just trying to find a delivery address."

Since the first time I met him outside of the event center, he'd always reminded me of a golden retriever, boyishly enthusiastic in a sometimes overbearing way. As I swept my gaze over his expression now, it was devoid of its usual friendliness. His blue eyes were cold, almost emotionless as he reached in through the open window to unlock the door before throwing it open.

My relief evaporated.

"Get out of the car, Esther," he said calmly.

When I hesitated, he lifted his other hand into view, holding up a serrated hunting knife that sent ice through my veins.

"Was that Theo you were talking to?"

I flinched at the sound of Theo's name—Drew's voice dripped malice, and I wondered if I could lie, but my reaction answered for me.

"Of course it was. Put down the phone and get out of the car, Esther."

I did as he ordered, my thoughts racing so fast they tripped over one another. "I told him where I was headed. He could be here any minute."

"Good. We won't even have to call him with his invitation."

"What are you doing, Drew?"

"We're going for a little drive. That address was hard to find, wasn't it? Don't worry, I'll take you there myself," he said, pointing the knife toward his car. "And I assure you Theo knows exactly where it is."

Even if I'd thought I could talk my way out of this, my teeth started chattering so hard during the twenty feet between the cars that I could barely speak. I might be able to make a run for it, but the lake lay on one side of the street and a field of deep snow drifts on the other. The temperature had to be below freezing by now, and I wasn't dressed for prolonged exposure to the cold.

"Put your hands on the roof of the car. I have big plans for you, so don't try anything stupid."

Though my fingers curled into fists at the command, I forced them to relax and set them on the top of the car. I didn't see what he did with the knife, but he grabbed one wrist, then the other, looped a plastic zip tie around them both, and yanked it tight. Before I could blink, he'd done the same to my ankles. Panic threatened to choke me as he opened the car's trunk and lifted me off my feet to drop me inside.

The entire trunk was lined in white lilies, the smell so horrifically overpowering that I nearly gagged. I thought back to the bouquet I'd received—not from a grateful customer or someone playing a prank, after all.

"Drew, I don't understand. Why are you doing this?" I whispered when he moved to close the trunk.

He studied me, his expression blank. "All in good time, Esther. We all have to reap what we sow."

Then he slammed the trunk shut, encompassing me in perfumed darkness, and I couldn't stop the bone-jarring shudders that wracked my limbs as the car started moving.

Chapter Thirty-Seven

THEO

As soon as Esther said the words *Peregrine Cove,* my brain jolted into action. I turned off the oven, dinner be damned, and yanked on a coat as I ran out to the truck. I dialed Alex's number as I pulled out of the driveway.

"Are you in Spruce Hill?" I asked as soon as he answered.

I could almost hear him frowning at the phone when he replied, "Yeah, I just finished plowing Mr. Ankarberg's parking lot at the north end of town. Why?"

"I need your help. Esther had a delivery this afternoon. She couldn't find the address, so I offered to help. She was headed to Peregrine Cove. Jesus, Alex, the call cut out but she said someone was walking up to her car."

"Shit," he whispered. "Okay, how far are you from the Ankarberg plaza? Should I head straight to her or should we go together?"

My hands were shaking, so I gripped the steering wheel so tight that my knuckles went white. "I'll be there in a minute. We go together. And Alex...thank you."

"Just shut up and focus on driving. I'll see you soon."

Peregrine Cove was a little community of cottages at the edge of town, mostly used as beach houses during the summer. The party on prom night had been at Number Seven.

And it was right next to the lighthouse.

I swung into the parking lot barely a minute later and stopped beside Alex's plow truck. He hopped into my passenger seat, still buckling his seatbelt as I pulled back onto the road.

"What the hell is happening?" he asked.

"I don't know," I replied, "but I think she's in danger. Can you call Chief Roberts or Hanson, get them to send someone out?"

Alex made the call, sounding so calm that it almost settled my nerves until I heard the undercurrent of fear when he spoke to me again. "They're on their way. You accused me of being behind the pranks—what pranks, Theo? What's going on?"

As I turned onto the road leading out of Spruce Hill, I told him about all of it: the flowers, the phone calls, the email, the box of peanuts, even the nude photos. Alex swore under his breath when I reached the end, rubbing both hands over his face.

"You think it's all connected to Peregrine?" he asked shakily.

I puffed out my cheeks. "I didn't until ten minutes ago. No one lives at Peregrine year round. Who the hell would order cupcakes out there in the dead of winter?"

Neither of us had an answer to that.

Even after eighteen years, I remembered the way there, though I couldn't quite recall whose family had owned the cottage we were at after prom. The area was one of those hidden gems only townies knew about, tucked away off the main road at a turn that non-locals barely even noticed. I wasn't surprised Esther had trouble finding it.

This stretch of road was poorly lit, apart from the eerie glow of the snow on either side of the black pavement. When my headlights washed over Esther's car on the side of the road, I pulled up beside it and hopped out, leaving the truck running. Alex moved to follow me, but I waved him back.

After grabbing Esther's phone and the purse containing her EpiPen from the floorboards, I jogged back to the truck. I wasn't sure what the hell we were going to find when we reached Peregrine Cove, but my imagination ran rampant.

Given the nature of those threats, I wanted to be armed with epinephrine just in case.

The turnoff was only a mile from Esther's car, but the lighthouse came into view first. I forced myself not to slow down as we drove by, though both my brother and I held our breath until we were beyond it. Alex let out a shaky sigh. I wished I could find the words to reassure him, then we were turning into the entrance of the abandoned row of cottages.

The driveway hadn't been plowed, but there were tire tracks leading straight to a house all the way down on the left.

"It's like a ghost town," my brother whispered. "Theo, what's the plan? We can't just go crashing in there if someone's got Esther inside."

I flipped off my headlights as we crept along the row of cottages, but apparently we were expected. The outside lights at Number Seven flipped on, nearly blinding us, and a silhouetted figure flung open the front door. I couldn't make out any features, but whoever it was gave a jaunty wave with a wicked-looking knife, as though inviting us in.

"Maybe you should stay in the truck," I said quietly. "I doubt he got a good look at us. You can send the police in when they get here."

Alex glared. "You're an idiot. No way are you going in there alone. The chief should be right behind us."

"There's no sense in us both walking into danger, Alex."

Though he didn't look any less annoyed, he gave a slow nod. "You go in the front. I'll wait until you're inside and then sneak around the back. You're not facing this on your own, brother."

"Fine. My toolbox is in the back, find yourself something to use as a weapon. Crouch down so he can't see you when the door lights go on."

"What will you use?" he asked, cramming himself in the space between the seat and the dashboard.

I said nothing as I got out of the car. If Esther was a hostage, I wouldn't give whoever was holding her here an excuse to hurt her, even if that meant walking in unarmed. Without a backward glance at the truck, in case anyone was watching from inside the house, I strode through the snow to the open door.

Whoever had waved me in was no longer standing in the doorway, so I took a deep breath, opened the creaking screen door, and went inside.

Chapter Thirty-Eight

ESTHER

E VEN AFTER THEO STEPPED into the little cottage, I was still convinced Drew had simply gone off the deep end because I turned down a date with him four years ago. I didn't think about why he cared that Theo would come for me—I was just really fucking grateful he did.

My hands and feet were numb from both the cold and lack of circulation. Though I'd stopped hyperventilating when Drew finally pulled me out of the trunk to bring me inside, my entire body still shook with the aftereffects of that panic. The cloying scent of lilies still permeated the air, wafting from my clothes and skin like I'd been doused in perfume.

Theo's eyes locked on my face as soon as he walked in. They softened with relief as he looked me over, checking for injuries, and under the warmth of his gaze, I felt the tremors begin to fade.

Drew had stepped into a darkened bedroom to Theo's left after he waved him down at the door, but not before telling me everything he would do to Theo if I gave any kind of warning.

There was no chance I would risk that.

I stayed silent, watching as Theo took slow, cautious steps toward me, trying to understand what was happening.

"Are you hurt?" he asked softly.

I shook my head, afraid to speak, but he only smiled like he understood. Once he was about ten feet from the chair Drew had shoved me into, my captor stepped out of the bedroom, still holding the stupid knife.

"Well, now we can get this party started, hmm? I thought I'd have to issue a personal invitation, but I guess you have a brain in your head after all. Welcome, Theo."

My breath stalled in my lungs at the words, but it was Theo's expression that made me question my assumption about why we were here. He stared at Drew like he was seeing a ghost, shook his head slightly, then said, "Andy? Andy McNulty?"

Drew gave a sharp laugh. "Oh no, Andy died the same night as Michelle. New town, new name, new me. I've been Drew for the past twenty years. Not a single person in this shithole town recognized me when I moved back."

"I don't understand," Theo said quietly.

"No, you wouldn't. Instead of admitting the truth, every-one talks about you like some tragic fucking hero." He paused, fondling the handle of the knife like it was precious to him as he moved toward me. "Do you like the house? When it went up for sale a few years ago, I knew I had to have it. It was destiny."

Theo held perfectly still. "It's me you want. Let Esther go. She had nothing to do with Michelle's death."

"No, she didn't, did she? Sometimes innocents are the ones to pay for our mistakes, though, Theo."

"Don't do this," Theo whispered.

"Michelle paid the price while you and your brother walked away, moved on, made a life for yourselves. You didn't pay a fucking cent. While you two were off living your lives, my mother swallowed a bottle of pills and my father drank himself to death. Did your parents share that news with you?"

Oh, Christ. This wasn't about me or the food truck at all.

Theo kept his gaze on Drew, but his muscles tensed like he was preparing to spring. I doubted he'd be able to reach us in time to keep the knife from making contact with my flesh.

"You were just a kid at the time, Drew," Theo said gently. "And so was Esther. You want me to pay? I will. Gladly. Just let her out of here unharmed. You don't want to hurt her, I can see it in your face."

Drew looked down at me. "No, I don't. I wanted her to be mine, but she wasn't ready. I even sent you lilies, Esther. Didn't you like them? They were the same type of flowers we had at Michelle's funeral. After that, I waited for you to come to me. I waited fucking years, and then you chose him over me."

I started to shake my head, but he laid the flat part of the blade against my cheek like a caress. A whimper slipped out before I could stop it. With a glimpse of that friendly smile he'd always given me in the past, he laid his finger over my lips.

It was only with the greatest effort that I managed not to flinch away from his touch.

"You should have chosen me, Esther. I would have treated you like a queen. Instead, you became his whore."

"Please don't do this," I whispered when he removed his finger. The knife was like ice against my cheek, but it was the flat, dead look in his eyes that chilled me to the bone.

"Drew," Theo said calmly. "Let her go. She's not involved in this."

Drew shook his head slowly. "Of course she is. I would have let her make it up to me, but she wouldn't give us that chance. Do you know who your whore's father is, Theo? The slimeball attorney who denied us an insurance payout, leaving us with *nothing.*"

The rest of my body went as cold as the knife.

"That's right, Esther. Did you know your family betrayed mine like that?"

"No. No, Drew, he didn't talk about work at home. I only knew he worked for an insurance company. I swear, I had no idea. I'd never even heard of Michelle until recently."

"Of course, the mighty Silvers were always tight with the chief of police," Drew went on. "They ruled it all an accident."

"It *was* an accident," Theo said quietly. "She tripped on her dress."

It was like he hadn't even spoken. "No criminal charges, no civil suit. Every last dime went to Michelle's funeral and paying the lawyer who promised it was a slam dunk to get that insurance money. I took care of him years ago, but I wanted to give you a chance to make reparations, Esther. All of this could have been avoided."

Theo shifted like he was going to throw himself between us when Drew tutted quietly and stroked the flat of the blade along my skin.

I hoped Theo had a plan, because I saw no way out of this.

Flashbacks to all those times he'd talked me down from a panic scrolled through my mind, but the chances of it working on Drew seemed terribly slim. Even if he didn't intentionally cut my throat, I'd started shivering again and was terrified I might simply vibrate my way into the blade.

Since Drew was still staring down at the knife against my cheek, he didn't see the swift glance Theo sent to something behind me.

"Drew," Theo repeated. "Look at me. We can settle this between us."

The second Drew lifted his gaze to Theo's face, something swung in the space over my head and struck Drew's shoulder with a thud. The knife clattered onto my lap as he screamed and spun around, but whoever was behind me grabbed him and

Theo dropped to his knees in front of me, using the knife to slice through the zip ties.

As soon as my wrists and ankles were free, he yanked me out of the chair and turned us so his body was blocking mine from whatever was happening behind him, pressing my back against the wall and shielding me with his larger frame. Shuddering sobs wracked my body even as he started murmuring soothing words into my ear.

When silence fell, I heard Alex's voice say, "It's okay, he's tied up."

Theo stared down at me like the world was still crumbling around us. "Are you hurt?" he asked, running his hands down my arms. I blinked at him until he repeated the question, this time more urgently.

"No," I said finally. "No, I'm not hurt."

In the next second, I was wrapped in his arms again, crushed against his chest. The steady thump of his heart wound through me like the sweetest melody. My hands, still tingling with numbness, gripped the front of his jacket.

When Alex waved the police inside, Theo finally turned our bodies back toward the room. Drew's arms were tied behind his back, though he was still howling about his shoulder. There was a metal garden stake on the floor that I assumed Alex had used to hit him. The hunting knife, glittering now with a reflection of the lights from the police cruisers outside, lay beside it.

Detective Hanson cuffed Drew and passed him to an officer I didn't know before coming over to us. "There's paramedics right behind us. We weren't sure what we'd be walking into here. I don't see any blood, but you should let them look you over, Esther."

Theo thanked her, then pulled back just enough to smooth my hair off my face and inspect me more closely. "Will you let them? For my sake, if not your own."

I laughed, though it sounded hoarse and a little bit hollow. "You just told a man with a giant ass knife to let me go and make you pay instead. I guess the least I can do is let an EMT check my vitals."

When Alex joined us outside, Theo released me to the care of the paramedic and pulled his brother into a tight hug. I watched them, blinking back a sheen of tears, as a woman named Casey checked my pulse. Her fingers were gentle against the red, raw marks the zip ties had left on my skin.

"You have someone to stay with tonight?" she asked.

Theo met my eyes over Alex's shoulder and smiled so tenderly that my tears spilled over, trailing unimpeded down my cheeks. I nodded, both at him and in response to her question.

"Yes, I do," I said softly.

"Good. Your vitals are all strong, though your pulse is a little high. Your wrists are scraped and irritated, but the skin isn't broken. I want you to go home and take it easy for the night, got it?"

I nodded, thanked her, and let Theo pull me back into his arms until Roberts came over to take our statements. Though I must have answered all of his questions adequately, I barely remembered any of it, only dimly aware of Theo eventually thanking Hanson and the chief.

The next thing I knew, I was bundled between Theo and Alex in the truck, each of them chafing one of my frozen hands between both of theirs while heat blasted from the vents. They were careful to avoid the red bands around my wrists, but as my digits came painfully back to life, the tears started to fall again.

"I know it hurts, but you're cold as ice," Theo murmured, kissing my temple.

"You two make quite a team," I choked out, trying for a smile. It wobbled, but they both smiled back at me.

"Can you forgive us for getting you into this mess?" Alex asked.

I met Theo's eyes and he lifted one hand to brush the tears from my cheek. "Of course," I whispered. "You saved my life. Both of you."

Alex released my other hand as Theo wrapped his arms around me. Though there was more to say, that simple statement trumped all of it. The brothers had forgiven each other, come to my rescue, and risked their lives for my own. I had a feeling that went a long way toward healing the hurt of the last few days for all of us.

"Can we go home now?" I asked, my voice muffled against Theo's jacket.

He reluctantly released me, though not before pressing a kiss first to my forehead and then to my lips.

"Yes, absolutely. Let's go home."

Chapter Thirty-Nine

THEO

WE DROPPED ALEX AT Esther's car, which he agreed to leave parked in the plaza where his plow truck was waiting for him. Before he slipped out of the truck, however, Esther caught his hand in a tight squeeze. I was ashamed of myself all over again for overreacting to their friendship, but Alex caught sight of my face and shook his head.

"Forgiven, brother. All of it. We're moving forward now."

I inclined my head in appreciation as Esther released his hand and nestled back into my side. "Thank you. For everything, Alex," I said, my throat tight with emotion.

He flashed us his standard grin, lifting a hand in farewell, and folded himself in half to fit in Esther's front seat before he was able to slide it backward.

Esther leaned across me to call to him, "There are two dozen cupcakes in the backseat. They're all yours! Payment for saving the day, and safe to share with Isabella and Dominic, to boot."

"You just made my night," he called back, then waved again and closed the car door.

We had to pull away so he could turn the car around, but I caught Esther watching the side mirror until the headlights appeared behind us. For the first time since we climbed into the truck, she relaxed, the remaining tension finally flowing out of her limbs.

I laced my fingers through hers and brought her knuckles to my lips. Soon, I would find out which *home* she wanted to go to—I wasn't willing to make any assumptions—but for now, I just wanted her to stop shaking like a leaf. The cab of the truck was warm and toasty, but her fingers were still cold against mine.

Half a mile from home, her teeth started chattering again. I wrapped my arm around her, driving one-handed down the familiar side streets until I finally had to release her to shift the truck into park. When the engine went off, the resulting silence enveloped us in a breathless moment of indecision.

Esther looked shaken and miserable, but I wanted this to be her choice. After a moment, she looked up at me, vulnerability written in every line of her beautiful face, and asked, "Can I stay with you tonight?"

Relief flooded my chest. "Of course. Let's get you inside."

In the mudroom, I helped her out of her boots, rubbing her hands again to try to warm her up. Aside from the chill that seemed to have taken residence in her veins, there was some-thing else dimming the brightness in her eyes, something that lodged like a boulder in my chest.

Our half-cooked meal sat in a casserole dish on the stove, the counter strewn with the vegetables I'd been about to start preparing when I called Esther to ask if coconut was okay. Thank fuck I had, otherwise I wouldn't have known she was in any danger, nor had any idea where to find her.

Before making it another step, I turned and pulled her into my arms. A violent shiver raced down her spine as her hands twisted in the back of my shirt. It took only another heartbeat for the sobs to work their way out of her chest with jarring intensity.

I held her, absorbing the impact as much as possible while I whispered reassurances against the top of her head.

"You're safe now, I promise. I'm right here with you." I shuddered and tightened my arms around her softness as the reality of how close I'd come to losing her sank in. "God, Esther, I love you."

With a hiccuping sob, she tipped her tear-stained face up to look at me in shock. I laughed a little as I tucked a loose strand of hair behind her ear. Her eyes glimmered like peridot in the kitchen light, searching my face like she needed to confirm the words were true.

"I love you," I said again. No going back now. "I had a whole lot of things to say to you tonight over dinner, and I'll say them when you're ready, but I want you to know that. Life is too short to miss the opportunity to tell you how I feel."

She buried her face against my chest, so I cradled the back of her head while my other hand rubbed soothing circles across her back. It was only when Toni strolled into the kitchen and started winding herself through our legs that I realized how late it had gotten.

"I'm afraid dinner is a bust, but I can throw something together if you're hungry," I offered.

Esther finally released her grip on my shirt and scrubbed at her face with both hands. "I don't think I can eat right now. I made a lemon cake for dessert, you know," she said, then another stray tear tumbled down her cheek. "I had a nice outfit picked out and everything."

I didn't want to laugh, but I couldn't hold back the chuckle that rumbled through my chest as I swiped my thumb across her cheekbone. "We'll just reschedule our fancy meal for tomorrow, then. Or I'll run over and get the cake. We can have it for breakfast."

Her own laugh was watery, but given that I'd been afraid I would never see her beautiful smile again when I walked into that cottage, I'd take it as a win. In the aftermath of the adrenaline, my empty stomach jumped for joy at the thought of the cake, but Esther looked about ten seconds from collapsing.

"If you're sure you don't want to eat something, why don't you go up and get into bed. I'll put this stuff away and be right up," I suggested, stroking my hand gently down the side of her face as though I could erase the memory of that bastard's knife.

She'd been precious to me before, but now? I wanted to wrap my arms around her and never let go.

Weaving slightly on her feet, Esther nodded. "I'll meet you upstairs," she said wearily, then turned to go up to the bedroom.

I waited until I heard her footsteps fade before moving to the stove to throw out the half-cooked dish that sat out all afternoon. Once I'd packed away all the vegetables on the counter, I fed the cat her dinner, threw together a small bowl of fresh fruit, checked ingredients on a package of crackers, and brought the selection of snacks up to the bedroom.

The overhead light was still on, but Esther was tucked up under the blankets, curled into a ball on her side. I'd planned to follow her lead as far as sleeping in our clothes or stripping down, so I waited until she shifted enough to reveal the bare skin of her shoulder and the upper swell of one breast before tugging off my clothes.

I flipped off the light and crawled under the covers, meeting her in the middle of the bed. Just as I reached for her, she turned into my embrace and pressed her face to the pulse in my throat. Though she'd stopped shaking, there was still a faint tremble in her fingers where they curled against my chest.

For a long time, we lay there in the dark. *She's safe,* some helpful part of my brain kept repeating, but it didn't feel quite real yet. There were too many alternate scenarios playing inside my head, ones where we didn't reach her in time, where my dead girlfriend's baby brother started slicing into Esther's beautiful body, where I ended up covered in the blood of the woman I loved.

With enormous effort, I forced it all away. Instead, I focused on the rise and fall of her chest and the tiny breaths that brushed over my throat. I ran my hands through her hair and over her soft skin. The shared heat of our bodies created a cocoon of warmth under the comforter, seeping its way back through my veins to replace the icy terror.

A long time later, well after I thought she'd fallen asleep, Esther whispered, "I'm so afraid."

"We're safe," I murmured against her temple, but she shook her head.

"I'm so afraid of loving you."

My muscles tensed, caught between the joy of this almost-admission and the pain of knowing I'd put her into this position. With a long exhale, I said, "You don't have to be afraid. Never, I promise you. Esther...I'm staying. Moving back to Spruce Hill."

Her head tipped up. "You're staying?"

"My partner is going to buy my half of the business. I'll have to wait for this Wylie project to be completed before the transfer, because of the contract, so I may need to go back and forth a few more times. I got an apartment over the Davies Soap Emporium."

"You got an apartment," she repeated. I couldn't see her face, but I felt her eyelashes brushing over my skin as she blinked, presumably processing that information. "You're moving back to Spruce Hill."

"Yes. I'm very much in love with you, Esther, but you're not responsible for choosing my future or finding my happiness. I wanted to prove to you I wasn't putting any of that on you or using this as some way to pressure you into forgiving me. Christ, I don't know if that makes any sense. I just wanted to show you I'm serious about this, all of it."

Silence fell again, stretching until I was sure this was the end of things. My heart clenched painfully in my chest and I tangled my fingers in her hair, certain it would be the last time she let me this close to her. Then, when I opened my mouth to speak, her nose nuzzled the hollow at the base of my throat, followed by the soft press of her lips.

"I didn't want to love you," she said quietly. "But tonight, all I could think about was wasting these last few days, losing that time with you."

I scooted down slightly in order to meet her eyes, glowing like silver discs in the darkness. "My days are yours. And my nights. All of them, from here on out."

"I'm sorry I freaked out on you."

"No," I replied, my tone firm, and kissed the tip of her nose. "I'm sorry I freaked you out. I had a lot of shit to work through with my brother, but I think...I think we're on our way to fixing things between us. I am so, so sorry, Esther, that I let that hurt you."

"I do love you, you know," she whispered.

With a shuddering sigh, she relaxed completely, her body melting into mine as though the confession had been a final wall that crumbled between us. I kissed the top of her head, tightened my arms around her, and held her until she finally fell asleep.

Epilogue

ESTHER

IT WASN'T QUITE CLEAR which news traveled faster—that Theo Silver was moving back to Spruce Hill, or that the only remaining member of the McNulty family had tried to kill me. Even the bustle of the last few days before Christmas couldn't quell the furor of gossip flying through town.

Those invitations we'd feared never actually materialized, aside from one for a New Year's Eve gathering at Sofia's place. When we told her we'd see how we were feeling after Christmas, she just yanked us both into a warm hug and left us with a teary smile.

Still, we weren't entirely without plans for the holidays. Theo asked if I was open to inviting Alex, Isabella, and Dominic over for a small celebration, and I enthusiastically agreed.

The three of them were driving out to Rochester to see her family on Christmas Day, so we scheduled our little get-together for Christmas Eve. Theo laughed at me for trying to toddler-proof the house as much as possible before their arrival, but I caught him moving a side table with sharp corners into the basement before they arrived. When I tried unsuccessfully to hide a smile, he only winked at me.

The day after the incident, Theo helped me string Christmas lights throughout the guest house with reckless abandon while we ate the lemon cake I'd made straight off the serving plate. The day after that, we turned our attention to the main house, hauling boxes of decorations from the basement. The artificial tree we put up in the living room was so tall that even Theo had to stand on a step stool to put the star on top. I cooed and Theo groaned over every handmade ornament his mother had saved from his childhood.

We'd just added a final ornament to the tree when the doorbell rang. For a beat, we stared at each other, then I followed him toward the front door. In all the times I'd been to the house, I'd never come in that way. We always used the side door by the driveway.

When Theo opened the door, he kept me behind him as though there was still some threat out there. I knew there wasn't—Detective Hanson had told us they'd tracked the prepaid phone to Drew McNulty and found another half dozen doctored photos on his laptop at home—but for once, I didn't mind letting Theo step between me and the unknown.

Except...on the other side of the threshold were my parents, holding a prettily wrapped box with a golden bow on top of it.

I shifted out from behind Theo and stared at them in surprise. For a second, I thought he might tell them to get the hell off his porch, but they were looking back at us with such contrition that we were both startled into silence.

"We're sorry," my mother said softly, blinking back tears. "So sorry. My beautiful girl."

I was frozen in place, barely aware of Theo's hand settling against the small of my back in a wordless show of support. As I looked back and forth between my parents, wondering what the hell was happening, my dad held out the gift.

"We didn't understand what you were dealing with back then, Esther. That's no excuse for turning you away, and I will regret it until my dying day. But we love you. I never thought my job might put you at risk, and I can't—"

When he broke off, choking on the words, I shook my head. "It wasn't your fault."

"I heard about what happened to that boy's family. I should have realized there was danger and shielded you from it."

Theo glanced down at me before asking, "Do you want to come in?"

"No, no. We didn't mean to intrude, but we wanted to bring this over. It's for the two of you," he said, waiting until Theo took the box from him.

"Merry Christmas, both of you," my mom said. She put her hand on my father's arm, but her gaze snagged on mine and she added, "If you're willing, we'll arrange a time to get together someday. If not, we understand."

They moved back down the steps and along the walk, shoulders curled forward and heads bowed. I'd never seen either one of them look so defeated, so small. The image tugged at my heart.

"Merry Christmas," I called out just before they reached their car. They both turned in surprise and smiled before getting in.

Theo waited until they were gone to close the door. He lifted one hand to my cheek, the other holding the gift. "Do you want to open it?"

"Not yet," I replied. I took it from him and returned to the living room to tuck it under the tree.

We managed to keep ourselves busy with decorating the entire first floor of the house until Alex and his crew arrived for an early dinner on Christmas Eve. Toni made herself scarce the second Dominic's little feet hit the kitchen floor. After a relaxed meal of homemade pizza, we moved our little group into the living room to watch Dominic inspect every ornament within reach. I knelt beside the little boy, showing him the most indestructible ones I could find.

It was impossibly beautiful. From a life of solitude, I'd suddenly become part of a family, surrounded by people who cared about me.

My gaze landed on Theo, sitting across from his brother and Isabelle. Though he was mid-conversation, his eyes caught mine and his lips curved into a soft smile before he returned his attention to what Alex was saying.

Dominic had just torn the wrapping paper from our gift to him, a shiny red tricycle, when the sound of the side door opening broke through the chaos of Christmas music and laughter.

Theo squeezed my shoulder as he started to stand, but the faces that appeared in the doorway caused him to drop back onto the couch beside me. An incredulous laugh slipped past his lips and his arm tightened around me as we watched his parents walk into the room with armfuls of gifts.

"Well, isn't this a cozy little scene!" Anita cried as Lou dropped down onto the floor beside Dominic, who threw his chubby arms around the older man. Alex and Theo rose to embrace their mother, but over Theo's shoulder, she caught my eye and winked.

One thing was certain—I would never again underestimate a member of the Silver family.

Also by

RACHEL FITZJAMES

Keep in touch! Sign up for Rachel's newsletter at https://rac helfitzjames.com/ for FREE bonus content, sneak peeks, sales, and news about upcoming releases!

SPRUCE HILL SERIES

Unpacking Secrets

A Lonely Road

Canvas of Lies

Crumbling Truth

Playing for Paradise

Sinister Returns

Treasured Legacy

Lucky Save

Wrenching Hearts

Flash of Danger

Acknowledgements

All of my books feel personal to me, but none more than this one. Food allergies have influenced every part of our lives for nearly two decades (and even longer for my husband), and Esther's past experiences with playdates and reactions all stem from our real-life experiences. From the time my kids could speak, they knew how to recite "peanuts, tree nuts, milk, and eggs" to keep my eldest safe. Things you'd expect from a toddler became suddenly terrifying—putting toys in their mouths, sharing sippy cups, accepting food from a well-meaning friend or caregiver. When we threw out a brand new 36-pack of Play-Doh after the peanut residue incident mentioned in the book, I don't think we used any again for months because the experience was so traumatic.

Food allergies impact an ever-growing number of individuals and even though Nutless Wonder *was* the name of the bakery business I considered starting when I was in the throes of baking vegan/nut-free cupcakes for every playdate and birthday party we attended, allergies are no joke. I hope I conveyed the seriousness of the topic with sensitivity but also impact, because what's safe for one individual can be deadly for another.

So, first and foremost, thank you from the bottom of my heart to all the friends and family who made sure my kids were not only welcomed but included and protected at every stage of the game. Thank you to those who tested cupcake flavors and offered to provide only allergy-friendly foods at events where they didn't have to go to those lengths, because it meant the world to us. You guys are the real rockstars in our lives.

Obviously, thank you to my firstborn, for inspiring Esther's food truck and for dealing with more than a kid should have to face, including our first EpiPen experience at the age of 17. Sorry I'm not better at decorating those vegan/nut-free cakes, but at least they've tasted pretty good. To my youngest, for being a fierce advocate, for understanding that safety had to come before preferences, and for baking a variety of Esther's creations so we could get content photos for this book release. I couldn't (okay, wouldn't) have done it without you.

To Genelea Barker, Heather Frances, Tobie Carter, Christina Brennan, and Melissa Rotert, thank you all for the insights that made this book what it is today. As always, to my other CPs, Christie and Bri, thanks for letting me ramble about this one as I adjusted everything this way and that.

And lastly, Melissa, I know this isn't the rom-com you wanted me to write, but this book wouldn't exist at all without your suggestion that I give it a go, even if it turned into something else entirely. Love you, and I'd be lost without you.

About the author

Rachel Fitzjames is the author of a contemporary romantic suspense series set in the fictional town of Spruce Hill, NY. She started writing on her brother's ancient computer back in the early 90s and never looked back, though her first short story about an underground cat thievery ring was sadly lost. With a degree in geography inspired by wanderlust, Rachel has a keen appreciation for the escape that the romance genre allows. She is a lifelong resident of Western NY and created Spruce Hill in order to give a little bit of home to all of her characters.

Connect with Rachel at her website, https://rachelfitzjames.com/, or on Instagram and Threads at @rachelfitzjames.